books by harry crews

scribner paperback fiction
Published by Simon & Schuster

the

harry crews

mulching

of america

a n o v e l

SCRIBNER PAPERBACK FICTION
Simon & Schuster Inc.
Rockefeller Center
1230 Avenue of the Americas
New York, NY 10020

First Scribner Paperback Fiction edition 1996
SCRIBNER PAPERBACK FICTION and design are trademarks of Simon & Schuster Inc.

Designed by Karolina Harris
Manufactured in the United States of America

10 9 8 7 6 5 4 3 2 1

The Library of Congress has cataloged the Simon & Schuster edition as follows:
Crews, Harry.
The mulching of America / Harry Crews.
p. cm.
I. Title.
PS3553.R46M84   1995
813'.54—dc20   95-11358
CIP

ISBN 0-684-80934-6
       0-684-82541-4 (Pbk)

This book is for George Kingson.
Abrazos.

chapter

one

the air was a shimmering of heat, and it felt to Hickum Looney as though with every step he took the weight of the sun on the top of his balding head and his thin shoulders became heavier. The long sidewalk in front of him was so hot that it shook and undulated in his eyes and made them feel cracked and gritty.

There was nothing unusual about that, though. Just another ordinary August day in Miami. Hickum had suffered through twenty-five years of such summers, and if he could survive five more, he could walk away from the only job he'd ever known—if he did not count the three years he had spent as a supply technician in the air force.

And he had never counted those years a job. He'd spent every hour of every working day in an air-conditioned office filing copies of supply requisitions. Those were pleasant, comfortable days, the kind of days during which a man could let his mind float where it would while he stood over an open file drawer, daydreaming and fantasizing, and no one would care because no one would notice whether he was actually filing anything or not.

He went into the air force a private and he came out a private. He never got any letters of commendation, but he never got any turds in his personnel file, either. Any way he figured it, it was an easy ride. And he did not know how much he had liked it until his hitch was up and he was a civilian again, looking for a job, and ended up as a door-to-door salesman for a company named Soaps For Life, and realized before the first month was out that he did not like being a door-to-door salesman talking to people day in and day out about soap.

It wasn't that he hated it, or anything nearly that strong. He just had never been able to make himself care for it very much, which he thought was worse than the promotions he had deserved in the air force but never got. Nor did he want to learn more about selling soap than he already knew, which he felt must be about as much as any sane man ought to know about anything, nor did he want to talk about it nonstop when two or more salesmen of Soaps For Life got together, which the Boss had gone to some trouble to let all the salesmen know was precisely what was expected of them.

The real horror of the whole thing was that Hickum had taken this job twenty-five years ago with the intention of quitting it the following week and going to work as an apprentice in a sheet metal shop. All he had to do was wait seven days for the sheet metal job to come open and he could kiss the door-to-door business good-bye. But it didn't work out that way. The morning before he was to start as an apprentice, a butane gas tank had blown up and left nothing of the sheet metal shop but flat ground and grieving widows.

He knew he ought to count himself lucky not to have been there when the tank blew up. But all he could seem to think of was that he had lost a job. In some screwy way he did not understand, it seemed to him that he had always missed every good job he had had a chance for. Except for Soaps For Life. So he had obsessively clung to it for a quarter of a century now, always secretly wishing he was doing something else.

One of the worst parts of having the job was going to the annual sales convention and listening to the harelipped little man who had founded the Company and who invariably spent three podium-pounding hours telling his salesmen—every one of whom, with the exception of Hickum Looney, seemed to want to be just like him—how he had single-handedly built his company. Over and over, he would hammer through his success story: one-man-and-one-dream-and-one-case-of-soap-samples-and-one-long-street-that-never-ended-until-that-one-man-and-that-one-dream-had-become-an-empire. *"Shoe leather,"* the little man would scream, *"shoe leather is the secret."*

Again and again during the interminable speech that at times seemed deranged and half out of control, the little man hopped about the stage as though he had hot coals in his shoes, often raising his hands above his head in what could have been surrender or supplication, and screamed: "You nink I nare if I not a narenip?"

He might not care, but God, did he have a harelip! It was by far the worst one Hickum had ever seen.

"My narenip was given na me by Nod!" Hysterical applause made him smile, and the smile would always show a single enormous, square, and badly stained tooth in the center of his face. Then he would raise his hands for silence. "Nu nink I non't know what people nall me? I know! I know plenty! But, now listen! I may be kind of strange and warped . . . " In this part of the speech, he often went into a kind of frenzied jitterbug: head snapping, arms flapping, and knees pumping like pistons. "Can nu near me? Can nu near me, brothers?"

After each question there was a responsive roar that shook the walls of the convention center: *Yes,* they could hear him. Then the Boss would abruptly become very still. When his voice came out of his mouth, it would come in a whisper, and yet the whisper reached every man and woman present. And that voice, so quiet and yet so strongly surging, gave them all gooseflesh.

"I am most awfully ugly. But! *Near me now!* I am standing in a nousand dollars' worth of suit!"

The roar of approval seemed it would take the plaster off the walls.

"Nand I may have wists and nurns in me na make a rattlesnake crazy. But I still drive a Cadillac car. Ne biggest Cadillac car nay build. Nand I got a nelephone in nat Cadillac, got it right by my knee. Nand finally, finally, I trade for me a new Cadillac car every year!"

It was then that the salesmen got loose and crazy, some of them bashing their heads together in an ecstasy of enthusiasm and longing. Hickum never felt like bashing heads with another salesman at the annual convention, and certainly he never felt ecstatic with joy by anything the Boss said from the podium. Hickum thought this to be some failing in himself that he could not identify. Nonetheless, he never doubted it was somehow his fault.

But if he dropped dead this very instant on the short flagstone walk leading to the house of his prospect of the day—a modest yellow cinder block house with a white roof—he would be recorded in the annals of the Company with an asterisk identifying him as one of the top salesmen it ever had. If it hadn't been for the Boss, Hickum would have been the champion salesman at Soaps For Life. But it was the Boss who held all selling records. Year after year, he remained unbeatable. So if Hickum Looney didn't feel an urge to bash heads every year at the convention, why didn't he at least feel a convulsive jolt of accomplishment? Why instead did he carry a cold fury and dread at the center of his chest, where he had always supposed his heart to be?

He knew why. Of course he did. He could not easily or graciously accept being second best. The Boss had somehow taught him to accept nothing less than being a winner and then—year after year—refused to allow him to win. This was the first day of August, the month of the contest for Salesman of the Year. Whoever sold the most soap this month would win a Cadillac, a trip to Disney World in Orlando, Florida, and $2,000 spending money.

There was only one problem. The Boss always entered the contest each year himself, always in a different part of the country, and he always won. To ensure it was absolutely honest, the Boss's completed sales forms were entrusted to an old and honorable CPA firm, which verified the accuracy of the sales. For the twenty-five years Hickum Looney had worked for the Company, the Boss had been the undisputed champion salesman. And finally, in a gesture that the Boss called magnificently generous, but a gesture that humbled and humiliated his salesmen all the same, humbled and humiliated them as nothing else in their lives could, he took the sum total of the winnings—the car, the trip, the spending money—and divided all of it evenly among his salesmen across the country. In all the years Hickum had been with Soaps For Life, the share for each salesman had never exceeded $4. Last year, Hickum's check had been for $3.36.

And yet every year, including last year, Hickum had fought his heart out to win. And in spite of himself, in spite of not wanting to bash heads with his fellow salesmen at the convention when the Boss spoke, he fully intended to walk the leather off as many pairs of shoes as it took to win. The Boss always told his men to think of the contest as a learning experience because, he said, that was why he had started it in the first place, and he also told them he always entered the contest himself to demonstrate to them that he was not asking the salesmen to do anything he would not and could not do himself. It was to strengthen the bond between them.

Hickum Looney shook his head violently to get rid of the unthinkable notion of strengthening the bond between himself and the little demented harelip. He had to make himself focus on the Selling Mode and at the same time try to get himself into it. The founder of the Company, known universally as the Boss, demanded that all his salesmen focus their concentration on getting into the Selling Mode before ever approaching the first prospect at the beginning of each working day. But even after all these years Hickum Looney still did not know exactly what that meant. He must be doing something right, though, because it was rare when one entire order book was not full, or nearly so, when he got back to the office in the evening.

He loosened his tie and tried to look haunted and full of stress. For a salesman to give a potential customer the impression that he was haunted and full of stress was called simply the Look in the official Sales Manual. When he felt everything was as it should be for him to make a quick sale, he walked up to the little yellow cinder block house and rang the bell. He had a habit of counting after the first ring of the doorbell or knock on the door.

"One hippopotamus, two hippopotamus, three hippopotamus . . . "

If nobody appears or he did not hear somebody moving behind the door by the time he got to *thirty hippopotamus*, he usually went back to *one hippopotamus* and counted to *twenty hippopotamus* before he rang or knocked again. But there were often times when he simply walked away. It all depended on what his instincts dictated that he do. He trusted his instincts and he trusted signs, and always tried to trust whatever signs he thought he saw or what his instincts were trying to tell him.

He had counted back to *fifteen hippopotamus* when the wooden door behind the screen eased open a little. He had heard no footsteps, no bolt sliding in a lock, no sound of hinges turning, nothing at all. There was no light in the room behind the door, which had slowly closed now to about six inches. The person, dim as a ghost behind the screen wire, was the size of a jockey with a cap of closely cropped gray hair twisted into wild tufts. Hickum had no idea if it was a man or a woman. But then one of the person's hands reached up and patted the twisted tufts of hair and then dropped and held a tiny gold locket suspended from a gold chain. The hand was full of blue veins under translucent skin marked with liver spots. It was a woman. No question in his mind at all.

"Good day, madam. My name's Hickum Looney and I represent Soaps For Life. Our headquarters are in Atlanta, Georgia, but we've got representation for our product in every state in the Union. The company that I represent makes exactly what you need, no matter what that need might be. I know that makes me sound just about too beautiful and too good for your ordinary citizen to accept. But all the representatives of Soaps For Life are one of a kind. Yes, madam, one of a kind. You might have seen our thirty-minute infomationals on television."

As Hickum talked, he watched one of the old lady's nearly fleshless hands float slowly but steadily upward and latch the screen door before floating in the same slow and steady way back to her side.

When he heard the latch fall into place, he looked down and rubbed the toe of his shoe in her welcome mat and said: "Aw, now how come you to do that, ma'am?"

"Because you might be a crazy person," said the little old lady in a dry rasping voice, "with murder in his heart and rape on his mind. Don't you read the papers? Happens every day."

Hickum smiled broadly. He always did when he was in the Selling Mode. It didn't matter at all what the prospect said to him. She'd need a hatchet to get the Selling Smile (treated at length in the Sales Manual) off his face, now that he was in the Selling Mode.

"I try never to dispute a lady," said Hickum, "but you are flat wrong is what you are. I come from a long line of honest, hardworking people. Back in east Tennessee my mother was a Hickum, so I got her maiden name. And Looney? My daddy's a Looney. Up in east Tennessee it's enough Hickums and Looneys to fight a war. Matter of fact it was a war between the Looneys and the Hickums off and on for nearly a hundred years, so the story goes. But then they got started marrying each other and such, as men and women are subject to do, and that kind of cooled things down, if you know what I mean."

the mulching of america   15

"I do not believe I would care to know what you mean now or any other time," said the little old lady. She had taken a half step back into the room and Hickum could hardly see her through the screen door. Her cap of gray hair bobbed and weaved in a way that made her head seem to move, in the deep shadowy light, as if free of a body.

"I don't believe I understand," said Hickum.

"Well, a fool can see you don't understand a whole lot," she said. "If you understood much of anything at all, you wouldn't be standing on my porch at my front door at this time of the morning holding a suitcase full of soap and expecting to be let into my house. That's the way us girls get raped, you know, strangers showing up on our doorstep carrying suitcases made out of tin and wanting to use our phones."

"I do not want to use your phone, ma'am. I never said one single word about using a phone of yours."

"They mostly never do, but that don't mean a thing." She clicked her false teeth in a little rhythm like castanets.

Hickum glanced down at his metal briefcase and then back to the old lady, who was growing more indistinct and harder to see as she moved deeper into the room. The old ones were usually either the easiest or the most difficult to sell. They had only a few years left and they weren't risking anything by opening the door for the wrong reason. On the other hand, nearly all of them were desperately lonely. That's the kind all the salesmen at Soaps For Life tried to search out when they could. Most people seemed not to notice it, but a salesman could not help but notice how many of the old ones were so desperately lonely they would let the devil through the front door if he promised to talk to them.

Hickum sighed. This was what door-to-door selling was all about. Anybody could sell who could somehow manage to get inside the house. Failed salesmen always got shut out on the steps before they could make their presentation. A man who could never find a way to make his presentation could never make a sale. But there was always a way to handle getting on the inside, and top-of-the-line door-to-door men like Hickum

harry crews

Looney always knew that, and given enough time, he could always find a way to go in.

Hickum lifted the metal briefcase and smiled for all he was worth. "Don't you think this is just a little small to be a suitcase?"

In a tight little voice that sounded like an infuriated schoolteacher, she said: "I try not to think of that which is of no concern to me."

"But this is your concern. This box holds life everlasting."

If someone had a gun to his head, Hickum Looney could not have explained why he had said his box held life everlasting. He didn't even know what such a statement might mean, or if it meant anything at all. But there was no denying that some days he was more creative than others. He had suspected for a long time now that the habit of meeting strangers at their doors, a habit stretching back over his entire working life, had taught him instinctively what to say. In any event, he had found out early on that simply saying something like that would not move the product, just as smelling good would never sell a bar of soap. Everybody that sold anything seemed to sing the same tired song. And no doubt that was why the Sales Manual had a whole chapter demonstrating that a good salesman could play a customer like a banjo: Pluck the right string, get the right sound, and get a sale. A door-to-door man simply had to find the string that said: *I'll buy.*

But there was no single string, no single tune, no single song a door-to-door man could use that would sell everybody. That was the Boss's great secret. Or he said it was. Read the customer like a road map and you'll go straight to his heart. That was what the Boss said he had built his company on, his company and his selling record, year in and year out. And where was the evidence to prove him wrong? He had his suit and his Cadillac car and men all over the country ready to follow him anywhere he led. What didn't he have? What?

The little lady came rushing out of the shadows until her nose was nearly pressed against the screen door. Her tiny eyes were black and shiny as a bird's.

"*Everlasting?* Did you say *life everlasting?* Young man, you keep on talking like that and sure as I'm standing here lightning will strike my house. And I'm not insured against lightning, and on top of that, I'm not even a Christian."

"Madam, could you unlatch the screen door? I wasn't raised to talk to a lady through a screen door."

"What was that you said?"

Hickum knew she had heard him, but he repeated it anyway, adding: "And I can just look at you and tell you're not the sort to have conversations through a screen door, either. Anybody can see that's way yonder too trashy for a lady like you."

She caught her bony little chin in her hand and seemed to think on that for a moment. "It's what's wrong with the world today, people doing business through screen doors. But you can't be too careful, am I right?"

"Right as rain. *Careful* is the watchword."

She squinted her eyes as though to see him better. "*Careful* is the watch . . . what?"

"Word," he said.

"Word? Is that what you said?"

Hickum had not been paying enough attention to what he had been saying. He had to stay focused or he would let himself slip onto automatic pilot and lose her after he already had her moving in his direction.

He nodded his head and said, "Yes, madam. I believe *watchword* is what I said."

"You've started spinning your wheels. You better quit while you're still ahead."

"No doubt the gospel truth. Yes, indeed, I . . . "

But even as he was talking, her hand drifted up and unlatched the door.

Without making a move, Hickum said: "You're a very wise lady. Not many in this old world's going to put one over on you. Noosirree!"

"You can count on it, buster. My face may be red but I wasn't born yesterday," she said.

Hickum gave the Hearty Company Laugh, and at the same time he eased the door open, not knowing if she would allow it or not. She did, though. She left it open while she kept her eye on his metal briefcase as he moved slowly to a low coffee table and set it down on its side.

He straightened up and put one of the Company's Looks on his face, a look that the manual called *the truth can be awful*.

He looked closely at her, judged her age as best he could, and said: "Let me ask you this, madam. Do you suffer from swelling of the joints? Night sweats? Failing eyesight? Thinning hair? Difficulty falling asleep? Or find it hard waking up?"

Was there a goddam woman her age in the whole sorry country who didn't suffer from at least one of the ailments he'd named?

"I don't know as I go around having conversations with total strangers about what I have and what I don't." But her voice had a tremor in it when she spoke, and Hickum knew he had caught the scent of blood spoor, the sweet fragrance of old mortality. And he had known for a long time now that getting mortality into the game could never hurt, no matter what game a man was playing.

"That's more gospel truth right there," he said. "People nowadays don't seem to know what's public and what's private. They just go ahead and tell anything and everything."

The old woman watched him but said nothing. Hickum focused his smile on her with ultimate intensity, and then winked, which made her head snap back as if she'd been slapped.

"I told you my name at the door, Hickum Looney, remember? Don't believe I got yours."

"Don't believe I gave it," she said.

Hickum Looney clasped his hands and remained standing. Every blind in the house was drawn, making the room very dark. She either didn't have any air-conditioning or did not have it on. He had to wait for his eyes to adjust before he could see very clearly. First dimly and then in sharp detail, Hickum saw a man standing in a corner of the room, and it made him jump and grunt as though he had been struck in the stomach. It was a

God's own wonder that it didn't make him scream and bolt for the door, leaving the briefcase behind, so badly did it unnerve him. But squinting harder showed it to be not a man but rather a rubber aspidistra plant. It was very old and very tired and the thick leaves were gray with a thin layer of dust. But it looked for all the world like an old man wearing a ruined hat.

"What's that?" she said. She had stopped on the other side of the coffee table and not taken her eyes off the briefcase.

"What's what?"

"You grunted," she said.

"Why would I grunt?"

"How would I know? Why'd you show up at my door with a suitcase full of soap?"

"Briefcase," he said.

"What?"

"That on the table there is not a suitcase, it's a briefcase."

"Full of soap?" she said.

"Full of soap."

"You still grunted."

"Not me. Not today."

She regarded him for a moment and then said, "If that was not a grunt I heard, maybe we better leave it alone and get on with the business at hand, because if what you say is true, I may be on the edge of the last deep hole and just about to slide in."

He said: "You're too hard on yourself. You're still a fine figure of a woman."

"I'll tell you, buddy boy, you make a move on me and I'll dial nine-one-one so fast it'll make your head swim. They've got a place for salesmen gone bad."

He dropped his eyes to her hands, joined over her stomach by twisted, large-jointed fingers. Then he called on a voice that was deep with authority, a voice that had been given him by the Boss, along with the soap, the metal briefcase, the *Manual for Presentation of Products*, and everything else that had made him the salesman he had become.

He pulled himself up but restrained his desire to go all the way to tiptoe, tilted his chin upward, and called on the voice that the Company Manual insisted would open the gates of heaven themselves. "I am an honorable man doing an honorable job with an honorable product. Now, would you please sit down, Mizz . . . , sit down, Mizz . . . ?"

"Ida Mae," she said in a curiously subdued voice hardly more than a whisper.

" . . . sit down, Mizz Ida Mae. There are other of God's children waiting."

"Waiting?" she said, her eyes going wide to show red broken veins at their edges.

"For me," he said, still in the Company voice, "for me and the soap to save them."

The business about soap and God's children waiting for him to save them was something that had only occurred to him once he got inside the house. It just seemed to go with the decor, with the dusty aspidistra plant wearing a hat, or something that looked like a hat, in the corner of the living room, crushed, dry, and hopeless. But now that the lie had come to him, there was nothing to do but see what he could squeeze out of it. The Boss would have been pleased that he noticed it and, further, that he planned to milk it.

He snapped the hasps in the front of his briefcase and lifted the lid. It was lined in red velvet. Round jars were held in round slots. Each jar had a different-colored lid on it. And on each lid of each jar was a single letter, each letter drawn in elaborate Germanic script.

Slowly, she traced out each of the letters with a rigid, thick-jointed finger. As she touched each letter there in the dim little room, she pronounced each of them as soft as breathing: "S-A-I-P-P-U-A-K-I-V-I-K-A-U-P-P-I-A-S."

chapter

two

It had been a good day, an unprecedented day, for Hickum Looney. As he eased his dirty yellow dented Dodge through bumper-to-bumper traffic, he whistled a gay little tune, his favorite. It had been a Coca-Cola kind of day and he was whistling a Coca-Cola commercial from a good while back—he couldn't remember how long—five or ten years, maybe even longer. And he loved it so much, he invariably saved it for those days when sickness, suffering, death, and the rankest kind of blasphemy—all subjects begging for confession and absolution—opened every door he knocked upon or responded to every bell he rang. But not one of his days over the last quarter century could match this one.

Without quite being able to help it, he suddenly pushed back in his seat, stretched his neck, and sang: "Co-o-oke is the *re-al* thing."

He pounded the steering wheel and bounced on the seat to

keep the beat and sang at the top of his voice: "And so is Hickum Looney!"

He was doing the commercial again while he was stopped at a red light, substituting his own name for Coca-Cola, when he looked over and saw four men in rumpled suits, ties loosened and crooked at their necks. Only one of them was pointing at him, but they were all stretching their faces in tired smiles. They looked suspiciously like salesmen themselves. Seedy, down at the heel, supplicants all. Even their smiles looked like pleas for help.

It embarrassed Hickum, and he covered his mouth with the back of his hand and yawned, his mouth pulled to its limits, until the light changed and they drove away. As soon as they were out of sight, Hickum tried the commercial again just to prove to himself that he could do it. Hell, he wasn't embarrassed. He tried the commercial jingle again but he found it impossible to do. He was more embarrassed than ever. Suddenly he felt like he would be embarrassed for the rest of his life.

It should not have been so. He should have been elated, but if he wasn't, so what? It had been, by any measure, his greatest day—ever. To his absolute delight, today had been like touring a huge neighborhood exclusively reserved for the sick and dying. Even the occasional cirrus cloud that floated across the blue Florida sky seemed stamped with a death's-head. Consequently, he had filled not one but twelve order books. An all-time record. He had never even dreamed of such a thing. The highest number he had ever heard of was nine filled order books in one working day. And it had taken the Boss himself to turn that trick.

Hickum Looney had been lucky enough to stumble onto Ida Mae and she had insisted on taking him through an unbroken string of tragedy. A gift. Nothing but a gift. It was damn near impossible to sell anything to a happy person. Serious injury or sickness or any near-death experience was another matter. Grief would pay any price to buy anything, no matter how absurd the thing for sale was. Such was the nature of hope, or of courage, depending on who was looking at it or who was putting the name on it.

If the grief was deep enough, the world and everything in it was transformed into salvation of one kind or another. Hickum had always thought that a man broken badly enough in body and spirit could be sold anything at any price, and the more broken and troubled he was, the easier it was to sell him. Who else but poor, broken, and troubled men and women could be sending all that money to all those preachers on television who daily told all the poverty-ridden, death-stricken listeners who could hear their voices that the first thing they had to do was quit taking their medicine and quit eating so much food and quit trying to stay warm in the winter and send every cent they had to the Service of God? Then magically the address of the Service of God appeared on the screen.

Ida Mae was the classic prospect. Hickum knew she would buy his soap the moment his gaze had fallen upon her arthritic fingers, which she held over her swollen stomach. From long experience, he could see there was so much hurt in her that she desperately needed to be rid of it. And after she was rid of it, she needed care. She needed hope. She needed love. And Hickum Looney had it all, or at least he had everything she needed, right there in the Company Manual in his metal briefcase. Hickum Looney believed that to be the truth. He had no alternative. Without belief, how could he get up every morning and go on with the work of Soaps For Life?

She had looked down at the briefcase. "What's in it?"

"I told you, soap."

"What kind?"

"The kind with wonder-working power," he said.

Her milk white face darkened. "I'm an atheist," she said. "Been one a long time. Hope to stay one. So don't try to work that one on me."

He leaned back on the couch and put his hands behind his head. Then he brought his hands down and put them between his knees, leaned forward, and looked serious. "I would have taken you for a believer of the gospel, the way you were talking at the door."

She leaned over the table. Her eyes were fixed on him and he could smell her. Her odor was thick and heavy, an odor that Hickum Looney always associated with things long enclosed.

"I'm not responsible for what you take or how you take it, but I'm an atheist. Believe it," she said, "because it's true. And they drove me to it is what they did. I've been sold more shit in the name of Jesus than there is rice in China. Oh yeah, I know that one. Give your money to Jesus but send it to my address."

Hickum Looney said: "Well said. "Yessireebob, well said! Me? I try to cover the waterfront. I'm everything to every man and to every God, dead and dying. I'm a believer and a disbeliever. I go out when I come in. Janus faced, too. At least they called it that in olden times, or at least that's what the Company has to say on the matter anyway. I'm also a man who never wanted much and at the same time a man who always wanted everything. Put your mind to working on that once in a while when you think the mystery has gone out of your life and out of this tired old planet we live on."

Everything he'd said had been a direct quote from the Company Sales Manual.

Ida Mae sat very still and appeared a little stunned. "I think I'd prefer not to. You're not making a whole lot of sense, either, you know that?"

"Sense and nonsense?" Hickum said. "It come to me a long time ago that entirely too much is made of the difference."

"I'm afraid I'll have to ask you to leave."

She breathed on him and he smelled the old friendly and final odor of death. It had never bothered him. Actually he had come to enjoy it. Everybody's breath to one degree or another smelled of death to Hickum Looney. Most people couldn't smell it because they were afraid of the truth. But if a man was not afraid of the truth but loved it instead, then the odor of death was heavy everywhere, ubiquitous as the air he breathed, and it kept his own mortality firmly fixed in his mind. Or at least that was what the Company Manual guaranteed in boldface print. And the salesmen believed, because believing was the first condition of employment.

"I can't," he said.

"Can't what?"

"Leave."

The quilted flesh of her face pulled tightly smooth: "You'll leave my house when I tell you to."

"Perhaps," he said. "But you wouldn't tell me to leave."

"And why, may I ask, would I not?"

"Because you're a lady." He held up his palm to stop her when she opened her mouth to answer. "No denials, please. We are both too mature for childish games. Breeding tells. It always tells."

"How tacky," she said. "You only want to sell me containers of soap that somebody has made you carry from door to door every day of your life like a beast of burden, and you have the nerve to talk to me about breeding. That is purely tacky."

"There," he said. "Don't you feel better now? Nothing clears the air like the truth."

"What would you know of the truth?" she said.

"Not nearly as much as some people. But just enough to know that you need to buy what I've got more than I need to sell it to you. The people who buy from me always do."

When the Boss was out giving a selling demonstration, he could deliver that line about people needing what he had to sell with such fiery passion that people often fainted, especially the afflicted and the very old.

Hickum indicated the chair directly across the coffee table from him. "Would you sit with me for a moment?"

"No."

"Oh, please don't be hard to get along with and make my day

harry crews

more difficult than it already is. Why wouldn't you sit with me for a moment?"

"You forget where you are," she said. "I am not required to give reasons or offer excuses for what I do in my own home."

"I know that," he said. "But you'll end up feeling compelled to explain it if you don't sit. Noblesse oblige."

"I would not have thought you to know such a phrase."

"I don't, not really," he said. "It's in the Company Manual."

"What else is in the manual?"

"Everything," he said. "Everything, even my heart's most secret desires."

"How delightfully corny," she said. "You manage to be disgusting without even trying."

"Actually, that was not in the manual," he said. "I made that one up myself."

"I thought as much."

She had thought wrong. It was on page 32, subhead B, the part that dealt with False Poetry. The Company thought—correctly, as it turned out—that it would not do for the manual to be too consistent, so they deliberately threw in errors and bad diction and greeting-card poetry in an effort to make the salesmen seem more nearly human. The crooked made the straight seem straighter. The rankly false made ordinary truth seem gospel, or so the Company Sales Manual insisted.

Hickum Looney had found out a long time ago, the Boss of the Company was nobody to fool around with. He'd nail you hand and foot every time and he didn't appear to give much thought to what he nailed you to or nailed you with or how long or how much you bled. He could be a kind and generous man, but he could also be a real sonofabitch, merciless and unforgiving, and there never seemed to be rhyme or reason to explain the kind of man he was at any given moment.

Ida Mae made a little sound in her throat, not a word exactly, just a little humming that was close to a word.

"What?" he said.

"I thought I heard my name."

"You might have heard it but not from me."

"Carrying that suitcase around in this weather may have touched you a little. The sun can cause an awful affliction, if you know what I mean."

"Perhaps."

"You like that word, don't you?"

"*Perhaps?*"

"You say it a lot."

"I mean it a lot. *Perhaps* is as close as I've ever been able to get to anything."

She pointed to the metal briefcase on the table. "What about that?"

"Perhaps it'll save you. Perhaps it won't. Then again perhaps it's all up to you. Perhaps you can see the problem."

"What makes you think I need saving?"

"It's not what I think, it's what you think. Do you know Shakespeare?"

"Never had the pleasure," she said.

"Aww, now come on, Miss Ida Mae, you know what I mean."

"As it happens, I do."

"Perhaps you'll remember this then: 'Nothing is true or false but thinking makes it so.' I've always thought it might be the truest thing he ever wrote."

"That's not a direct quote. He didn't write it that way. What you quoted was really a kind of sloppy paraphrase. Did you get that out of the Company Manual, too?"

"Yep."

"No, you didn't."

"Miss Ida Mae, you must be able to read minds. You've caught me again."

"I knew there wasn't a Company Manual in the Western world that quoted Shakespeare—even badly."

She was wrong, again. He had quoted from chapter 10, page 23. Ten was the Shakespeare chapter. And it was invaluable.

Shakespeare was a source of total contradiction. If you wanted to prove the truth of any subject, go to Shakespeare. If you wanted to disprove what Shakespeare had just got through proving, go back to Shakespeare. If you knew where to look he would always obligingly disprove himself for you.

Shakespeare was like the Bible that way. He could and would go either way on any subject. If you didn't like his position on a subject, keep reading. Sooner or later he'd change. Shakespeare did not seem to give much thought to what might or might not be true. He only wanted to win the point at issue.

The Boss of Soaps For Life loved Christ the same way he loved Shakespeare. Christ himself would go either way on any issue. The Boss loved him for that if for nothing else. In some of his three-hour tirades from the podium at the annual convention, the Boss would completely break down and cry.

"Nu couldn't pay a man nike Nesus Christ what he was worth. If I had Nesus, I could rule ne world. Wit Nesus, I'd be bigger nan Wal-Mart and IBM both together. I know in my heart nat Nesus Christ could write more orders nan all my other salesmen put together. Nat's one goddam ning I know about Nesus Christ."

Had he been religious, Hickum would have thought it blasphemous the way the Boss carried on, but since he himself believed that every man everywhere was only flesh that would eventually return to the nitrogen cycle, he did not spend too much time thinking about it.

Things did happen, though. They did happen, things did. The business with the dime and Ida Mae and what Hickum had done was brand new. It had amazed Hickum as much as it had Ida Mae. When he took the dime out of his pocket, he didn't have the slightest notion of what he meant to do with it. The dime lay in his open palm with Ida Mae looking at it. Hickum was staring at it too. He could not have done otherwise.

"Your left wrist hurts very badly, doesn't it?" he said.

"You wouldn't believe how I suffer with it," she whispered, as though to keep a secret.

"You're wrong there," he said. "I believed it when I stepped through the door." Her left wrist was badly discolored and swollen half again as big as the right one. "But," he said without raising his eyes from the dime, "the only real bedrock problem we have here is whether or not you believe."

She stared at the dime. "It's got to where I can't even lift my frying pan with that arm and it's aluminum, too. I haven't been able to lift my good cast iron one in years."

"Rub a little bit of this soap on the dime," he said.

There was silence during which they did not raise their eyes from the dime.

When Ida Mae did speak, her voice fell between them in a soft, uninflected monotone. "Which one of the bottles you want me to get the soap from?"

"You'll get it from the right place," he said. "I wouldn't worry about it."

She'd get it from the right place? He wouldn't worry about it? What was he saying and what on earth had he meant by it? But then he made himself calm down by reminding himself that the manual clearly stated that each customer's pain was different, and the Boss himself emphasized that it did not matter what the salesman said or promised as long as he sold the product. He was only trying to sell, sell as much as he could. That was the way it had always been. That and nothing else. Selling as much as he could day in and day out, the salesman served not only the Boss but the customer as well.

"I'm not so sure about this," she said.

"It's not my wrist," he said. "I believe you'll get the right soap. That's what I believe. What do you believe, Ida Mae?"

She touched the lids of several bottles before her finger stopped on a yellow one decorated with an elaborate S.

"This is the one," she said. Then: "I believe."

"Open it," he said.

"Could you hold the bottle for me while I do the lid? I don't think my bad wrist can hold it."

"That's what I'm here for," he said, "to help."

harry crews

He held the jar and she unscrewed the lid. It was only then that she raised her eyes from the dime to look at him.

"What?" she said.

"Touch the soap with your finger and then touch the dime with the soap."

She did as he told her. Hickum took up the dime. "Let me have your hand."

She gave him her hand and he drew it toward him and placed the dime soap side down on the swollen place where he could see the pulse beating under her fine, nearly translucent skin. He could not even guess at what might be going on in her mind, much less the turmoil in her tired old heart, and he was completely at a loss about what he ought to do next. Fear splashed over him as quickly and totally as if it had been water thrown from a bucket.

He heard himself say: "The dime is warm and growing warmer. That heat's spreading." He felt totally absurd and he wondered if she felt how essentially crazy all this was. "Your entire wrist is hot now, not uncomfortable, but still hot." He didn't know how long he could go on with this. He was making it all up and had no notion at all where it might lead. But this was the way it was supposed to work. With every customer he had to reinvent the way to sell the soap. The Boss called it creative salesmanship, and it was covered in detail in the manual.

"Oh, sacred Mary, Mother of God!" she said in a rushing whisper. "Look at my wrist."

He looked at it and it looked exactly as it had before. The swelling and the discoloration were still as they had been. Nothing had changed. Nothing.

She said: "On the holy eyes of Jesus, you've cured me."

He was addled and startled, and more than that, he was frightened. "Be careful with that Jesus business," said Hickum in a voice that sounded in his own ears like that of a beggar. "You're the atheist, remember?"

"Not anymore," she said.

He threw his hands out between them, his palms facing her.

"I'm a soap-selling fool from east Tennessee, but I never signed on for anything like fooling with Jesus."

The Boss would not have approved. But Jesus scared the hell out of Hickum, not because he was a believer but because he was superstitious.

"You know where I've got to take you?" she said, a little breathless. "I've got to take you to meet my friends."

"Ida Mae, I'm selling soap today."

"They'll buy." Her old, milky, quilted skin had gone grayer still. "I will testify for this product and the rewards it brings. I'll testify and they'll buy."

"You'd do that for me?"

"I'll do that for the soap," she said in a whisper, and then after a moment of thinking, still in a whisper: "I'll do that for you too." Another silence as her brow drew together and her skin broke into a fine web of wrinkles. "But you and the soap are the same thing, if you know what I mean."

Hickum nodded vigorously although he did not have the slightest notion what she meant. Still, he shuddered at the thought it might be true.

She gave him a coy, sly look that, despite her age, reminded Hickum of the look of a young girl when she first feels her sexuality begin to beat in her blood.

"I saw that the word was a palindrome when I spelled it out," she whispered. "I saw that it spelled the same backward as it does forward: S-A-I-P-P-U-A-K-I-V-I-K-A-U-P-P-I-A-S. I'm betting it's the longest one-word palindrome in the world."

He felt the skin over his heart go cold. She was, of course, right. Although he had never told anyone, he himself believed the word to be wonderfully incredible, totally impossible, and at the same time silly beyond saying, because the word meant *door-to-door soap salesman.*

She opened her mouth and showed him the tip of her old dry tongue that was as gray as death. She closed her mouth and said, still in a dry whisper: "A palindrome ends where it begins, and lives inside itself, a self-contained, self-justifying madness." She waited a moment, her dry tongue tracing her thin desiccated lips that now held a smile he did not like and that he thought might not even be a smile. "Be careful, Hickum Looney," she said. "Take nothing for granted."

"I'll try. God knows I'll try."

chapter

three

Hickum turned into an asphalt parking lot in front of a blindingly white three-story building of some brutal design, full of sharp edges and abrupt angles. Sloping away from either end of the building was a carefully tended, geometrically designed garden of beautiful, varicolored flowers. But the lovely, delicate flowers only served to make the brutal design of the building seem even more brutal. Perhaps that was why it always reminded Hickum of a bunker on a battlefield, even though he had never seen a bunker or been on a battlefield. Every regional office of the Company throughout the country was of this design. The design had originated with the Boss. The little harelipped demon had his touch on the pulse of everything in the Company. He was a pushing, pounding, probing, hands-on kind of owner as he never tired of writing in memos and directives and screaming at the annual sales convention.

He would cat-dance across the convention stage in a frantic little jig, moving as though the soles of his feet were on fire, stop at the podium, smiling, a single great square tooth gleaming through the inverted V of his upper lip, and thunder: "I'm a nand's-on nind of an owner. I push, I probe, nand I pound. I do it because I nove nu. By Nod and by damn I *do* nove each and every one of nu nat carry my soap through all the long streets of ne great cities of ne country. Net all ne people everywhere know what I've fabricated for ne fullness of nair lives!" His salesmen always went a little nuts when he told them he loved them. "Nure my troops nand I mean na take nu na levels of greatness nu never imagined."

And the salesmen would roar their approval. Several throughout the enormous convention hall would enthusiastically bash their heads together, not because they liked doing it but because they could not help doing it, much as football players on a playing field bashed one another's heads about in uncontainable spasms of joy.

As Hickum eased his dented yellow Dodge into slot number eleven, he realized just how tired he was. Even his bones seemed to hurt with exhaustion. He could not remember a day when he had covered more ground, worked harder. But the entire surface of his skin tingled when he let himself think about the fact that he had done that day what had never been done in the history of the Company by anybody. Not even the Boss on his best day ever had brought in twelve completed order books.

Despite his mutilated mouth, or perhaps because of it, the little man would sometimes show up unannounced at regional offices throughout the country to take an inexperienced young salesman or sometimes one of the older experienced salesmen out for a day of selling. But nobody had ever filled twelve books of new orders. Hickum Looney had crossed into virgin territory.

Hickum got out and stood thinking beside the open door of the car. It would never have happened without Ida Mae. Hers was the energy of a buzz saw out of control. Amazing! She, not he, had made it happen. She had taken him through enclaves of men and women who were sick and dying from the same incurable disease: *age*.

They had tramped from one elderly village to the next elderly village, from one home to the next home. Some of the homes and villages were run for profit and some of them were not. Some of them were affiliated with one of the Protestant denominations and some of them were not. Some of them were supported by the mother church in Rome and some of them not. But Ida Mae had worked each and every one of them with equal fervor while Hickum Looney carried the display case of soap and watched, utterly amazed.

And he was a man who believed in giving credit where credit was due. If anybody wanted to know how such an incredible feat of selling had been accomplished (as all the salesmen might, every last one of them), Hickum was prepared to give Ida Mae the credit, all of it if necessary, simply because she deserved it. At least he thought he would give her the credit. He paused and looked off toward the west, where the sun had not yet gone down into the waveless water of the Gulf of Mexico. He was late, but with twelve order books filled, he didn't care.

Of course he would give Ida Mae credit. Wasn't he a fair man who always played by the rules? No answer came behind his question, and he stood very still watching dark thunderheads beginning to rise on the western horizon. He listened carefully for the little voice that always spoke in his head at times like these, the same voice that—in rare moments of doubt—assured him of his own basically decent morality. And the voice might have come if the macadam that had been soaking up the sun all day had not suddenly made him aware that his tender feet were cooking through the thin soles of his shoes.

Hickum grabbed the metal briefcase out of his car and hurried toward the Company office. No one was allowed to go home in the afternoon until all the salesmen had reported in. Every last one of the parking slots had been filled with the exception of Hickum Looney's, filled with the dented and yellow Dodges the

harry crews

salesmen had no alternative but to drive. The Boss thought driving dented and dirty yellow Dodges generated sympathy for his salesmen and made the work of selling easier.

When it was pointed out to him that American businessmen and their salesmen always tried to look like millionaires, particularly if they were on the edge of bankruptcy and dying of despair, the Boss would scream: "I made my fortune nand built my nompany nand my name doing everything my way!" He would go into a characteristic rapid spin on his tiny and fiery little feet, and then suddenly stop and point one of his long, spoon-shaped fingers at the person nearest him. "Neep ne bastards guessing! Near me? *Do nu near me?*"

And not only did everyone hear him, but everyone also believed him too. Because even if he was small, ugly, and handicapped by his speech impediment, he was also a millionaire many times over. And his being a millionaire made them forgive him every fault he may have had in the past, had now, or might have in the future. His salesmen loved him simply because he had made money, and that had made believers of them all.

But as Hickum found out, there were believers and there were believers. It had taken Ida Mae with her twisted little-girl curls and her pleated Gypsy skirt and her mincing little-girl walk to make a more profound believer out of Hickum than he had ever been before—not in God, which he dismissed as a hoax and a fraud, but in his own powers to control what happened in his life.

What he was most deeply and immediately interested in at the moment was doubling the amount of soap he sold in a day. He'd done that and more with Ida Mae's help, and up until the very moment he started through the door of his office building, he had taken it for granted that he would tell everyone about her and all that she had done. But now he was not so sure, and the knowledge that he might not do what was right made his face burn with shame. Along with everyone else, he thought himself to be a deeply moral man.

The interior of the Soaps For Life building always reminded

Looney of a public restroom. It had, the first day he had set foot in it, and after all these years it still did. He tried not to think about it because he was frightened by what thinking such a thing might imply about himself. But he thought about it anyway. He always did. For all he knew, every other salesman thought the same thing. He wished he knew. But he had never asked. He had wanted to but he had not. He tried to force himself to think about Ida Mae and all the credit he was going to heap upon her old graying head. Then it occurred to him that he might not heap credit or anything else on her graying head. He had begun to suspect that he might not even mention her.

To keep his mind off that ignominious thought, he looked at all the smooth tile and plaster and plastic and glass and fake marble and remarked again the total absence of decoration— not a single framed print or picture, not a plant of any kind, whether hanging or potted, fake or real—and told himself that, goddammit, he was not only entitled to think anything he wanted to about such a place but also about the people in it. But all he got for his trouble was the abrupt, almost overwhelming aware- ness of a ubiquitous odor that lingered everywhere about the building, in every room, hallway, and closet. The odor was of a particular and peculiar disinfectant. The only other place Looney had ever smelled it was in the urinal of a public restroom. He lowered his head and hurried for the stairs.

There were no elevators in any of the Soaps For Life buildings because that was the way the Boss wanted it. And he never explained the reason. He didn't have to. His employees had figured it out to their own satisfaction. The Boss had certain notions about physical fitness, never fully articulated by him and consequently never fully understood by his employees. Every worker in the Company, though, knew the Boss's position on how information ought to pass between him and the people who worked for him.

"If I want nu na know something, I'll tell nu. If I want na know something, I'll ask nu."

Everybody at Soaps For Life knew this, but nobody had ever

harry crews

seen it written anywhere and nobody could ever recall hearing the Boss say it.

But some facts were not in dispute. All company office buildings were three stories, no more, no less. The salesmen's offices and the big conference room were always on the third floor. All the secretaries had cubicles on the first floor. The Boss believed in keeping the salesmen away from their secretaries as much as possible. Although a short man, the Boss invariably took the stairs two at a time going up and two at a time coming down. Nobody had ever successfully kept up with him, not even the very young and the very strong, although many had tried. He was nothing but a blur once he had his full stride, and when he visited a regional office, he sometimes stood about with a stop-watch timing his workers as they went up and came down the stairs. Sometimes on one of his random visits he took up his position on the stairs with his stopwatch for an entire day, shout-ing encouragement while salesmen and janitors flew past him. Without it ever being stated, the assumption was that whether the Boss was visiting or not, everyone was expected to take the stairs in a full-bore sprint.

Some did, others did not. Hickum Looney always tried his best to give his best. So even today, with the soles of his feet tender from the hot sidewalks and the even hotter parking lot, the very marrow of his bones aching from exhaustion, and his vision blurring from sweat and the reflected glare of the sun, he attacked the stairs in a hip-hop stride with his briefcase banging against his thin legs. But after two flights he was gasping for breath and he had to slow to a walk.

The conference room was at the end of the hall. The door was open and Hickum knew the salesmen were all waiting for him. So why was there no sound—none at all—coming from the room? He stopped and cocked his head to listen. Nothing. But tobacco smoke was boiling out of the room, so the salesmen had to still be in there. Hickum eased up to the door and looked in.

The salesmen sat with their fingers tented under their chins, their elbows on the desktops in front of them and thick cigars stuck in their faces. It was a physical attitude the Boss took and sometimes held for as long as half an hour, each minute of which seemed insufferably long, as though each of them was trying to see who could hold his breath the longest. The room was so full of blue smoke that Hickum thought it could probably be cut up and made into work shirts. On the teleconference screen at the front of the room sat the Boss, fingers tented under his chin and his elbows on the desk in front of him and smoke boiling from around the cigar jammed deeply into his mouth through his split upper lip.

Each of the salesmen's faces held an expression that was a copy of the look that hardened on the Boss's face when he wanted to signify that after long thought he had decided that there was no hope for his salesmen, his company, or himself. He often reminded them at such times that if this were Japan there would be no honorable option left the entire sales force but a collective gut ripping. Every last one of them would have to commit ritual seppuku and watch dispassionately as their entrails and blood spilled onto the floor in front of them. The Boss often wondered aloud why he could not command the loyalty of a single one of his employees the way a goddam Jap could. If only one of his people would disembowel himself, sales would quadruple in a month. It was his opinion that there was nothing like blood and guts spilling onto the floor to light a fire under everybody else. But so far, he'd had no luck with that, nor did he expect to. He said Americans had not grown soft, they had always been soft.

Peering in the door through the cloud of blue smoke, Hickum stood very still watching the salesmen with their tented fingers under their chins and their defeated faces, and Hickum was watching, too—the Boss, on the teleconference screen. Hickum Looney knew he had just missed the Japanese-gut-ripping lecture. And besides that, Hickum knew that the length of the teleconference had been extended, to wait for him to show up. Thank God for Ida Mae. Thank God that in his briefcase were twelve completed and signed order books, a new and incredible company record, because the truth was he had forgotten this was a tele-conference day.

From his inner jacket pocket he took a long, thick cigar—a cigar supplied to him and the other salesmen by the Boss—bit the end of it off, lit it, coughed, and then puffed like a bellows until he was nearly hidden in smoke, even though he was always afraid he would puke on his shoes when he had to light one up, because he had never even smoked cigarettes and he generally became light-headed with a storming attack of nausea by the second or third puff of a cigar.

And if that were not bad enough, an uncontrollable bout of diarrhea often appeared unannounced. Not always, but often. The random nature of these green-apple two-steps made it all the worse. With everything else he had to live with in his life, he knew that at any moment and totally without warning he might feel the hot juice of his bowels running down his legs and filling his shoes if he lit a cigar. Whether or not he lit one, however, was not in his control.

He had no choice. For reasons nobody understood, cigars had become fashionable, so fashionable in fact that it caused movie actresses and actors (whom the Boss inevitably referred to as triumphs of advertising over good sense, which made him love them all the more) to come together for cigar-smoking parties that apparently had no other purpose than for the sleek, golden, blindingly beautiful men and women who graced the silver screen to sit around and blow smoke in one another's faces and cough and laugh and generally have a good time.

The Boss, a student—amateur though he was, he was still a rabid student—of physical behavior in men and women, would immediately pick up any fad or fashion that raged through the movie colony, and his salesmen, without ever being told or asked, would immediately do as the Boss had done. In his earlier days he had been in the habit of taking his salesmen to the ballet every night of their yearly sales conference, which lasted a full week. He had been overwhelmed by the long-limbed bodies impossibly soaring through the air, hanging there at times as if they never meant to come down.

But somebody, somewhere, had mentioned that they were all fags and lesbians, so none of what they did counted for anything in the world of real men and women. Nobody knew who had the nerve to tell the Boss such a thing. But that was the rumor, and since in the Soaps For Life Company, rumor was all anybody had to go on, it became the truth. When the cigar craze came along, the Boss knew he had found something that would give his Company and everybody in it a boost. But then he saw Stacy Keach with a cigar clamped in his slightly mismatched lips and he started to shut down the entire experiment in smoking.

Then it was pointed out to the Boss that Stacy Keach was only one of the thousands of beautiful people—and besides, Keach wasn't really very beautiful, looked about half sick actually. He could easily be discounted. Since the Boss was truly fond of the cigars—not smoking them, but using them to plug the unseemly split in his lip—he decided doing something Stacy Keach did was a small price to pay for a partial disguise for his devastated mouth, a mouth he talked about constantly because (or so Hickum Looney was convinced) he hated it constantly.

Hickum Looney crept into the room and eased his thin shanks into a chair. His chair was of the sort that schoolchildren use, as were all the other chairs in the room. The salesmen sat hunkered over their desktops as if in deep thought, steadily puffing on their cigars. Their order books for the day were stacked neatly in front of them. Hickum opened his briefcase and carefully placed his own order books in front of him in two separate stacks. The other salesmen's heads swung slowly to watch him. The more order books he took from his briefcase, the harder they puffed their cigars. By the time he pulled out the twelfth order book from his briefcase, the ends of their cigars were all glowing with red ash and their faces were entirely leached of color.

"We're all present now, Boss," one of the salesmen said.

It could have been anybody who spoke. They were all equals

at Soaps For Life. They all supervised one another and reported directly to the Boss. There were no managers or office heads or organizers or overseers of any kind. At least that was the theory. But since it was only a theory—along with everything else—nobody was really sure. The Boss stayed on top of things through random, unannounced visits and through the use of teleconferencing, which he was using right now and which none of the salesmen really understood, but which they all pretended to understand, and each of them would have died and gone to hell with his back broken before admitting ignorance about the teleconference, the Boss's toy.

From the Boss to the salesmen there was video and audio. From the salesmen to him there was only audio, provided by an open mike for the entire room. That meant there could be no coughing, sneezing, shuffling of feet, clearing of throats, or any other noise that the open mike might pick up. They had to sit as quietly as schoolchildren, which was exactly the analogy used by the Boss: They were the children, he was the teacher.

On the enormous screen at the front of the room, the Boss untented his fingers, then laced them together and cracked all his knuckles. He moved very slowly, and everything about him suggested that he was very tired, tired to the point of being on the verge of falling asleep. Except for his eyes, which never looked anything but angry. They were shot with veins and they bulged from their sockets in a way that suggested madness. But his salesmen were used to his eyes looking like those of a madman. Being used to them, though, did not mean they weren't still terrified by them. They did not know quite what to make of them. The single thing they all agreed upon was that his eyes were not the eyes of a normal man.

"We are a nittle nate, are we not, Nickum?" asked the Boss, speaking with his inverted, misshapen mouth clamped tightly about his cigar.

"Yessir," Hickum said.

"Do nu know what its nosts ne Company na keep nis tele-nomference awaiting nour pleasure, Nooney?"

"Yessir."

They all knew what the teleconference cost. He had lectured them at great length about the small fortune he was forced to spend for the uplink at his mansion in Atlanta, the downlinks at the individual regional offices, the rent for satellite time, the cost of dishes that were necessary to receive the signal from the satellites, and the capital outlay for every other component of teleconferencing, not the least of which—he was always careful to emphasize—was his own time.

"Nand now was it out nair for nu today, Nooney?"

The Boss's voice had dropped abruptly out of its gritty, insistent tone and into that of a concerned parent. It always did when he was talking about the actual business of selling and how much money a salesman might have made for Soaps For Life in a given day.

"Good, sir. It was good."

"Nood? One nerd? Nu nive us a single nerd after keeping us waiting an unseemly length of nime? Nell me. How nood was it?"

Hickum Looney looked at his order pads stacked neatly in two piles in front of him. He raised his right hand and gently placed it on the pads. Too bad the Boss couldn't see what he had done that day.

"It was very good," Hickum said.

"And now nood might nat be?"

Hickum Looney could feel the other salesmen staring at him. He could feel them frantically sucking and puffing on their cigars. His own cigar had gone out. It often did. Through the dense fog of smoke, the Boss's face seemed not to be on a screen at all but to float there at the front of the room.

Hickum squinted at the wavering face of the Boss and slowly tapped his stack of order pads. He wished the Boss could see what he had there in front of him. It was an all-time company record, but he could see the other salesmen refused to believe it. They no doubt thought that half the orders in the books were blank.

"I sold more than I've ever sold before. That's why I'm late. I was selling like a house burning down. It's a record."

The Boss stiffened. He snatched the cigar out of his mouth. It came out of his lips with a sucking *pop.*

"I always have na use a whip na drive all nu people about nike beasts, and nu have na nerve na nell me nure late because nu stayed out nair and sold of nure own free will?"

This was as good a time as any to tell him about Ida Mae. Hickum had not stayed out selling of his own free will; Ida Mae had kept him out. But he thought it best—at least for now—to leave Ida Mae out of it.

"I don't think anybody would have quit and come into the office if they were selling the way I was selling." He patted the order books stacked in front of him. "There's the proof of what I've done, right in front of me."

The Boss sighed and mumbled something under his breath. "Nooney, nis damn ning only noes one way. When will nu learn I nan't see nu? What is it new've got?"

"Twelve books. I filled twelve books of orders."

The Boss sat very still for a long time. A tic that none of them had ever seen before developed in his right cheek. The longer he sat, the faster the cheek jumped, until finally the Boss reached up with his right hand and pinched the cheek with the tic in it for a long time, and when he removed his hand, his thumbprint was clearly apparent where the tic had been, and the whole side of his face was mottled.

"Now, Nooney, now? Now nid new do nis ning?"

"It's a long story."

The Boss let his eyes sweep over his other salesmen. "Gentlemen," the Boss said softly.

The entire group turned toward Hickum and in a single voice that was brutally loud, roared: *"Cut the bullshit and the story'll get shorter!"*

It was what the Boss had taught them to scream in order to get to the truth when the Boss suspected one of their kind of lying and, worse, beating about the bush to do it. The point was what he wanted, and the point was all that he would settle for.

Hickum, feeling himself wanting to cry, said: "I'm not lying. The truth's right here in front of me. There's not a lie in anything I've said."

Again the Boss's eyes swept the room. "Gentlemen."

All the other salesmen's heads swung to look at Hickum. Their faces were mottled and twisted. Hickum knew they were only tired and hungry and wanted to go home, but they looked like they wanted to kill him. In a single voice they roared, *"There are lies everywhere and in everything."*

That was something else the Boss believed with all his heart and demanded that his salesmen believe too. Hickum could only shake his head. He was angry but he knew there was nothing to be gained by showing it because he was outnumbered. They'd only beat him down and exhaust him until they made him admit to a lie whether, in fact, he had told one or not. It wasn't their fault. It was only the way the Boss had trained them. Hickum thought of Ida Mae. He may never tell any of these bastards about her now. They didn't deserve her.

"Bickle," said the Boss.

Bickle struggled and bucked, bucked and struggled, until he was able to get out of the child's desk into which he had somehow managed to wedge himself. By the time he got to his feet, he was sweating and his breathing was rapid and shallow as that of a Chihuahua dog. His every attitude clearly showed he was not pleased. Bickle had been with Soaps For Life longer than any other salesman. And he was legendary in what he would attempt in order to sell a kit of Soaps For Life. Nothing was too ridiculous, nothing too dangerous, nothing too cruel. Year in and year out it was either he or Hickum who was the top salesman. Top salesman after the Boss, of course.

Maybe he managed it simply by being so ugly, so monstrous. Over six feet tall and a biscuit away from three hundred pounds, he was the biggest man Hickum had ever seen. A slab of fat nearly a foot thick hung over his belt. His tits were heavy and

harry crews

pendulous under the linen shirts he always wore. And to make everything about him seem even bigger than it was, his head was so tiny that it seemed hardly larger than a cue ball. And the way his features were set into his face frightened Hickum. Bickle's eyes, nose, and mouth were pushed tightly together and buried so deeply in thick red fat that they were hardly distinguishable one from the other.

When a meeting got tedious or in any other way upset the Boss, he turned things over to Bickle, who in the most ordinary of times kept his hands clenched into fists and was known—in moments of extreme agitation—to pound on his dependent breasts until his diminutive face was screwed into a point of what appeared a murderous rage.

"Looney," said Bickle in a high-pitched, lilting voice.

"Yes, Bickle," Hickum answered.

Bickle reached up and wiped at a white froth that had bubbled out of his mouth and hung at his chin. Watching Bickle bring away the froth with the back of his hand, Hickum thought he looked like a rabid dog, but the truth was that underneath all that blustering threat, Hickum knew him to be even worse than a rabid dog and absolutely nobody to mess with.

In a voice that made him sound as though he thought he was talking to an idiot, Bickle demanded: "What are you?"

Hickum Looney knew the answer to that. They all did. It was part of what the Boss called Company Esprit and perhaps the single point the Boss pounded most relentlessly.

"I'm a team player," Looney said.

"You've got your fucking nerve saying you're a team player."

"I said it because it's the truth." He was so afraid of Bickle that it felt like the very marrow in his bones was trembling, but he was doing his best not to show it. He knew what would happen if he did let it show. Hell, it might happen even if he didn't.

"The truth?" A huge bubble of froth swelled between Bickle's lips. "You wouldn't know the truth if it came up and bit you in the ass. For your information, you stupid prick, the truth does not make the Boss unhappy. Does he look happy to you?"

the mulching of america   47

Looney refused to look at the Boss on the television screen.

"No. The answer is *no*, he is not happy." Bickle crossed his thick, meaty arms over his chest. "I'm waiting for you to defend yourself."

"I don't have to defend myself. I haven't done anything wrong," Hickum said.

"Then why is the Boss not happy?" When Hickum Looney kept his eyes on his desk and did not answer, Bickle said: "I'll tell you why he's not happy. You've displeased him mightily. What made you think you could do that and get away with it?"

Hickum kept his eyes averted and did not answer. He could think of nothing to say without mentioning Ida Mae, and he did not want to do that because it would sound like Ida Mae had caused Hickum to set the sales record, which she had.

And if he admitted that, where did that leave him? It left him the way he always thought of himself: a plodder, a peddler of soap who should have been something else, anything else. But he had poured all his life and energy into his briefcase of soap, and it was too late now. A smirk crept over Bickle's tiny, crowded face and he looked around at the other salesmen. As if on prearranged signal, they all smirked too. On the television screen the Boss stoically puffed on his cigar as though he were no part of any of this, could hear none of it.

"And what color underwear are you wearing today, Hickum?"

Hickum could feel the blood rush to his face and his spine stiffen. "You wouldn't dare!"

Bickle looked around the room at his fellow salesmen. As a single voice, they shouted: *"To hell he wouldn't!"*

Hickum looked at the television screen although he knew the Boss could not see him. "Bo-osss . . . "

The Boss took his cigar out of his mouth and examined the well-chewed end of it. "As I nated previously, nand as we all knew anyway, nis is a neam. And dis happens to be a neam decision." He looked up and as if by magic his eyes locked directly on Hickum's. "Nand as even nu must be aware, Nooney, I make nevry neffort na nay out of neam decisions. Nand non't whine, Nooney. Whining is never helpful."

"This isn't right. I sold twelve books of orders, for God's sake," Looney said and realized that he was still whining.

"So new say."

"They're right here in front of me," said Looney, trying to keep himself from screaming, because Bickle was coming toward him and he could not remember what color his drawers were or what shape they were in. He almost never bought any clothes and on the rare occasions when he did, he never bought underwear. He only stopped wearing a pair of drawers when they were so ragged they would no longer hold together.

Hickum lifted his twelve order books toward the television screen. "They're right here! Right in front of me!"

"Nu know nas well nas I know nat I can't see what's in front of nu."

Massive, his face clinched tighter than a fist, Bickle was towering over Hickum now.

"Bickle's here, Boss," said Looney. When he got dressed this morning, he'd never counted on having to show his drawers to the assembled sales staff. "Let Bickle look at the orders and he can tell you."

"I'm ne only one who needs to nook. Nand I will when dey come in."

"Then you're going to call off Bickle, right?"

The Boss kept his cigar in his mouth and held up one hand. He counted off on his fingers. "Number none, new cost nus many man hours by neeping us waiting. Number two, nu say nu shattered the Soaps For Life nail's record—*my record*. I asked nu how. Nid nu nell me? No. Nu give me nome shit about a long story nis what new nid. Nat dog won't hunt, Nickum Nooney."

"Wait a minute. Hell, I'll tell you how it happened. I *want* to tell you."

"Nu had nure chance, Nooney. Now it's Bickle's bidness."

Hickum surprised himself by looking up at Bickle and saying

with genuine anger: "You get away from me, you fucking freak."

Bickle said: "You know how this is played out. Get to it. We're about to find out who the fucking freak is."

"Never in twenty-five years of service to Soaps For Life have I ever been forced to do this." He was whining again but he knew it didn't matter now. Whatever chance he'd had was gone. Bickle looked slowly around the room at the other salesmen. "It's up to you. How is it going to be?"

"Make him give 'em up," growled the other salesmen in a single savage voice.

On the television screen, the Boss, smiling to show a single square tooth, stained and very large, said, "No options, Nickum. Try to nearn from it." Still holding his crazed smile, the Boss got up and walked off camera, leaving nothing on the television screen but an empty chair at an empty table.

From somewhere a large brown paper sack appeared. It had served as somebody's lunch bag and was greasy with dark patches on the sides and bottom. Without a word, the sack was passed from salesman to salesman across the room to Bickle.

Bickle held open the top of the bag. "Personal effects?"

"Get away from me." Hickum's voice was full of outrage, but he felt himself on the edge of tears.

"You heard the Boss say you had no options, and you know it's true." Hickum knew it was true, but he still did not move. Bickle's voice dropped a register and was almost kind when he said, "Make it light on yourself." Bickle waited while Hickum felt the blood beating in his temples. "This happened to me, you know," said Bickle. "It was a long, long time ago. Before you even came to work here. I was nothing but a kid. Can you imagine this happening to you when you're a kid?"

"I can't imagine it happening to anybody."

"But that never caused you to try to help anybody that had to do it, did it?"

In a voice that was little more than a whisper, he said, "No."

From somewhere in the room, a salesman, in a tired, angry

voice, said: "The son of a bitch's kept us waiting too goddam long already. Either he gives 'em up or we take 'em from him."

Hickum Looney got slowly to his feet, unbuckled his belt, took it off, folded it, and put it in the sack. The coins from his front pocket followed that, and then his wallet. He had been looking at the grease-stained sack, but now he raised his eyes to Bickle's face, which was relaxed and held an expression that was not unkindly.

"You'd better put your watch in too. Some really strange things have happened to some of our people who've been put out there without their pants. Mostly they've just made a run for their car and then drove on home and into their garage and it was over. But you'd be surprised how many have had to literally fight for their lives. It seems most people don't quite know what to do with a half-naked man except bash him over the head. But you'll be all right as soon as you make it to your garage."

"I don't have a garage. I live in an apartment."

"I'm sorry to hear that, Looney." And it sounded to Looney as though he really was sorry.

"Then why don't you just let me go?" And Hickum heard in his voice a deeper whine than ever and hated himself for it.

"You know I can't do that. The Boss let the team decide and, well, you know what that means."

"Why on earth does the Boss do this?"

"He thinks a man ought to know what he's made of."

Hickum could feel actual tears in his eyes. "I know what I'm made of. And I'm entirely unsuited for this."

"You may surprise yourself."

"I've forgotten how this actually works. Do I get to keep my shoes?"

"Oh yes," Bickle said. "Now get on with it. The quicker the better. You'll have to carry your car keys in your hand. And be careful not to drop them. It won't be safe to bend over out there. And for God's sake, whatever you do, don't let a cop stop you on the way home. You'll never be able to convince him you're not a pervert looking for little girls to flash." Bickle started grinning when he made the remark about bending over, and by the time he got to the part about the cop and the pervert, he was giggling and he didn't seem to be able to stop. "Sorry," he said. "I know it's not funny."

"No, it's not funny," Hickum Looney said, unzipping his trousers and quickly stepping out of them.

Bickle opened Looney's metal briefcase and put the sack and trousers inside it. "You'll have to leave this here, I'm afraid. And your jacket too. You might use them to cover up with." As though he couldn't quite help it, Bickle looked down. "My God, is that your dick?"

"Of course it's his dick," said one of the salesmen, and the entire room burst into laughter. "What there is of it."

Someone else said, "It's barely bigger than a peanut, a dirty, wrinkled little peanut."

The laughter rose to a kind of scream and Hickum Looney thought it was the kind of sound a lynch mob might make. It frightened him terribly and he bolted for the door and left the entire sales force screaming behind him. Just as he reached the stairs, he felt a thin hot stream of shit slip down the inside of both his legs and into the tops of his over-the-calf socks. Hickum Looney didn't know what was waiting for him on the other side of the door leading to the parking lot, but whatever it was, he knew it had to be better than this. But then a voice as plain as he had ever heard said: *But of course you've been wrong before.*

He wished he could wait for the dark, but he could not. With the way his luck had been running, some of the cleaning crew that worked only at night would come in early and see him lounging about at the door wearing not a pair of pants but ragged drawers that exposed as much as they covered. That would never do. It simply wouldn't. He took a deep breath, pushed the door open, and stepped out into the parking lot, where the air was so heavy with humidity, it felt as though a thick, damp blanket had been thrown over him. The sun had disappeared behind the high, dark thunderheads building in the west. It would not be long before dark. He could be thankful for that, if nothing else. He moved away from the door and stood with his back pressed against the building. He stared off toward one of the gardens of blood red flowers and wondered how long he would have to wait before he found the courage to get to his car.

chapter

four

even with the sun already behind the broken skyline, the parking lot was like a furnace after the air-conditioned building. A raging heat that he did not know if he could bear beat upon his eyes and skin with a palpable force. He instinctively hunkered and held his palms over his raggedy shorts, which his dick insisted upon bouncing out of as he went over the blistering asphalt. He didn't actually walk, and neither did he run. He got along in a kind of hip-hop bounce because the asphalt, made nearly soft now by a long day under an unrelenting sun, was cooking the bottoms of his feet right through the thin soles of his shoes, shoes that he had been meaning to replace for some long time now without quite getting around to it. He made a mental note that he absolutely had to get new shoes and new drawers the first opportunity he had. He must never be caught in this predicament again.

The heat had driven everybody who could afford it into an

air-conditioned building. Strain as he would to see, he could not make out another person anywhere. Not that it mattered very much. There was little that he could make out in any detail, after being in the indirect lighting of Soaps For Life. The whole world exploded now into a blur of colors. He could not make out a single thing that was hard edged and clear.

Ever since he had managed to buy a Lincoln Town Car he had been parking it while he was working directly across the street from his office in the huge semicircle lot of a shopping mall. It was better lighted at night, and during the day, when the weather would allow, filled with foot traffic, all of which made it safer than the Soaps For Life lot. He also did not want the other salesmen to know he had it, or even the Boss for that matter, even though the Boss had repeatedly told the people who worked for him they only had to be in dirty dented yellow Dodges during working hours. Their own private vehicles for their own private use were none of his affair. Hickum had his Lincoln Town Car hidden for one reason: He didn't believe the boss.

Hickum was so blinded and exhausted that if he had not been parking his own private car in the same spot for almost two years, he might never have found it. But he knew the exact place in the exact row it would be in. He looked down the aisle between cars and there was his Lincoln Town Car no more than forty yards away. It had been a demonstrator and then a lease car before he managed to buy it, at a fraction of what it would have cost new. It had twenty-five thousand miles on it when he drove it off the lot, but it was a quality-built automobile and with the proper care—which Hickum Looney was determined to give it even if he had to go hungry himself—it would give him a hundred thousand miles of good service.

Just to look at it made Hickum Looney proud to be an American. Forgetting entirely for the moment that he was half naked, he stood tall, threw his shoulders back, took a good deep breath, and felt himself at one with his luxury car. It was a starburst of light sitting there with the neon lights of the mall reflected off the custom Simonized finish. It was ready to roll. The gas tank was topped off, and the engine was filled with Quaker State motor oil, oil that he changed so often it always looked clean and clear enough for a man to drink. And the whole thing sat on four top-of-the-line gangster whitewalls, each of them filled with air to exactly thirty-two pounds per square inch.

The damn car was perfect. Only perfect. And the United States of America was probably the only place on the entire planet where an average man could have anything that was perfect, especially a perfect luxury car that was so big he could easily imagine that an Oriental family of six could live in it comfortably as well as indefinitely. In ways he could not have named, the Lincoln was a defense against the Boss.

He strode proudly down the aisle of cars to the Lincoln, having completely forgotten that his dick was leading the way by approximately an inch—a brown, wrinkled inch—or that behind him the white cheeks of his ass were flashing like semaphores through his ragged drawers.

Hickum was on the driver's side of the car unlocking the door when he did not so much hear somebody as feel somebody just there on the other side of the Lincoln. He looked up and directly into the eyes of a tall slender girl with a long tight face, freckled and full of fine lines at her temples. She looked no more than eighteen, but her eyes were hard and flat and set deep under her brow. But despite the tight face that was perhaps too long and the fine lines at her temples, Hickum thought her beautiful.

In spite of himself, Hickum instinctively looked down at the nub of his dick poking through his drawers and, below that, his legs, naked except for the black crusty streaks where fear had turned his bowels loose upon him after his encounter with Bickle. The streaks had dried in the heat of the day and looked almost like scars running down the inside of his legs and into the tops of his over-the-calf socks.

"You know which direction is the Wal-Mart in?" Her lips were thin and very nearly immobile even when she was talking.

She made talking look like some kind of showman's trick, as

harry crews

though a ventriloquist might have his hand under the back of her blouse. For the first time Hickum smelled himself. Probably the heat, he supposed. He had no answer for the woman on the other side of the car, because he could no longer remember the question. The heat was cooking all sense and reason out of his skull. Her face had grown steadily darker with rising blood and the corner of her lips pulled up to show square, flat teeth, white and impossibly even.

"You deef and dumb or just what?" she growled.

Hickum knew it was time to pull his professional rabbit out of the hat. He gave her his full frontal selling smile, his deepest, his warmest, the one that showed all of his teeth, right back to his darkened molars. A smile could sometimes win them over when nothing else could.

"My grandmother used to say that," he said, because it was apparent he had to say something, and that was the first thing that came to mind.

She flinched as though he had hit her with a stick. But Hickum had seen that reaction enough times over the last twenty-five years to recognize it for what it was. Anger had made her do it.

"Well, damn my soul to hell," she said in a nasty little voice that made her sound like a young dog barking. "Your own grandmother used to tell you you was deef and dumb? That's a by-God good one!" She looked as though she might bend over and slap her knee, but she didn't.

"No," Hickum said.

"No?" Her lips were tight again and she looked like she had never been pleased by anything in her entire life. "You playing with me?" she said. "Because if you are, you might oughta quit. Do you get my drift? I ain't the sort of person just every Tom, Dick, and Harry plays with."

"I bet you're not," he said, "not a woman like you."

The woman dropped her head straight back again and looked at the solid, darkened sky. "Now he's being sarcastic," she said, "and all I ever asked for or wanted in the first place was for him to tell me the direction the goddam Wal-Mart is in at."

It suddenly occurred to Hickum that he was standing out here talking to a woman in a public parking lot with no trousers on, actually wearing nothing but a pair of drawers that wouldn't keep his privates safely out of the public eye.

"What I meant was," Hickum said, "my grandmother always said *deef*, too. Just like you do."

"And?" demanded the woman.

"Well, it's just been a long time since I've heard the word said that way, that's all."

She only stared at him from the other side of the car, random drops of sweat running off the end of her pointed nose.

"*Deef* is not correct," he said. "What I mean is, that's not the way to say it." Once he had started with this business of how to say the word, he wished he had left it alone. But it was too late to go back. There was nothing to do now but push on with it. "The word is pronounced *deaf*, not *deef*. But half the people in the South say it the way you just said it, so don't worry about it."

Once again, she dropped her head back and addressed the sky. "I only wanted to know where the goddam Wal-Mart is at, and this guy is trying to give me a English lesson." She bent over where he could not see her but he could still hear her high, sharp voice. "Just let me get this leash off and I'll give you a frigging lesson you won't forget real soon."

"I wasn't looking for any trouble, lady," said Hickum and immediately realized he was whining.

Still bent over where he could not see her, she said: "I don't know what you were looking for, asshole, but I know what you found."

"Don't make me call the authorities," said Hickum, trying to get a little more punch into his voice.

He was struggling to get the key in the car door, but his hands were full of sweat and the keys were full of sweat, and he simply could not get the key into the lock.

But then, as if by magic, the key slipped into the door, and at the very same time, the woman on the other side of the car stood up so he could see her and said: "Sic the son of a bitch, Bubba! Chew him a new one!"

Hickum heard no bark, no growl, but when he turned his head, coming around the front bumper of his car was a bandy-legged, heavy-chested pit bull, his teeth bared in his flat face, and slobber that looked like shaving cream hanging from his jaw.

Hickum made one last try to turn the key before he took off around the car, screaming, "Please, Jesus! Jesus, make 'im stop!"

When he passed her, the woman was a study in unconcern and appeared to be engrossed in filing her nails. She did not even look up when she said: "My name ain't Jesus. It's Gaye Nell Odell, and I told you I was nobody to play with. I guess you probably believe it now."

"I believe! You have made me a believer." Hickum tried to scream but he didn't have the breath left for a scream. He was coming around the car for the third time and his lungs were burning and, worse, his bowels had turned loose again.

When he came by the next time, she said: "You might better see a doctor about that sewer of yours. I don't believe it's working just like it's suppose to."

"Call off the dog, lady!" screamed Hickum. "Call off the goddam dog and I'll do anything you say!"

"That's more like it," she said. "Bubba! Leash!"

The pit bull skidded to a stop and trotted over to her and picked up the leash where she had dropped it on the macadam. He stood looking up at Gaye Nell Odell with the leash hanging from his broken yellow teeth and his tail whipping the air so fast it was nothing but a blur.

"You got him trained good," gasped Hickum. "I'll say that for you."

"You better thank God I took the time to train him. Otherwise, it's no doubt in my mind, you'd be dead meat about now. You got to thank God for your blessings where you find 'em, I always say."

"Believe me, I always do. I really and sincerely do exactly that, lady."

"I'm not a lady and my name is Gaye Nell Odell, I told you one time. What's yours?"

He said: "Hickum Looney."

"Good Lord," she said, "that sounds like the name of somebody that's afflicted."

"Nope," said Hickum. "It's my name, all right. And as far as I have ever been told, there is no affliction that runs in my family." He looked down at the dog for a moment, watching it contentedly licking its ass. Hickum twisted to look at the backs of his legs and said: "Two or three more jumps and that dog would of had me."

His black silk socks, the only pair he had, were torn, and both calves were bleeding where the dog had managed to nip him. The adrenaline rush that he got right behind the nips was the only thing that had kept Hickum going. He had been about ready to pass out from heat and exhaustion when he felt the dog's teeth take his calf, and that was enough to get him immediately up to speed again.

"Where in the name of God is your pants at?" She had come around the end of the car and stopped to watch him.

"It's a long story," he said and thought for the first time that this terrible evening had started because he had done his job better than any other salesman had ever done it, including the man who had founded the Company.

She cocked her head to regard his drawers for a moment. "Is that what I think it is?" she asked.

He reached down and palmed his dick back behind his tattered drawers. "Sorry," he said.

"You ought to be," she said. And then: "Not for the unseemly size of the thing either, but for letting it flip-flop in the breeze that away. Even if it was of a normal size, I wouldn't want every Tom, Dick, and Harry who come down the pike to get a look at it."

He felt his face go hot with anger. "You seem to be mighty close with Tom, Dick, and Harry."

"Now just what's that supposed to mean? If I was named Hickum Looney and standing around in a public parking lot without my britches, I think the last thing I'd do was get caught saying things about other people. And I still don't know what you said about Tom et cetera means."

"Nothing," he said. It meant nothing." He had to disengage from this beast of a woman and her savage pet and get the hell off this parking lot before some cop came cruising by and locked him up for public nakedness, if there was such a crime. And somehow he was sure there was.

She slapped the top of the Lincoln. "These your wheels?"

"No. I was stealing it."

She closed one eye and sighted him with the other as if down a gun barrel. "A man walking around in public after he has shit on hisself can't afford to be a wiseass, either."

"Sorry," he said, "it's just been a terrible day."

"Isn't every day?" she said with some satisfaction.

That stopped him right in the middle of the plan he was trying to work up to get away from her and the pit bull.

"I don't think about such as that," he said.

"I've thought about it all my life," she said. "Trust me, every day is terrible. We're just lucky none of us knows how terrible the days ahead of us are going to be. The past is bad enough. None of us could live with the future."

"We could stand it," said Hickum. "We don't have a choice."

"Oh, it's a choice, old son," she said. "The choice is called eating a bullet."

Hickum took a step back. "I don't think I want to talk to you."

"I didn't ask you anything about talking to me. I asked you where the goddam Wal-Mart was at." She looked down at her dog and then back at Hickum. "You didn't answer my question. This your car?"

He blinked, tried to think of something clever to say. Couldn't. So he answered her question. "Yes, this is my car."

"Nice," she said. "A really nice car."

"Thank you. It's the only thing I own, though. Everything I've got in the world is tied up in it."

"Nothing wrong with that. It's the American way," she said brightly. Then: "Take me and Bubba back over to my van, could you?"

"Thought you were going to the Wal-Mart."

"I thought so too. But I don't see one from here and you don't seem to know where one is at. And it's so goddam hot I believe I smell my hair burning. So screw the Wal-Mart. I might as well go back to my van with Bubba."

Hickum looked at the dog still working himself over with his tongue. "I guess that's Bubba," he said, pointing to the dog.

"You're getting cute again."

"No," he said. "I just never much wanted a dog in my Lincoln, that's all."

"You don't want Bubba to ride in your car," she said, "but you aim to get on the front seat after you've befouled yourself the way you have."

He stuck out one shoe, turned it slightly, and checked his leg. Then he did the same thing with the other leg. He knew she was watching him, and he did not know what to say. But he felt an overwhelming need to defend himself.

"I don't believe I've done anything like this to myself since I was a real little boy."

"Well, you made up for lost time today. What got your bowels tore up like that, anyway?"

"This awful day! I believe I've managed to jangle my nerves is what I believe I've done. The day's just about killed me."

"We keep baking here in this parking lot and it'll kill us both for sure."

Hickum was trying to figure out how he was going to get into his Lincoln with shit all over himself. He wasn't even thinking about the dog anymore.

"I believe I can help you out," she said.

"Help me out?"

"That's what I said."

"With what?"

"You got to quit trying to be cute. I don't like it. You don't need nothing but a pair of eyes to see what your trouble is. And if you didn't have eyes, your nose could probably get the job done."

"Oh, you mean . . . "

"Shit," she said.

With everything that had happened today, he still felt himself blushing again. Apparently there was no limit to the number of times a grown man could blush in one day.

She pointed to the dog and said, "Not caring to have Bubba ride in your car, I wouldn't think you'd want to just slide under the wheel with . . . "

"Okay, okay, *goddammit*, I understand."

She smiled and her thin lips looked strangely beautiful to Hickum. "You don't have to get hot about it. Think about it this way—the good Lord didn't make one single, solitary human being on the whole face of the earth that doesn't shit."

He watched her steadily for a very long time and then slowly sighed.

"Gaye Nell Odell, why would you tell me something like that?"

"I just thought you'd feel better if you thought about it that way."

"How'd it be if I didn't think about it at all?"

"Not possible. It's there. You got to deal with it."

"Some things are easier to deal with than others. I'm not magic, you know."

"I told you I believed I could help you out."

"And how might you do that?"

"Don't take the uppity tone with me. You the one need help, not me."

He started to say something back but thought better of it. She was bent over rummaging through an enormous handbag that had been lying at her feet. When she straightened up, she had a box that at first he thought was Kleenex.

"Ever use any Handi Wipes?" she said.

"Suffering Jesus," he said.

"Don't be putting it on Jesus. He didn't shit all over you. It was you done that."

He stood watching her. He did not reach for the box she had taken out of her purse. He could not endure even thinking what she meant for him to do with it.

"Do you have anything in the trunk of your car you could use to sit on?"

Her voice was calm, straightforward. She might have been asking him how he liked his steak cooked.

"No," he said and was ashamed of the guilt he managed to get into that one tiny word.

In the same straightforward tone, she said: "Take them rag-gedy-ass drawers off and throw them away. They won't do. And here." She handed him the box. "Clean up with these. You won't be able to do much. Just give it a lick and a promise. That's better than nothing."

"A lick and a promise?"

"Just a saying we got back home."

"We got the same one in east Tennessee, but I wouldn't have thought to use it under the circumstances."

"Don't be so damn precious. I'm burning up standing here on this frying pan. Get to it."

He stood unmoving.

"Now what?" she said.

"I can't just take off my drawers right out here."

She turned in a complete circle, stretching her neck. "I don't see another human being in the whole damn place. Anybody with any sense is somewheres it's cool."

He shifted from foot to foot, looked as though he might scratch himself but didn't, and finally ended up staring off toward the far horizon where the setting sun cast pillars of light into the dark sky.

"Damn, what is it now?"

"You're here."

She threw up her hands and rolled her eyes. "You've had your pants off since we met. You had shit on yourself to start with and then done it on yourself again. Your dick's popped loose and looked me dead in the eye two or three times and you . . . you . . . " She put her fists on her hips. " . . . and after all that you don't want to get out of a ruined pair of drawers in front of me?" She snorted loudly. "By God, that beats all I ever heard of in my life!"

"It's the principle of the thing," he said softly.

"No comment," she said. "Would it help if I turned my back?"

"If I take off my drawers, what am I going to sit on in my Town Car with?"

She sighed now and seemed to grow smaller in a crush of defeat. "This ain't twenty goddam questions you think we're playing out here, is it?" she asked in the quietest of voices. "Hickum, I don't have a fucking answer for every question you can think of."

"You like that word entirely too much. I wouldn't have thought a woman like you to even know a word like that."

"Hickum, every woman on earth knows that word or none of us would be here."

"That's the second time you've used my name, Gaye Nell."

"And it's the second time you've used mine, so I guess that makes it official."

"What?"

"We're engaged." Laughing, she said: "You silly bastard."

"I guess it's just as cheap to laugh."

"I guess," she said. "But could we wait on the laughs till later? We've got more important things to take care of than bullshitting about our names. Like, for instance, you getting in this thing and turning on the A/C."

"I don't see how we mean to do it without ruining my seats."

"I figured it out," she said. "I'm turning my back." He watched her turn. "Now turn your back," she said. She waited a moment. "You turned your back yet?"

"Well, I have, but—"

"I don't need you to talk, I need you to do what I say. I'll keep an eye out best I can from all directions and you do the same. Now whip off them drawers and give yourself that lick and a promise with them Handi Wipes."

"But what about—?"

"One thing at a time, Hickum,"she said. "One goddam thing at a time."

He took his crusty drawers off and threw them behind the car where Bubba caught them in midflight and sank onto his plump belly to give them a good chewing while Looney wiped and scrubbed, scrubbed and wiped as best he could.

"Bubba is making me sick," he said.

"What's he doing?"

"You know."

"I guess I do. Try not to look."

"I can't help it."

"Yeah, ain't that a wonder?"

"What?"

"You can't help watching what you can't stand watching. That's people for you, though. Only a human being could come up with something like, 'You can catch more flies with honey than you can with vinegar,' but if they had put a little more thought to it, they would have said, 'You can catch more flies with shit than you can with honey.' "

"Godamighty. Your mouth is a piece of work," he said.

"I know. Ain't it something how it tells the truth every chance it gets?"

"You tell the truth one more time," he said, "and I'm not giving you and Bubba a ride to your van."

"I was just trying to pass the time," she said.

"No need to. I'm as through as I can get."

"Use all the Handi Wipes, did you?"

"I did," he said, "and this disgusting dog of yours eat every one of them as soon as I threw it down."

"Quit saying things like that in front of Bubba," Gaye Nell said. "He understands more than you think he does."

"All right, then," he said, "let's get on with this."

When he turned around he was holding the cardboard Handi Wipe box in front of his privates, but as soon as he saw she didn't have her blouse on, he quickly raised the box to cover his eyes, saying as he did, "That's the damnedest thing I have ever seen!"

She said: "I've had a few bad reactions about how I'm built, but I think *that* one may have gone right off the scale."

"You got your blouse off right here in the middle of a public parking lot."

"And you've got your drawers off, but I don't know that either of us had a choice."

"Well, whereabouts is your bra?" he said.

"Don't own one. Do I look like I need one?"

"I don't know. I'm not looking."

"You know you're peeping around that box and I know it too. Why are you lying to me?"

He was caught. He *was* peeping, but he didn't know she could tell. But more than that, he didn't know what to say now that he was caught. So he told the truth. "You're . . . you're . . . they're beautiful."

"My tits." She made it a simple statement.

"Breasts," he said, staring in a way that he wished he could stop but could not. They were small, cantilevered, and full of freckles. The breasts of a young girl, as best he could remember young girls' breasts being anyway.

"Call 'em what you want," she said, "but whatever you call 'em, don't forget I'm standing here naked from the navel up in a public parking lot with you naked from the navel down." She tossed him her blouse. "You throw that in the front seat and sit on it and let's see if we can't make a timely departure."

He giggled. "Timely departure. I like that."

From the other side of the car where she was opening the door to get in, she said, "There may be other of my odds and ends you'll come to like."

"I've never said I wouldn't. I know your odds and ends must be special."

"Pervert," she said as he fired up the powerful motor of the car.

Driving off, he said, "Now that's an ugly word—sounds ugly, is ugly—but dogged if you don't make it sound kind of pretty when you say it to me."

"I noticed that myself," she said, her thin mouth smiling, a thin mouth that had started looking beautiful to him at some point, but he couldn't remember when. She looked at him and for no reason he could think of, she winked, "I don't know if I like me making an ugly word pretty or not, I mean making it pretty just because I called you by it, I mean."

He stared straight ahead and drove carefully.

After a minute he asked, "Did you wink at me?"

After a minute or two, she said, "Yes, I did." Then, when he didn't say any more, she asked, "Do you want to know why?"

Now he was smiling, although he didn't look back at her. "No, thank you," he said, "I don't believe I do. I'd just rather sit here and think about it."

Now she looked entirely away from him through the window on her side and said, "Jesus H. Christ! I don't think I like the way this is going between us at all."

Even though he knew she tried to make her voice rough, he could hear it sliding toward laughter.

Looking straight ahead, Hickum said, in the meanest voice he could find: "I *know* I don't like the way things are going between us."

The last word had hardly left his mouth before they both broke down in howling, violent laughter, so violent Hickum had to stop the car so he could lean against the steering wheel.

Finally, the laughter died down to nothing but sniffles, and when he turned to look at her, she had entirely twisted toward him, and while there were tears of laughter on her cheeks, her face was not smiling but was solemn, even sad.

"You sure are a pretty woman," he said before he knew he was going to say it.

She looked down at her naked chest. With the tiniest flicker

harry crews

of a smile, she said, "You mean my tits," making it a statement.

"Breasts," he said. "I think I'd like to say *breasts*, if you don't mind."

They were talking in such hushed voices now that he almost didn't hear her when she said: "I don't mind."

"That's good," he said. "That's real good."

"Would you like to hug me?" she asked.

"It's been a long time since I hugged anybody," he said, "and besides, you . . . well . . . You don't have anything on your . . . " He made an awkward gesture toward her chest.

She took one of her breasts in each of her hands. "You mean these?" she said, her eyes averted, the color suddenly high in her thin cheeks.

"Don't do that," he said.

"Then you do it," she said.

And they came together in silence, over the quiet hum of the idling Lincoln engine.

chapter

five

The last blaze of light from a setting sun
cast the very tops of the tallest buildings in Atlanta, Georgia,
in a red haze that made them seem indistinct and unsteady in
the wavering lines of rising heat. There was not a single bird
flying anywhere over the city, and the intensely blue, arching
sky appeared artificial and dreamlike without a cloud in it. A
Rolls-Royce the color of pearl swept silently down a wide tho-
roughfare considerably above the speed limit and did not stop
or even slow down at any of the stoplights. A vanity plate on
the front and rear bumper carried the legend THE BOSS.

Every four blocks there was a sign that said the lights were set
for traffic traveling at thirty-five miles per hour. The engine of
the Rolls was silent as a child's toy in the early evening hours
of the city as it maintained a steady eighty miles per hour. A
cop on a Harley-Davidson motorcycle sat parked just off the

broad avenue beside a billboard with foot-high white letters on a solid black ground that read JUST SAY NO TO DRUGS.

As the Rolls blew past, the cop looked up from a pad he was writing on and touched the ends of his fingers to his white helmet in a brief and familiar salute. Inside the car, its glass was tinted so deeply that everything outside seemed very nearly dark as night. But the little man in the rear seat wearing a royal blue, pin-striped suit and Harvard Club tie saw the motorcycle cop clearly enough.

In a gesture so casual it almost looked tired, he gave the cop the pope's salute: hand palm up and gently cupped, tipping once, twice, toward the motorcycle. The little man knew that the cop could not see him through the tinted glass of the car. But that did not matter. He always returned a salute from one of his people. And all of them knew it. And that—as the Boss himself liked to say—was as true as anything carved in the tablets Moses brought down from the mountain.

Do the job well and do it on time—especially on time—and nobody could believe how good the Boss could be. Do not do the job at all or do it late—especially very late—and nobody could believe how ruthless the Boss could be. He was a legend, a myth, and totally unpredictable. Everyone seemed to have a radically different notion of who and what he was, but the single constant that remained true in every heart whose life the Boss touched was that he was one of the chosen.

The reason was simple enough. The Boss lived in a madness of money. The rumor that everyone had somehow heard but nobody ever talked about was that there was no problem in the whole world that the Boss could not solve by simply throwing money in sufficient quantity at it. And the Boss always had a sufficient quantity. Whether or not this was true or, in fact, a baseless rumor was beside the point, because everyone usually believed it.

And their collective belief made him invincible and necessary for them to love. Their only wish was to be as he was. They wanted only fame, money that was too much to count, and finally, what they wanted most was to be able to control, control absolutely, the world they lived in and, therefore, their own destiny. The Boss knew all this and thought of it as a considerable asset, and since he also believed an asset unused was no asset at all, he tried to use it as often as he could in his business and his daily life, which he considered one and the same.

The Boss took two cigars out of the inside pocket of his jacket. They were fat golden Havanas that made their way to him through Canada. He removed each one from the aluminum cylinder that held it, snipped the ends with specifically designed golden clippers, leaned forward, and tapped his uniformed driver on the shoulder with one of the cigars.

"Here. Moke nis," said the Boss.

It was not a question but a command, and it sounded like a command. Without looking back, the chauffeur reached up and took the cigar. Both men sucked and licked them until they were sufficiently wet and then, as if their movements had been choreographed, they simultaneously touched the ends of their cigars at the same instant with the glowing ends of lighters that popped from the leather panels of the car. The Boss and the chauffeur stared straight ahead and never touched their cigars again once they had plugged them into their mouths. Instead they puffed with a single-minded passion as if in a contest with each other. It was only a matter of minutes before the Boss could no longer see the back of his driver's head through the heavily layered fog of blue cigar smoke.

"I am mad enough na kill ne bastard," the Boss said.

"Yessir," said the driver without the slightest notion of who the Boss was mad enough to kill.

"It's a nigger in ne woodpile numwhere."

"Yessir."

"Nomody mut nomody can meet my record of nine mooks of orders."

"No, sir."

"We'll yust see, my Nod. We'll yust see."

"Yessir."

"Order a plane ready for nakeoff as soon as I get a massage na calm me down."

"Yessir," said the driver, picking up the car phone.

"If I non't get a massage first, I know I'll kill ne bastard."

The driver put his hand over the phone into which he was discreetly speaking and said, "Yessir."

The driver put the phone back down in its cradle and coughed once. The Boss said, "No." The chauffeur coughed no more.

When the car stopped, the Boss sat completely immobile while the driver got out, sprinted around to the other side and opened the back door, and stood at attention beside it. The Boss's arm shot straight out of the Rolls-Royce, his hand holding the Havana, ragged now, caught between thumb and forefinger. The driver took it and at the same time took his own out of his mouth. He dropped both of them on the asphalt and discreetly stepped on them with his booted foot.

The Boss got out and jerked imaginary wrinkles out of his coat, adjusted the already perfectly adjusted Windsor knot in his tie, and used his thumb to test the creases in his trousers, creases that he touched as though they might be razor blades. While the Boss was preoccupied with his clothing, the chauffeur dived into the backseat and came out of the car a moment later with a metal briefcase in his hand and a stack of papers under his arm. The Boss was already halfway across the parking lot walking very fast toward a building that had SOAPS FOR LIFE in letters six feet high stretched across the entire top of it. The chauffeur had to run to catch up just in time to hold a door open for him. The building they went into was white, full of angled edges, and three stories high. Terraced gardens of bright flowers fell away from either side of it. Once inside the building, still carrying the rolled-up bundle of papers and the metal briefcase, the chauffeur followed the Boss from two yards behind, exactly in step with him, and matching him stride for stride as though the two of them marched to a cadence called by someone only they could hear. The corridor they went down, their heels striking smartly and in unison on the terrazzo floor, had very small cubicles on either side of it. The doors to the offices stood open and in each one a young woman stared as if in a trance at the screen of a computer while her fingers flashed over the keyboard.

There were three shifts of young women who kept the computers going twenty-four hours a day. They were all blond, blue eyed, and wore no makeup on the pale flesh of their faces, faces that looked as though they had never seen the sun. Not one of them glanced away from her computer screen, and there was not a single hitch in the rhythmic flash of their long, slender fingers. And yet at the precise moment the Boss was opposite one of the open doors, the young women, without as much as a glance in his direction, called: "Good morning, Boss." They always wished him a good morning, even if he came in at midnight, which he often did.

Without expression or even glancing in her direction, each time he was spoken to, the Boss replied: "Morgue, Newness."

The young women had talked at great length about what the Boss might be saying when he spoke back to them, which he always did. Was he saying, "Morning, Eunice," to each of them? It certainly sounded like that was what he might be saying, but if that was true, then there were at least two major problems. One, even allowing for his unfortunate mouth (*unfortunate* was one of the words they used if they absolutely had to make direct reference to it in conversation with one another), even allowing for *the lip* (another phrase they sometimes used for his deformity), it was still almost impossible to get *morning* out of *morgue*. And, two, *Eunice* was the only name they could think of that even came close to *Newness*, but as luck would have it, none of them was named Eunice.

One of them sooner or later would have come right out and asked him what he was saying to them if every one of them had not been mortally terrified of him. They had caught the terror after only two or three days in the building. There was no escaping it; the air was alive with it. These women had been hired for the typing pool and it was in the pool they would remain until they were fired, quit, or fell dead at their machines. There was no one to complain to and no system in place for redress of any grievance. They were treated exactly like slaves. Consequently, they came to feel like slaves without ever knowing it.

There was not a woman in the company that held any position higher than that of a clerk mindlessly punching the keys of a computer. Not a single woman was invited to the annual conference. And finally, *finally*, every newly hired female employee was humiliated beyond saying when, on her first day at work, she looked around and saw that every other woman at Soaps For Life was blond and blue eyed just as she was. And they were all real blondes. My God! What they had submitted to! But they had no choice if they wanted to work at Soaps For Life. The Boss's personnel department had its instructions, and by God the department followed them to the letter.

There were little groups of women that got together and talked of *revolt*, *takeover*, and *vengeance*, but they were unsure exactly what they meant by *revolt*, *takeover*, and *vengeance*. But what they did know was that every goddam hiring practice of Soaps For Life was against the law. It was *unfuckingconstitutional!* But so far it had all been talk and only talk among the women. Sooner or later, though, sooner or later there would be justice at Soaps For Life. Or there would be no Soaps For Life. The women didn't talk much about it but each woman, in her most secret heart, had no doubts that someday there would be justice at Soaps For Life. When the day came, they would take no prisoners.

The Boss and the chauffeur turned a corner, and at the end of a short corridor was a flight of stairs. The chauffeur immediately increased his pace and moved up even with the Boss. Every two or three strides the chauffeur's head turned almost imperceptibly as he glanced nervously out of the corner of his eye at the Boss. The chauffeur's breathing had increased also until he was nearly panting. His face was beginning to redden.

Nothing whatsoever changed about the Boss. His gaze was steady and straight ahead. His stride, if anything, had shortened.

But he still stayed dead even with the chauffeur, who had moved the square metal briefcase to his right hand and clamped the stack of papers more tightly under his left arm.

Suddenly, in a quiet, secretive voice, the Boss said: "On *free.*"

The chauffeur's whole body tensed and his head stuck forward on his long neck.

Casually, quietly, the Boss said: "None . . . new . . . *free!*"

The Boss already had a stride on the chauffeur before the *three* was completely out of his mouth. He always got the jump because it was he calling the signals. They both knew it but there was nothing the chauffeur could do about it, and they both knew that too. But the chauffeur showed the strength and form and sheer grit that had made him the only white boy to ever hold the state one-hundred-meter sprint championship in the state of Mississippi. But that was twenty years ago, when his daddy had always referred to him as "my goddam little nigger beater" all through the tenth, eleventh, and twelfth grades while he was outrunning every black kid that would come to the line with him.

But he couldn't beat the Boss, who beat him by two strides on the last four stairs at the third floor. The race over, the Boss hesitated only for an instant and shook himself like a dog coming out of water. The chauffeur's face turned redder still as he looked away from the Boss toward the windows that gave onto a view of the asphalt parking lot. Neither man spoke as they walked to the end of a corridor, where the chauffeur leapt forward to open an oaken door marked PRIVATE. The Boss didn't have to alter his stride at all as he stepped through the door, the chauffeur right behind him.

A huge man with a tiny waist and a chest broad enough to easily accommodate *SAIPPUAKIVIKAUPPIAS* spelled out on a tight T-shirt in large block letters leapt to his feet from the chair he had been lounging in, leafing through a fitness magazine. He stood at rigid attention while the chauffeur helped the Boss out of his clothes, putting them on the rack of a silent valet as he did: first the coat, then the tie, and then the job of unbuttoning the stiffly starched shirt, all of which the chauffeur went at slowly and methodically.

The Boss raised an eyebrow at the large man and said, "Now nu nis morning, Meterbilt?"

"I'm fine, Boss," the huge man said after frowning a moment as if trying to determine exactly how he was this morning.

"Nodnam teleconferencing today has got me out of my grooves. I need a really nood rubnown bad . . . "

"That's what I'm here for, Boss. I live to work you over."

The Boss's eyebrows shot up and the edges of his damaged mouth turned down. "Watch nure mouth."

"Yessir . . . I didn't mean nothing."

The Boss watched him for a long time, during which the massage parlor filled up with the ticking of a clock the size of a basketball that was fastened to the wall over the massage table, each tick of the clock seeming louder than the one that preceded it as the three men stood watching one another, not one of them seeming to breathe.

"Right," the Boss said. "Nu rememor nat. Nu don't mean *nothing. Nothing.* Unnerstan*!*"

"Yessir."

With the chauffeur holding his shorts, the Boss stepped out of them and he was naked except for his alligator shoes and his black silk socks monogrammed with THE BOSS. The Boss was no bigger than a jockey and he carried a jockey's weight, a constant one hundred pounds. Every muscle in his body showed as clearly as if it had been etched in metal by acid. Neither the chauffeur nor the masseur could keep from staring at him. Naked, he was a living anatomy chart.

The Boss turned to his chauffeur. "Drop 'em nan grab ne nodnam table. Winner kicks."

The chauffeur dropped his trousers and his shorts to his ankles, bent over, and put his hands on the massage table.

The Boss stepped behind him, set himself, and kicked him soccer style squarely in the ass. The chauffeur went flying over the table and, turning in the air, landed on the other side on his back. The chauffeur had partly propelled himself over the table, but at least half of the ride had been provided by the Boss's kick. As the chauffeur got slowly to his feet, the masseur started enthusiastically applauding.

The Boss whirled and slapped the huge masseur. The surprise and force of the blow collapsed the masseur onto a straight-back chair. The print of most of the Boss's hand was outlined in red on the masseur's face and blood was running from both nostrils.

"Who nold *nu* to clap, nasshole?"

On the other side of the table the chauffeur was hurriedly pushing his shirt into his trousers.

The huge masseur sat very still on his chair, a look of raw terror in his eyes. "But, Boss," he said, and then stopped, a thousand-yard stare in his terrorized eyes. It was as though he was trying to find the answer to his predicament written on the far wall. Then he shook his head and without looking at the Boss, said: "It's what I'm supposed to do."

The Boss slapped him again and a spot of blood appeared in the ear on which he was struck. "Not ne question I asked, nasshole." The Boss leapt into the air and with balletlike precision came down on the instep of both the masseur's feet. The masseur screamed and somehow bit deeply into his tongue at the same time. A fine spray of blood blew out of his mouth.

The Boss turned to his chauffeur, who was standing by the door with his hand on the knob. Almost gently, he said to the trembling chauffeur: "Nu wait noutside in ne hall while I nake care of nis."

The chauffeur popped through the door, closed it, and stood leaning against it. He looked as though he had died on the spot where he stood. His eyes were closed. His lips slowly turned blue as if he might not be breathing. Through the door he could hear something thick and flat slamming into something that sounded like a side of beef. And each time the thick flat thing landed there was a noise that was obviously human and that was obviously not, something terrible and impossible.

Finally the noise behind the door stopped as suddenly as it

began. The chauffeur did not move. He held tightly to the door frame on either side of himself and looked neither to the left nor the right, but he was blinking rapidly and the blue color of his lips had spread upward until it now marked his nostrils.

The dead bolt on the door slid open and the Boss's voice, full of emotion, the kind of voice that the chauffeur had heard only from people at funerals, said: Come nin here and clean nis up. I'll be nin ne neamroom. I non't have nime for a massage now. I not to nit to Miami."

The chauffeur listened carefully until he could no longer hear the sharp click of the built-up heels of the Boss's shoes. Then he turned and gave the door a gentle push. The masseur was lying on his back on the massage table. His head was slick with blood. Even his crosstrainer shoes had splashes of blood on them.

Without moving, he asked, "Is the little motherfucker gone?"

"He's gone."

The masseur sat up on the table and when he did, a long fraternity paddle with holes drilled in it slid onto the floor.

The chauffeur had heard rumors of these beatings. Everybody had. But he had never been this close to one. The masseur turned to look at him, and the chauffeur felt his gorge rise and he fully expected to puke. But he couldn't. And he couldn't quit staring at the masseur, either. His eyes were completely bloodshot. And the bridge of his nose was swelling.

The chauffeur's mouth opened and closed several times before he could speak. "What the fuck is this, man? I've put up with some nasty shit from that little fuck, but if he ever bloodied me anywhere, in any way, I . . . " It was a moment before the chauffeur could go on, he was sputtering so badly. "True, I let him kick me in the ass and I jump over the table for him. It's business, only business. I get a nice little bonus in my paycheck every time he does it. And I got a wife, three kids, and a fucking dog to support. So you can see why I gotta go through with it." He spread his arms wide as though he would embrace Meterbilt where he sat. "But this kinda shit right here . . . I mean, it's fucking barbaric, man."

Meterbilt did the best he could with a smile. "For money. I do this for money. What else can I do? I don't know jack shit about nothing. I ain't even a fucking masseur." He paused and held up a finger. "When I was young, I was one of the world's great iron freaks, you know, a bodybuilding champion. It made me a good living, too, but the years caught up with me and I went to the only place I could go, professional wrestling. Believe me, I was taking a hell of a lot worse beatings than this for a hell of a lot less money. Then I met the Lip—in a gym, actually— and he brought me here. Had no fucking choice. None. What you're looking at is not really bad. I got a cut in my scalp. All the blood's coming from that.

"Not that it's any of your goddam business, but I do what I do to make a living the only way I know how to make it. Everything's about fucking money. Can you understand that?"

Very softly, and looking at the wall behind Russell Muscle's head to keep from looking at him, the chauffeur said: "Yeah, I understand. A lot of things I don't understand in this world, but I do understand money. That little split-lip motherfucker took me to college about money."

"Well, don't just stand there and watch me bleed to death. Get the doctor up here. I've got to get cleaned up. The Boss'll be back out here any minute."

"I know," said the chauffeur, picking up the telephone to call the Boss's personal doctor.

chapter

six

In the Lincoln, Hickum sat on Gaye Nell's blouse with the Handi Wipes box on his lap, praying he would not get excited, because he knew the Handi Wipes box could never hold down a hard-on. She was sitting beside him, her breasts cast in silhouette by the dash lights, and he could not keep from looking at her out of the corner of his eye. The memory of her breasts lived in the palms of his hands, and the shape of them seemed a miracle. He did not have much to compare them with, though, because he had never had much luck with women.

He could not remember the last time he'd been laid. He could vaguely remember the woman's face, but not her name or how she smelled or the place or how they had come to do what they had done. He could have had more women, he supposed, if he had done things differently, been a different man. There were always an extraordinary number of sexual opportunities when he was making his rounds from door to door. But Hickum Looney had a strict rule about using his position representing Soaps For Life as a way to seduce women.

He couldn't remember when or how he had made the decision or if there had actually been a conscious decision, but somewhere in the dim past, masturbation had become a way of life. It had become an effortless solution to a very large problem. At least his good right hand never had a headache or a period or bad breath, and it would never sue him for child support or alimony, and most of all, it would never, ever break his heart. His only defense against Gaye Nell Odell was anger, an anger he did not truly feel.

"I'm thinking about slapping this goddam dog," Hickum said, staring straight ahead at the automobile lights sweeping toward him out of the darkness.

"That'd be the worst move you've made all day."

"You don't know what this awful day's been like. Slapping a dog wouldn't even come close to the worst move I've made today."

"That's not just a dog you're talking about. That's a Bubba."

Bubba was somehow managing to stand with his back feet on the rear seat of the Lincoln and hold his front legs over each of Hickum's shoulders. For no apparent reason, the dog had started licking the back of Hickum's neck and had never stopped.

"I'm not telling you again to make him stop slobbering on my neck like he is."

"It's not my fault your neck is salty," she said. "And it's not his fault he likes salt. You sweated all that salt out today, and Bubba just naturally loves him a salty neck."

Hickum held on to the steering wheel as though it might save his life. He had only known this woman for less than two hours and it seemed to him that he'd had more thoughts of mutilation and death during that short time than he'd had in all the rest of his life put together. But that was not the worst part. The worst part was that he thought she was beautiful and funny and he thought her breasts were eminently suckable, although he couldn't imagine his mouth on one of them, and he also thought—no, he knew—that he would be willing to permanently mutilate himself or commit suicide for her. Back on the side of the road, they'd never got beyond sweaty wrestling and a little kissing. He wondered if he'd ever forgive himself. He also wondered if he'd have been able to pull it off if he had got her entirely naked on her back.

Still without looking at her, he said: "I know you could have got us something to wear so we wouldn't be naked like this if a cop stops us. One stops us, we automatically get arrested, you know that, don't you?"

In a mocking little voice, she said, "And I told you how it was back there at my van. You know that, don't you?"

Now he turned quickly, meaning to growl something at her, but his eyes locked onto her naked breasts and never made it to her face, and instead of a growl, his voice was a sick whisper: "Yes, I know."

Hickum, sitting on her blouse with the Handi Wipes box on his lap, had driven Gaye Nell and Bubba across the parking lot to a badly battered Volkswagen bus that was rusted out along the door panels and had a nearly perfect cross cracked into the left half of the windshield.

He pulled up beside it and stopped as she had told him to do and for a long time said nothing, only sat looking at it and very slowly shaking his head.

"Mother of God," he said, "is that what you intend to drive away from here in? That thing'll never make it out of the lot."

"Me and Bubba lived in that vehicle all the way from California. That ought to tell you something about it."

Hickum had turned off the ignition of the Lincoln and killed its lights. A heavy moon that seemed hot as the sun hung low on the horizon and lighted them where they sat, while Bubba scrambled out of the backseat to sit between them.

"I wouldn't want to be driving that thing around," he said. "I don't like to get left on the road."

"I never cared for the kind of Detroit monster you're driving, either."

"I just never like to be left on the road."

"So you said."

"I don't much like sitting out here half naked, either. It's cops that patrol these lots."

She opened the door and Bubba went right over her lap to the asphalt. Gaye Nell looked back at Hickum.

"Could you give me a little light until I get it started?"

She sat looking at him as though she would say more, but she did not. Hickum felt somehow something was missing, something he ought to say or do, but he could not imagine what it might be. He could ask her for an address or a telephone number, but every time he had ever tried that, it turned out badly. No woman had ever even come close to giving Hickum Looney any kind of number, not house or phone or even a P.O. box. His long experience on that score was sour, very sour. Being refused always made him feel bad and he felt bad enough today already.

As she was getting out, she leaned back in and patted him reassuringly on the knee. "Don't worry about a thing, we'll get together again before you know it."

He had no notion at all what she meant, but he turned the motor over and got it idling before he turned the lights on. When she walked in front of the car on the way to the van, the tight tremble of her heavy-nippled little breasts started a jolt of sadness as powerful as any he had ever known. For as long as he could remember, women had been a blight on his life, and he told himself he ought to be happy that he was rid of her. And he thought he was. But at the same time he was happy, he was also sad and utterly undone with melancholy.

He struck the steering wheel with the heel of his hand so hard it hurt. Goddammit! Why was he so surprised? Every time he talked to a woman about anything other than soap, some awful thing like this happened.

He had waited in the Lincoln, the lights on, the air conditioner humming, and his patience wearing thin. Why the hell didn't she fire up the Volkswagen van and turn the headlights on?

He could see her dark shadow moving behind the wheel. Suddenly, the window on the driver's side of the van slid back and her head popped out. The moonlight cast much of her face in shadow. Bubba's head came through the window right beside hers. Dark slobber dripped from his darker tongue.

Gaye Nell made a winding motion with her hand. He saw her lips move and knew that she was saying something, but he couldn't tell what.

He touched a button and his window slid down. "Make this good," he said. "I don't have strength for much more."

"You got any jumper cables?"

"Gaye Nell, people who drive Lincolns don't own jumper cables."

"Elitist bastard," she said.

Hickum wasn't sure what *elitist* meant. *Bastard* he knew.

"Fine," he said, starting his window sliding up. "Have a good walk. Me and my elitist Town Car are gone."

Her voice, when she spoke, sounded louder than it was becuase it was cold and hard as stone. "You wouldn't fucking leave me like this!"

He took his finger off the window button and watched her furious eyes flare in the heavy moonlight. She was right. He wouldn't leave her. But she didn't know why. Or maybe she did.

"All right," he said, "but hurry up, dammit." He could at least pump up his fake anger with a little foul language, the sort of words that he was not accustomed to using. "And don't fucking forget to bring me something to cover myself up with."

But when she burst through his headlights coming back, she was still half naked in the same old way. And she carried nothing for him to wear. She opened the backdoor for Bubba and then got in beside Hickum.

"Do you ever hear anything I say?" he asked.

"Now what's wrong?" she said, making a little pouty mouth that made him think of kissing her.

"Clothes. I told you to get clothes."

"It's dark as a bat's ass in there, for Christ's sake. I couldn't see shit, so don't start screaming."

"Anything would have been better than nothing. Towels, anything."

"I did what I could. But it's too dark. Lucky I didn't get killed. The place is a jungle, everything piled everywhere. I guess I didn't tell you, I'm not a good housekeeper. Messy as hell is what I am. There, you got your confession. Satisfied?"

"I never asked for a confession. I asked for something to put on."

She turned to look at him. Her face was tight and without expression. And her teeth were a strange color in the light from the dash. "You drive out of here. Now! Not one more word about how I do or do not measure up. You ain't exactly the king of fucking Siam, you know."

Hickum didn't know what he had been expecting, but whatever it was, it wasn't what she had said to him. It startled him so, he left a little rubber when he floored the accelerator driving away from the Volkswagen.

As they were leaving the parking lot, Gaye Nell asked: "Is it far to where you live?"

"With the traffic this time of evening, about forty-five minutes."

"God, that seems like forever."

"Where we're going is not that far."

"We're not going to your place?"

"We've got to get something to put on to make it in to where I live." He stared straight ahead at the stream of headlights coming at them in the other lane. "Since you couldn't go to the trouble to get something out of the van."

"I did what I could," she said in a small voice, a voice that for the first time was full of apology.

He didn't want to go on about it, but he couldn't seem to leave it alone. "Looks to me like anybody who had been in something as small as a van all the way from California could find anything they wanted with their eyes closed."

"I didn't drive it from California."

"Well, from wherever you did drive it from."

"I didn't drive it from anywhere."

He didn't mind that she had lied about California. Hell, everybody fudges a little now and then. But now he was confused. Did she say she did not drive it from anywhere? Is that what she said?

"Then how did it get to be where it's at back there?"

"You'd have to ask somebody else about that. Bubba and I found it. Right where it is."

He wondered vaguely whether or not driving down the road with nothing to cover his nakedness but a Handi Wipes box had affected his sanity. Something had gone terribly wrong with this conversation.

"You don't just *find* a VW van, Gaye Nell. You have to make a contract and then pay for the—"

"I don't care what the rest of the world does, but Bubba and I found it. Parked right there. I don't guess you noticed the tires were flat."

"No."

"I was afraid you would. I thought you'd see 'em flat and jump up my ass about it."

A horrible image flashed in his eyes. "You won't go far in life talking like that."

"Just a manner of speaking. Sorry if it bothered you. To tell the truth, though, I've pretty much quit caring if I bother other people or not. Living in an abandoned VW will do that to you."

"You live in that van?"

"Me and Bubba. For the last two weeks. Yeah."

Caught in early evening traffic, they rode along in silence for several slow blocks. Every few minutes Gaye Nell looked over at Hickum in quick little glances. He could feel her eyes when they turned on him, but he only gripped the steering wheel more tightly and stared straight ahead.

"Go ahead and say what you've got to say," she said.

"I don't know that I have anything to say."

And he really didn't. He had never known anybody who lived in a car. He felt strange. It was the kind of dirty life you read about in the newspaper. You read about it and then asked yourself, Who are these people? How does anybody, especially here in the U.S. of A., land of the free, home of the brave, and breadbasket to the rest of the world—in such a country, how does anybody manage to end up living in a ruined vehicle? A foreign vehicle at that. A goddam German vehicle. You glance at the story again, fold the paper, and try not to think about it.

Now he had such a person in his Lincoln Town Car. It was more than strange, Hickum thought, it was scary.

She said: "Sure, you got something to say about it. Everybody and his brother has something to say about it. They all want to tell you how you went wrong. It's a strange thing, but if you're out of work, it pisses everybody off."

"Not me," Hickum said. "I don't know a thing about you going wrong, or even if you did go wrong, which I doubt. No, you're talking about somebody else, not me."

"If you say so, but you'll get around to it before it's over. Hell, it's all right with me. I've heard so much about it already, it just flies right past."

Hickum had turned his rearview mirror so he could see her. He cut his eyes away from traffic and into the mirror just in time to see her take hold of a nipple between thumb and forefinger and give it a long, slow, absentminded pull, the way she might pull a lock of her hair. The car swerved badly and almost got away from him.

"You better hold this lane a little better if you don't want to have to try to explain to a cop how you happen to be driving without any pants on."

"This day has just about wrecked my nerves."

"That wouldn't seem like a good enough reason to rip up your ass, too."

"It's too much foul talk in the world already. I wish you wouldn't keep on with it like you do."

"I got a few wishes myself. I wish I knew how much longer I have to sit in this car and I wish I knew where we were going, if we're not going to your place."

"We're almost there. Traffic was heavier than I thought. We're going to a friend of mine's house."

"I hope it's a damn good friend. I mean we're not exactly dressed for a party."

"She's a good friend, I think."

"You think she's a good friend. You think? You're bringing a woman with you whose boobs are hanging out, bringing a woman like that to her door and you without any pants on, and you're saying shit about thinking she's a good friend? How long have you known her?"

Hickum looked at Gaye Nell and then back to the street. He put his fist to his mouth, coughed, and mumbled something.

"Don't play with me, Hickum Looney! How long?"

"I met her this morning."

"You met her this morning?"

"Right. Early, I met her early."

"Did you say *early?*"

"Yes."

"Well, hell, that makes all the difference in the world."

They drove a block in silence.

"Why is it," he said, "that when I think I'm beginning to understand you, something shifts and I don't know what gear we're in? Why is that?"

"Because we're not on the same page."

He looked at her. She was not smiling.

"Just like that right there," he said. "I don't understand that and never will."

"You might come to understand it," she said. "You never can tell."

"Maybe," he said. They drove in silence until finally he glanced over at her. "You mind telling me why you didn't at least get yourself a blouse when we were back at the . . . back where you've been living?"

She stared straight ahead and her voice was very small when she said, "The only blouse I've got is the one you're sitting on. We ain't all rich."

Hickum opened his mouth to say something, but an unfamiliar feeling flooded his chest and he could not speak.

chapter

seven

They sat for a few minutes in front of the yellow cinder block house alternately looking at each other and back at the house. The lights were on in the living room and the shadow of a woman passed slowly, very slowly, in front of the drawn shades. Even through the shades of the window they could see a hitch, a little limp, in the way she walked.

Hickum thought it might be his imagination, but every time he glanced at Gaye Nell, her eyes seemed to be a little brighter, a little shinier in the lights from the dash. Was that anger? What the hell did she have to be angry about? He had to be wrong, and even if he was right, he surely wasn't going to be the first to mention it.

"That her?" said Gaye Nell.

"Has to be," Hickum said. "Lives alone."

"Crippled?"

"No."

"Her walk looks crippled to me."

"If you'd walked as far as she had today, you'd move like that too."

"She old?"

"What?"

"Old?"

"Well, she's not young."

"You didn't tell me that."

"You didn't ask," he said, turning to Bubba at his shoulder. "Are you going to make this beast quit slobbering on me? Or am I going to have to slap his ears off his head?"

"You start thinking you can slap my dog and you might start thinking you can slap me the same way."

"I didn't say one word about slapping you."

"Men that slap women usually don't talk about it."

"One thing I'm not going to do is sit out here and see which one of us dies of boredom first. We need clothes and I need to get some sleep. I've got a bad day tomorrow. The Boss is mad as hell at me already."

"The Boss? Who's that?"

"Take too long to tell with me not wearing any trousers. He's just the maniac I work for. And that's not just a manner of speaking. Sometimes I really do think he's nuts. Besides, all we need is a cop to ride by and see you sitting here with naked tits."

"*Tits?* I thought you preferred *breasts.*"

"I'm getting to know you better, and I've changed my mind." He smiled and patted her on the shoulder. "Believe me, forget about *breasts*, you're a *tits* kind of person. All the way."

"I'll take that as a compliment."

"My mama didn't raise me to say such as that as a compliment, but the truth's the truth."

They both turned to look at Ida Mae's house.

"Now that we've got it settled that I'm a tits kind of person, how are we going to get inside of her house with both of us naked?"

"Easy."

"I'm glad you think so."

Hickum pointed to something that she could not quite make out. "We'll call her up and take the edge of her shock off."

Gaye Nell said: "Don't tell me that's a telephone?"

"It sure as hell's not a microwave."

"Wiseass."

"The Boss has got a phone just like it."

"Good for him. But I expect he's semirich while you have to grind yours out door to door."

"A telephone is basic to your Lincoln Town Car. You wouldn't want to own this car without a phone. I don't imagine they would even want to sell it to you. It's a package deal. If you know what I mean."

"I don't know what you mean and I don't think you do, either."

"I don't, but the good part is I don't have to make the call. I was thinking it might be better if you called."

"Why on earth would I do that?"

"To explain things."

"What things do you think I could explain?"

"That we're parked in front of her house inappropriately dressed."

"You want me to call a woman I don't even know and tell her that me and a naked man I don't know either would like to come into her house."

"You don't have to mention coming in the house right away. Just tell her we're parked outside."

"Naked?"

"*Inappropriately dressed* might be better. Don't worry, she's real easy to get to know."

After watching him quietly for a moment, she said, "I thought you were a little odd—I thought that from the beginning. But I was wrong. You're stone crazy."

Hickum picked up the phone and dialed. They could hear the ring inside the house. The moving shadow behind the window shades stopped still. They listened to the ring coming through the receiver.

"She's not going to answer it."

"She'll answer it," he said. "She is a deliberate and careful woman."

"How deliberate and careful do you need to be to answer a goddam telephone in your own house?"

"I hate to hear a woman sit in a car and continually cuss. It's not a seemly thing for a woman to do."

"I hate to sit in a car with my tits hanging out like decorations on a Christmas tree."

"See, there you go again . . . Ida Mae, this is Hickum Looney." There was a silence. Then: "But you must remember me. You spent the whole day with me." Another silence, a little longer this time. Then he shot a brief glance at Gaye Nell. "You're embarrassing me, Ida Mae. Hickum. H-I-C-K-U-M. Looney. L-O-O-N-E-Y. You satisfied now?" Another silence. "My God, why not? What'll it take to convince you that I'm me and that I'm not just playing here, either? The truth is we're pretty desperate for some clothes to put on. *We?* There's a woman with me. What? I brought her here because I didn't have any other place to go and I thought you were my friend. What's that you're saying? You're Hickum Looney's friend, not mine." Very slowly and quietly, he said, "Listen, Ida Mae, please just listen carefully. It's not but one Hickum Looney and I'm him. Always been him, always gonna be him. Where am I calling from? Hell, I'm right in front of your house," he said, his voice rising in triumph. "I've got a telephone in this baby I'm driving." A silence followed, about twenty seconds longer than any of the others. "Sure, I'll hold the phone. Ida Mae, I'll hold the phone as long as you want me to." A bladder that had seen the service Ida Mae's had seen no longer held very much for very long. He didn't mind a bathroom run.

Gaye Nell grabbed his arm with thin little fingers and they cut into his flesh like wire cable.

"What's she doing? In the name of Lucifer, will you kindly tell me what is taking so long?" Gaye Nell was looking toward the house and Hickum turned to look with her. One of the shades was rolled up and there was Ida Mae, gray twisted tufts of hair sprouting at all angles. Abruptly the shade went down.

Hickum immediately snatched up the phone and put it to his ear. "Ida Mae," he said.

"You know what nine-one-one means, sonny?"

"Everybody knows. But nine-one-one has nothing to do with this."

"You drive on out of here and take that woman with you. Don't and you'll have nine-one-one all over you, stuck clear to the bone."

Ida Mae was shouting now and Gaye Nell took the phone. "Mizz Ida Mae," she said.

"Who is this talking to me?"

"My name is Gaye Nell Odell and I'm a girl over her head and about to drown. Hickum said you were a Christian lady who might help us. We don't need much."

"Christian lady?" demanded Ida Mae. "Whoever is with you is off his rocker. They don't know me if they said that."

Ida Mae was shouting so loudly that it had caused Hickum to start squirming in his seat and shaking his head no.

"All I know is what he told me," said Gaye Nell. "And if you doubt him telling me that, I'm willing to be struck dead right where I'm sitting."

"You don't have to be willing. You'll be struck soon enough. And let me tell you something else, the real Hickum Looney drives a yellow dented dirty Dodge, real dirty. I wouldn't imagine the real Hickum ever was inside of a car like the one in front of my house."

"Mizz Ida Mae, that's not why Hickum drove his car to your house and that's not why I come with him."

"Then why'd you come?"

"We didn't have a choice."

"You always have a choice. A twenty-two-caliber pistol will send you to the place where there are no more good-byes—or hellos, either, for that matter."

"You're just poking fun."

"No more trouble out of the barrel of a gun is cheap at the price and nothing to joke about."

"Gimme the phone," Hickum said.

"No."

"What do you mean, *no?*"

"When did *no* start meaning more than the one thing?"

Ida Mae said: "Don't let him push you around, honey."

"This is none of your business, Ida Mae."

"I might just mean to make it some."

"I've got to talk to you," said Gaye Nell.

"Well, go on," said Hickum. "Talk."

"Not you, her." Gaye Nell looked through her window and across the little space and then through Ida Mae's window.

"Well, go ahead, child," Ida Mae said. "What's on your mind?"

"I need to come in."

"In?"

"Your house."

"Me, too," said Hickum.

"Well, come on in then."

"We can't," said Gaye Nell.

"Why?"

"We naked."

"Naked?"

"Naked. Semi, anyway. I don't have anything on top and Hickum, he don't have anything on the bottom."

"If you're with Hickum Looney of east Tennessee, you're not naked. Hickum's not that kind of man. *Whoever* you with, don't let that sumbitch drive off before I can call nine-one-one."

The phone went dead. The two of them sat looking at each other and then both turned to look at the house.

"Will she do it?" asked Gaye Nell.

"She'll do it."

"Well, get in there and stop her."

"You want me to walk in that door with this dick hanging out?"

"You're right. It's not much of a dick."

"I didn't mean that and you know it."

"If you didn't mean that, what did you mean?"

Hickum looked down at his wrinkled dick, that even uncircumcised didn't measure over two inches.

Exasperated, Hickum said: "Do you know you can do jail time for exposing one of these things?"

"You're shittin' me, Hickum Looney."

"You never heard of indecent exposure?"

With some indignation, she said: "I'm not an ignorant person. Of course I heard of indecent exposure. But I never once thought they meant that little raggedy-ass Vienna sausage you showing right there in your lap. It's so damn short, it won't fall over."

"While you're out here insulting me, she's talking to the nine-one-one people. Get in there and stop her."

"If you'll think back a minute, you'll remember I didn't drive us here in the first place. If you want something done, do it yourself."

Nodding his head vigorously and slapping the steering wheel with both hands, Hickum yelled: "I mighta known. I mighta seen it coming. Well, you just watch me take over this crisis situation we got ourselves in."

Hickum popped the door open and bounded out of the car, leaving the door open behind him. Bubba was right at his heels, snapping and growling. Hickum's blood was so high that he did not notice the dog, nor could he think about the white cheeks of his ass flashing and blinking as he loped across the lawn.

When he got to the door, he looked back at Gaye Nell, who was getting out of the car to follow him, and called angrily: "You just goddam watch this." With the pit bull growling and drooling at his heels, Hickum slammed on the door with the heel of his hand.

"You might as well open up because—"

The door jerked open and Hickum was hit square in the face with a wet mop. Soiled shreds of string flew in all directions.

"And I've dialed nine-one-one, too. You're in shit too deep to stir with a stick."

Before she had the first words out of her mouth, Bubba dashed between her legs and attacked the rubber aspidistra plant that looked like a man wearing a hat. Specifically, he went for the hat. Bubba went for the hat and held it between his front feet while ripping it to pieces. Ida Mae looked over Hickum's shoulder and said, "Never trust an old man, specially one that's stained about the crotch."

Gaye Nell cocked her head and said, "What we say back home is it's better to be an old man's sweetheart than a young man's slave."

"I don't know how you can say that standing there with your jugos swinging in the breeze like they are."

"*Jugos?*"

"That's what we called 'em when I was just a yearling girl like you."

"First my jugos were swinging in the breeze and now you say I'm a yearling girl."

Ida Mae said: "Now you got everything right."

"I don't mean to break a heavy discussion about what is or is not hanging in the breeze—do you think you got anything in the house I could wear?"

"Wouldn't mind a shirt of some kind myself."

Ida Mae stood looking at the two of them: "Let me tell you something, Gaye Nell, because you obviously have not caught on yet. A man has *the right* to lose his pants. No woman ever has the right to lose any part of her clothes, not even a kerchief tied round her head. If a man sees her riding out with a young man on a Sunday afternoon with a kerchief tied round her head and she comes back two hours later without that kerchief, she'll be a whore in the whole county before sunup the next morning. That's the way the fucking—and I use the word deliberately— world is. Understand?

"I already understood that."

"You did?"

"I knew that the whole time I was growing up."

"Did you have any brothers?"

"Three."

"The swine. One is too many. Three is a herd."

"I always thought so myself."

"You on the road."

"Almost a year now."

"You don't seem hardly old enough to stay alive on the road that long."

"Don't guess I would be if it weren't for him." She pointed to Bubba sitting at her feet with his tongue hanging over his broken teeth. "Seen 'im tear the leg right off a man, the whole thing."

"That'd take a whole lot of tearing."

"He was a right little feller, the man was. But I let Bubba go on with it. Figured it'd be good practice for the future."

"Come on in here, girl. I believe you my kind of people."

Hickum Looney, who had been shifting from foot to foot as they talked, said: "Whatever it was you two were talking about went right over my head." He put his hand on Ida Mae's shoulder. "You didn't really dial nine-one-one, did you?"

"No, but it's never too late. I didn't tell you, did I, Hickum," said Ida Mae, "but I am a student of the human skull and I knew right off the minute I saw the configuration of your head that it was made of the stuff that everything went right over."

Hickum, obviously a little embarrassed, said, "Why thank you, ma'am. That's mighty kind of you." He didn't understand what she had said, but it seemed like a compliment because of the word *configuration*, which struck him as a mighty fine word indeed.

"I'd like to get some clothes, if I could," Gaye Nell said.

Hickum said: "I'd be obliged myself for a little something to put on. It's a long way from being proper for me to be standing here talking to a lady naked down the front like this."

"Never told you I was a nurse, did I, Hickum? Was, though. And if you had every finger and toe in the world, you still couldn't count the dicks I've seen in my life. Big, small, all colors of the rainbow, and every shape you can imagine and some you couldn't!"

"All colors of the rainbow," Gaye Nell said in a musing voice. "That's near 'bout po'try."

"Everybody that speaks the truth that's close to the bone is pretty nearly always talking poetry."

"See," said Gaye Nell, "that's po'try right there."

Hickum said: "I hope nobody gives a damn about that plant in the corner, because while the two of you've been going on about poetry, Bubba's chewed that thing with the hat down to a nub."

Gaye Nell twisted to face the corner and at the same time screamed, *"Bubba, damn you."* Bubba paid her no mind and continued to chew at the pieces of the hat. "You need your ass blistered, mister, that's what you need."

Ida Mae caught Gaye Nell's arm as she started toward the dog. "Let him have it. Damn thing's been standing there twenty-four years, the hat too, without a soul touching it."

Hickum's loose mouth stretched into a grin. "I bet it's a good story behind that."

"And I bet it's not any of your business," Gaye Nell said.

Ida Mae stopped her as she started toward the ruined tree and Hickum. "Let it go. I don't care. Did once, don't anymore. That belonged to my former husband, Clyde. He used to toss his hat on top of that plant when he came in, sit down in front of the TV, drink fifteen or so beers, fart a few times, and go to bed. One evening he got out of his chair without drinking all his beers, said he was going to the corner for cigarettes, and never came back." She stared at the hat Bubba had reduced to pieces the size of a quarter. "I should have known something was wrong when he went out without his hat. Hell, he used to put on his hat to go to the bathroom. Said it made him concentrate better. Which I don't doubt it did."

chapter

eight

"Take your pick," said Ida Mae, opening the folding doors of a closet. It was packed with clothes from wall to wall. There was not space for another single hanger.

"Just any old thing'll do . . ."

"Then just get any old thing."

"I'd settle for a towel," said Hickum. "This is not funny. In case it hasn't occurred to either of you, this is an embarrassing situation for me."

Ida Mae and Gaye Nell turned to regard him for a long moment. Then Ida Mae said: "I hope you don't think it's fun for us girls to have to . . . well . . . to watch you swing and flop."

Gaye Nell, who had just pulled a silk blouse out of the closet, said, "There's not enough of him to swing and flop."

"Gaye Nell, try to remember," said Hickum, "where you'd be if it wasn't for me."

"You two can fight after you get your clothes on," said Ida

Mae. "Come on, Hickum, I'll show you where you can find some pants."

Behind them, Gaye Nell had slipped into the blouse. "I thought this was yours."

Ida Mae didn't even look back. "I never throw away anything: Waste not, want not, as the philosopher said. Thirty-five years ago, all that stuff fit me perfect." That was when she stopped and looked back. She stood very still looking at Gaye Nell before saying, "It fit me better'n it does you. You're what used to be called a itty-bitty-titty queen. Me? I had football players and every other kind of celeb tell me I had huds bigger'n their nephew's head."

"*Huds?*" said Hickum.

"Tits," said Ida Mae. "Any other questions?"

Neither Gaye Nell nor Hickum spoke. Hickum, his mouth slightly ajar, followed Ida Mae down the dimly lit hallway. She stopped and opened a closet similar to the one she had opened for Gaye Nell. Hanging neatly on one side were trousers of every fabric: polyester, khaki, denim, and other kinds of cloth that Hickum did not recognize. On the other side, shirts on hangers were packed as tightly as the trousers.

"Your husband?"

"They were his for a long time," she said, "before he ran off and left 'em. God knows where he's at. For all I know he's making the grass greener somewhere in a cemetery. If he is, it's the first proper work he's ever done."

"Apparently he didn't throw away anything either."

"Never let him," she said. "Waste not . . ."

". . . want not," said Hickum. "You already said." He snatched a pair of trousers off a hanger and pulled them on. "Your husband was a good-size fella, wasn't he?"

"I think you kind of look cute in them," Gaye Nell said as she came down the hall to meet them. "Floppy just naturally looks good on some people. It's called the layered look."

With more heat than he intended, Hickum said, "I don't say

anything about your blouse, you don't say anything about my pants. Deal?"

"Deal," she said.

"You took them off the wrong end of the rack, hon," said Ida Mae. "Get a pair off the other end and they'll fit better. My big old nasty husband blew up like a pig before he left. If you know what I mean."

"I don't know what you mean," said Gaye Nell. "And that's not a very kind thing to say."

"I'm not a very kind person. Didn't Hickum tell you that?"

"How could I tell her?" Hickum said. "It's a little hard to get in a word edgewise when you're talking to her."

"Clyde was a little thick that way too."

"What?"

"She was just pointing out that you're stupid like her husband," Gaye Nell said harshly.

"I don't know as I ever said I wasn't."

"You're a truthful man. I never said you lied."

Hickum stared at the old lady and thought of the Company Manual. Practically everything that had ever come out of his mouth was influenced by the manual. Hickum was suspect of its truthfulness, and he was not the only salesman who had such doubts about it. The Boss countered these doubts as best he could. Every three months or so he used the teleconference time to drive home the point that the Company Manual was only a series of perceptions on a different kind of product, all for the good of the Company's clients and clients-to-be. For people like that, you had to come at them with a sales pitch from an extreme angle. The straight, the direct, and the true would never do.

The bedrock on which the Boss's Theory of Salesmanship was built was that the consumer in America was the world's most terrified individual. Therefore, a little lying in the name of a product was not really lying at all. Anybody could make an excellent product and sell it. But it took a genius to make a piece of shit and sell it. And that was what the Boss pointed out again and again: He was a genius, and his exhortations to buy were nothing but pure patriotism, love of country in the purest form. Hickum always believed every word when he was listening to the Boss saying it. He had no alternative. But as soon as he was walking away from the lecture, he doubted every word he had heard. He had no alternative.

The doorbell chimed throughout the house just as Hickum was putting on a pair of overlarge khaki pants.

"You need to go down a size or two, hon," said Ida Mae.

"Somebody's at the door."

"I have many ailments," said Ida Mae, "but deafness is not one of them. Whoever's at the door will stay or leave, one or the other. We've got another matter at hand right now."

"I like the fit of these right here fine."

"Hickum likes his clothes loose," said Gaye Nell, looking toward the living room, where somebody was still leaning on the doorbell.

"He looks like he fell off a horse and was dragged about a mile or two," said Ida Mae.

Hickum couldn't very well tell her that was how the Boss wanted him to look. A white shirt, tie, and jacket were mandatory, but it all had to look tired. Very tired.

"That sumbitch at the door's doing a full-tilt boogie now," Gaye Nell said. "Want me to see who it is?"

"Might as well. It doesn't look like the fool means to stop," said Ida Mae. "Maybe I can get Hickum into a smaller size while you're gone."

Gaye Nell thought: I wouldn't count on it, old girl.

When Gaye Nell opened the door, she could not see the stoop because the man standing there completely shut out anything on the other side of the screen door, which Ida Mae had thoughtfully secured with the latch. The man's size caught Gaye Nell by such surprise that when she opened her mouth, she could not speak.

"Bickle," he said.

"What?"

"Bickle's my name."

"Congratulations," said Gaye Nell.

"The world is full of wiseasses," he said. "Even female children are wiseasses."

Gaye Nell said: "Get lost and take your mouth with you."

"Give me Hickum and I'll go."

"What's a hickum? Jesus, you're not asking for a hickey, are you?"

"I don't know a Hickey."

"Looking at you, it figures."

"But I know a Hickum and I know he's here. The Boss sent me and I want him."

Gaye Nell thought about that for a moment before saying, "And the Boss is pretty serious shit, right?"

"Wrong," he said. "The Boss is wicked shit entirely beyond the imagination of a person your age."

Gaye Nell turned and walked back to the closet where Ida Mae was trying to get Hickum into another pair of trousers that fit him a little better.

"Quit with the measuring," said Gaye Nell. "We've got wicked shit entirely beyond the imagination of a person my age at the door."

"Young lady," Ida Mae said, "I never have anything serious at my front door. I forbid it."

"Tell 'er, Hickum. His name is Bickle."

"Oh, my God, that's serious shit at the front door."

"The problem with standards is not having them, it's keeping them," said Ida Mae.

"He's bigger than a nightmare," Gaye Nell said, "and uglier than birth."

"Tell him we'll dial nine-one-one on him," Ida Mae said.

Hickum said, "Somehow I don't think he'd care one way or the other about nine-one-one."

"Then how do you handle him?"

"Humor him and hope for the best."

"What kind of thing might he do?"

"He's the reason I showed up at your door with no pants on."

"What were you doing to lose your pants?"

"Humoring him."

"But he actually did take your trousers?"

Hickum hesitated. "To give him his due, he didn't have much choice."

"How much choice did he have?"

"The truth?"

"Yes."

"None. He was only doing what the Boss told him to do."

"The Boss wanted your pants?"

"Yes."

"Why?"

"Punishment."

"I think that's as far as I want to go with this," Ida Mae said. "I think I'd like to see Mr. Bickle."

"Trust me," said Gaye Nell. "You won't like to."

Hickum let the women precede him, hanging back in the dimness of the living room.

Bickle, huge in the doorway, said, "Hickum, get out here."

Hickum did not answer and took a step back.

"Come on out or I'm comin' in."

In the tiniest voice, Gaye Nell said, "You can't come in. Mizz Ida Mae has latched the screen door."

Ida Mae and Hickum looked at her with a certain horror while Bickle showed the dark hollow of his mouth, smiling. His random teeth, square, almost black, appeared to be driven into his gums rather than growing out of them.

Bickle reached out with his thick, square-fingered hand and tore the screen door entirely off its hinges. He put his long narrow shoe over the threshold, stepping into the living room.

"How do you like that?" he asked, the grinning hollow of his face growing larger.

Nobody saw the weapon come out of Gaye Nell's new silk blouse and nobody saw her aim the .38 snub-nosed special and shoot the entire big toe off the foot that was in the living room.

"How do you like that?" Gaye Nell said.

Bickle howled not unlike a dog, and his momentum brought his other foot on into the living room too, whereupon Gaye Nell blasted the big toe off the end of it.

"Just keep on coming, sumbitch, there's a lot more slugs where that come from."

Instead of coming, though, Bickle fell onto his thick, meaty rump, stopped screaming, and began to cry great gasping sobs that made Hickum think of a huge baby.

In a very calm voice, Ida Mae said: "Are you going to shoot him again?"

Simultaneously with the end of the question, Bickle stopped crying and screamed again. Hickum wanted to demand that Gaye Nell stop, but he was afraid. He wanted to start talking about the police and jails and how cruel the world was to felons, but he was afraid. Really afraid. This girl had almost killed him with a dog; what might she be capable of with a gun? Bickle was still rocking and sobbing, though quietly now, and watching the pools of thick blood spread from the ends of his boots.

Gaye Nell said: "I may have to kill him if he keeps on with that noise. I've got my own nerves to think of, you know."

Bickle quit making sounds as suddenly as if his heart had quit beating.

"Better," Gaye Nell said. "Don't you think that's better, Hickum?"

Hickum would have liked to answer her, but he could not speak.

"That's much better," said Ida Mae, because she did not want Bickle shot again in her front door, and in her heart she was certain Gaye Nell was capable of doing just that, and for reasons she could not name, she was equally certain of the next shot being lethal.

"Bubba," Gaye Nell said so loudly that it caused Hickum to lose a few drops of urine down the leg of Ida Mae's husband's pants. The dog appeared as if by magic at her feet, resting easily on his haunches, looking up at Gaye Nell with his long red tongue dripping strings of saliva. "Fix," she commanded, pointing at Bickle who was trying to reach forward and hold his bleeding feet. On the command *fix*, Bubba's thick bony head swung to look at Bickle, his scarred ears went forward, and a ridge of hair leapt up along his spine. His tail stiffened above his back and the only thing that moved on him was his ribs as he panted and snorted through his foreshortened nose.

Gaye Nell looked at Bickle whimpering and trying not to touch his bleeding feet. "Those shot-up feet are nothing compared to what you'll get if I tell Bubba to do you."

"Damn," said Hickum, choking on the word.

Gaye Nell, in a voice that might have been discussing how to best fertilize roses, said: "It sounds worse than it is, if he'll do as he's told. *Attack* means to chew the living hell out of him if he moves. *Kill* means to take him all the way out."

"That doesn't sound worse than what it is. It's worse than it sounds."

"Your voice is coming around, Hickum" Ida Mae said. "You becoming a little more accustomed to the way things are going, are you?"

"In a word, no. Why do you put up with this?" He was pointing at Bickle.

"Seems about right to me," said Ida Mae. "I didn't tell the sumbitch to jerk my door off the hinges."

"The man has been shot twice in your house. In case you're interested, that's a felony."

Gaye Nell said: "Maybe, maybe not. We can always drag him on in the house and put another round between his eyes. That way we're shooting an intruder. I'm not going to do serious time because this guy's acted like an asshole."

"Jesus have mercy," gasped Bickle.

"It's not Jesus you want to be talkin' to. I own this animal. My name is Gaye Nell Odell. I got the dog and I got the mercy."

"God have mercy, show a little mercy."

"I think that may be blasphemous."

"Can't I do anything right?" he asked behind a sobbing hiccup.

"Doesn't much look that way," she said.

"I only did what I was told to do," Bickle said, his voice almost steady.

"Don't start with that," she said.

"I never had an option," said Bickle. "Go on, Hickum, tell her."

"He's right. No option." Hickum and Gaye Nell stood quietly balanced in each other's gaze. Finally Hickum said: "Why did you have that gun? You never told me you had a gun."

Gaye Nell looked at her dog, in whose thick throat a low growl had started and whose purplish lips had lifted tautly from his broken teeth.

"Steady, Bubba," she said.

The growl stopped and the dog's rigid lips went slack. But his eyes never wavered from Bickle's soft mottled throat, and the ridge of hair remained lifted on his back.

"What's the matter with him?" Hickum asked.

Gaye Nell said: "He wants Bickle to give him an excuse to kill him."

Hickum did not spit, but the sound of his voice made it seem he had it on his mind. "You," said Hickum, "you out there with a killer dog and a goddam pistol in your belt."

Bubba's huge, bony head swung in Hickum's direction. "Bubba don't much like people to cuss when they talkin' about me."

"I didn't cuss at all till I met you."

"Right," she said. "I understand. Now I'd shut up about it if I was you." There was a silence while everybody watched Bubba watching Bickle. Finally Gaye Nell said, "What now?"

"Somebody owes me a screen door and it mounted," Ida Mae said.

Gaye Nell pointed to Bickle and said, "There he sits, right there."

"I don't want the office boy. I want the sonofabitch who sent him."

Bickle sat straight up. "You've got that wrong, lady. If you think you want to meet the Boss, you're nuts."

"He's right," Hickum said. "That's the last human being on the face of the earth you want to get close enough to see."

Ida Mae fisted her malformed hands on her nonexistent hips and said, looking first to Bickle, "You're the only one in the crowd who appears to be bleeding to death, and . . . ," she turned to Hickum, "you can't even keep track of your own pants." She paused. "Thank both of you, but I think I'll decline the advice of both of you."

"You've got to take me to the hospital," said Bickle. "I'm bleeding to death here . . . And the pain . . . God, the pain."

Gaye Nell stepped over and kicked him on the bottom of his bloodiest shoe. Bickle screamed.

"That's just to show you things are not as bad as they can be," she said.

Bickle had never stopped screaming, and the second kick only made him take it up another level.

Gaye Nell reached behind her and got the .38 out of her waistband, where she wore it in the small of her back. "Your trouble, Bickle, is you're not familiar with pain. You don't know what real pain is until you've had a kneecap blown off."

"You might as well go on and kill him if you're going to mess him up like that," said Ida Mae. "Damn, I do hate a cripple."

Hickum took a step back. "The two of you have lost your minds."

"Blame it on him," said Gaye Nell, raising her voice to get over Bickle's screaming. "His hollering is making me crazy. Ida Mae might have the best idea I've heard today, just go on and kill him."

When the hand holding the pistol at her side started to rise, Bickle's scream stopped as suddenly as if a cork had been driven into his mouth.

The silence was startling. And the three of them stared at Bickle to see if he meant to start up again.

"I guess we ought to look at the poor bastard's feet," said Ida Mae. She gestured at the pool of blood spreading around his shoes. "A little pressure bandage ought to stop some of that."

While she talked, she had taken a first aid kit out of the drawer of a heavy antique chest beside the wall. She took a gleaming scalpel and with six strokes—three for each shoe—she stripped his feet naked. Blood poured out of the shoes where they had been cut.

"Holy Jesus, I'll be crippled for life," wailed Bickle.

"Don't excite them, Bickle. Keep quiet," said Hickum. "We've fallen in with two crazy ones here."

"You haven't seen crazy yet," Gaye Nell said. "Before this is over, I'll show you crazy."

"For God sake, don't," said Hickum. "I can't stand crazy."

"How can you say that, when you're neck deep in crazy all the time. From what I know so far, your whole life has been neck deep in crazy."

Hickum had no notion at all of what she meant, so he couldn't think of a reply.

Ida Mae had leaned back from the job of work she had done on Bickle's feet. All his toes were spread and stuffed now with gauze and cotton. Neither of his big toes seemed to be there.

"Ever had any trouble walking?" asked Ida Mae.

"No," said Bickle.

"You will," she said with some satisfaction. "And every time you have trouble with your feet, think of my goddam door you ripped off trying to get in here to my friends."

"None of it was my idea."

"So you say. But an idea won't tear the door off a widder woman's house. It takes a goddam wrongheaded man to do that."

In a small, apologetic voice, Bickle said: "You a widder woman?"

"I don't know, and I don't care." Ida Mae's voice was strident, her face red. "What if I am? Give me an answer to that, you . . . you . . . man. Can you? Can you give me an answer?"

"No, ma'am."

Gaye Nell and Hickum stood very quietly watching Ida Mae jerk Bickle's bloody feet around, pretending she was not through with them yet, and watching, also, Bickle chewing his lower lip until it was bloody in an effort to keep from screaming. But he could not keep tears from coursing down his cheeks.

"I should have let her shoot your kneecaps off and then killed you." She stood up and leaned over him. "You say one more word you haven't been asked for, and if she doesn't blow your chest out with that pistol, I will. Nod your head if you agree, shake it if you don't. But don't stretch me any thinner with that wretched voice your own mother cursed you with."

Bickle nodded his head and kept nodding it.

"All right, fool!" she said. "Stop." Then she turned to Hickum and Gaye Nell. "Let's get on the road. I want to see the little bastard that sent this dickhead to mess up my house."

"How do we know where to go?"

"Maybe he's at the office."

Hickum said, "That wouldn't be like him."

"Where's he stay when he comes to town?"

Hickum said: "I've only heard him call the places he stays various shit-holes."

Ida Mae said: "You mean to tell me that a man who owns a company with offices all over the country refers to the places he stays as *various shit-holes*?"

"His exact words," said Hickum.

Bickle, still sitting on the floor, said, "It's just part of the Grand Overview scene to help all of us salesmen get in the selling mode. It's all in the Company Manual."

Gaye Nell turned to Ida Mae. "Did you understand a word of that?"

"No, I didn't," said Ida Mae. "He may be in shock. Sometimes that'll make you babble."

"He's not in shock," Hickum said. "And he's not babbling. It just takes a little getting used to. Bickle, you know talking about what's in the Company Manual is cause for severe punishment."

"Severe punishment?" said Gaye Nell. "We're talking about a grown man here. Who the hell's going to punish him?"

"The little bastard we're about to go see," said Ida Mae.

Hickum tried to stay calm and keep his face without expression. During the long day of selling soap with Ida Mae's help, he had got started talking about the Boss and had said entirely too much.

Ida Mae was crouched and shaking her twisted forefinger in Bickle's face. "The same one who sent this mad dog to growl and slobber at my front door."

"I was just doing a job, lady," said Bickle, rocking back and to with the pain in his feet. "Nothing personal. It was only business."

Ida Mae straightened up and said, "You ugly wop, you're Mafia. I knew it. We've got a friggin' mafioso on our hands."

Gaye Nell sighed and said: "Turn it off, Mabel. What we've got on our hands is a regular old American addicted to watching television."

"But the way he talked just seemed—"

"Forget it. Even little kids talk like the Corleone family these days. Mario Puzo turned the whole fucking country into bogus Sicilian assassins."

Hickum said: "I never thought about it like that—*The Godfather* and all that. You could be right."

"Try not to think, it'll give you a hernia."

She looked at Hickum who was doing his best to avoid eye contact with everybody, including Bubba, who was still on point with Bickle. The sight of blood had stiffened his tail over his back like a thin, curling saber and raised more of his hair.

"Bring the car up on the lawn, Hickum," Gaye Nell said. "This meat is too big and awkward to think about carrying."

"You're not putting this bastard in my car. He's bleeding like a half-butchered pig."

"I'll put 'im wherever I want to put him. Unfortunately, at the moment, I own him."

"Put 'im anywhere but in my car."

"Before you two get into a fight here, could you call off the dog? You're going to get me killed by accident. I don't like the way he's looking at me."

"He only wants you to run so he can kill you. Believe me, if you die because of Bubba it will not be an accident. He has far too much pride for his work to be that sloppy."

Hickum said: "I don't see how Bickle is standing the pain with his feet busted up the way they are."

"Terror is a wonderful sedative," said Ida Mae. "But we can't keep him here like this. That Percocet is not going to hold 'im much longer."

"Before we go over to see the Lip, we'll drop 'im at an emergency room, where he's going to say he was shot in the feet and robbed."

"Because if you don't," said Gaye Nell, "I will personally see you dropped in Biscayne Bay."

"I can swim," said Bickle.

"Not with a thirty-eight round in your head."

"You wouldn't do that."

"I shot you in the feet, didn't I?"

"There's too much bullshit going on around here and too little being done. We going or not?"

"We're going."

"We'll do it in the Dodge Bickle is driving. The Lincoln's too fine a car to mess up with blood."

"Thank you," said Hickum.

"Shut up. You did me and now I'm doing you. This makes us even. You're big enough, but much too tender to run with me and Bubba."

"I agree," said Hickum. "I really do agree. I'm definitely too tender."

Gaye Nell looked at Hickum for a long moment and then cut her eyes to Ida Mae: "You believe this guy?"

"I can, but I have to work really hard to do it." She walked over and squeezed herself into Hickum's side. "But I don't mind," she said. "At my age anything male smells pretty damn good."

"Why you rank and randy old broad," said Gaye Nell.

"I know. It's hard to believe what a bitch I am. And at my age, too."

"Not all that hard," said Gaye Nell and winked. Then she turned to Hickum. "Let's see how fast you can get out there and back that yellow piece of shit Bickle drove up here in to the door."

Hickum went out the door, tripped on a screen lying across the walk, caught himself just before he went down, and backed the dirty yellow Dodge across the lawn, the tires spinning.

He came stumbling back into the light of the living room gasping for breath. "How's that?"

"It only shows how fast the lame can move when their ass is on the line."

Hickum's disappointment with her answer showed in his face before she finished speaking.

Ida Mae leaned closer to Gaye Nell and said: "Being kind of hard on him, aren't you, girl?"

"He helped me out of a hard place, but it's been all downhill from there."

"Ah, the history of the world since the thing got started."

Bickle gave a long gargling sound that was pure pain.

"We are moving," said Ida Mae, leaving the room and coming back immediately with a sheet. "Roll on, Bickle."

He looked at the sheet she had spread out beside him. "I been shot twice and you're asking me to roll?"

"You weren't shot in the ass, and I'm telling, not asking."

Bickle got himself onto the sheet with much groaning, grunting, and cursing under his breath.

"Hickum, grab that corner, I'll take this one. We'll slide his ass out the door like a side of beef."

Bickle was about to warn them not to bump him down the two concrete steps when they bumped him down the two concrete steps. Ida Mae jerked open the backdoor of the Dodge and said: "Get yourself in there."

"I can't get in there. I don't have any feet, for God sakes."

"I don't care how you do it, but do it, or else you won't have anything to make wee wee with."

"Did you say *wee wee?*"

"Think it'd be easier to shoot off a dick than two big toes." She looked at Gaye Nell.

Gaye Nell took a pistol out of the back of her waistband and said: "We'll never know until I try it."

But she had already put the weapon behind her waistband before she got through speaking. Bickle was hustling as much as a wounded man could hustle. He couldn't take to his feet, but he rolled over and like a giant slug he squirmed and wiggled on his knees and belly and elbows, glancing now and again up at Gaye Nell, his eyes rolling, until he had worked his way on the backseat.

It was then that Gaye Nell turned to Ida Mae and said: "You got to stay here with my dog, darling. You can't take Bubba on a thing like this. He'll either hurt somebody or get killed by some fool with a gun. I'll owe you forever if you do this for me."

"Damn, girl. I wanted to see the big man that's got everybody running scared."

"You'll see him," said Gaye Nell. "I'll make sure you do. You've got to be exhausted. Hickum told me what a day you had."

"I wouldn't do this for anybody but you. Truth is, I *am* tired, totally beat."

Gaye Nell sat in the back with Bickle. Hickum ground the old car into gear and tore up some lawn getting out of the yard and actually left a little rubber when he double-clutched into second gear.

"This old jalopy's got pretty good power," said Gaye Nell. "And you're not a bad wheel man for the basic nerdish type."

Hickum said: "When my selling don't do as good as I want it to, I moonlight as a cabbie."

"Now that's some pretty sad shit," said Gaye Nell.

"Where we going?" Hickum said. "You know where we going?"

"Ask the trouble in the backseat," said Gaye Nell.

"You know the Motel Ten, north on the Seventy-ninth Street Causeway?" asked Bickle.

"You're shitting me," said Hickum.

"That's where he called from when he told me to go get you and bring you in. He gave me this address in case you didn't answer at your place."

"How did he know I might be here if I wasn't home?"

"He got it when we faxed our orders in to him. You put Ida Mae Milk and her address down as the referral agent for every sale. You poor dumb shit, he's waiting at the motel right now."

"What's wrong with Motel Ten?"

"Nothing wrong with it," said Hickum. "I tried to stay in one once."

"Tried?"

"Turned back the corners to go to bed and there was hair in the sheet."

"I'm not going to touch that," said Gaye Nell.

"Hair?"

"Don't tell me anything else."

Hickum turned back to look straight ahead and swung the old Dodge into the fast lane.

"Where's the nearest hospital?" asked Gaye Nell.

"What?"

"I don't intend to say everything I say tonight twice."

"Jackson Memorial, about a half mile away."

"Drive through the emergency entrance. We'll dump Bickle."

Bickle twisted on the seat and said, "You can't—"

"Who's got the gun?"

"You do," he said in a defeated voice.

"Then shut up and listen. Here's your story. You were on your way home, forced off the road, shot in the feet, and robbed."

"That'll never fly," said Bickle, very nearly screaming. "How did my feet get bandaged?"

"Good Samaritan. The same one who dumped you at the emergency room."

"Why did he bandage me and then dump me?" He couldn't help screaming now.

"This is Miami. You can't tell a story that hasn't happened here and won't happen again. And if you raise your voice one more time you can crawl to the hospital."

Bickle started to cry, openly and loudly.

Hickum said, "We ought not just dump Bickle like this. I've known him over twenty years."

"I've already shot him in both feet," said Gaye Nell. "After that, kicking him out of a moving vehicle at the hospital is a kindness."

The neon EMERGENCY sign for the hospital blazed out of the darkness. There was a squad car, two cops, a handcuffed Cuban who might have been a Haitian, an ambulance, and three attendants all crowded around the swinging glass doors. Hickum slowed the old Dodge and Gaye Nell threw Bickle out onto the concrete. He landed on his bleeding feet and screamed. Nobody but the handcuffed Cuban looked their way as Hickum put the old Dodge in gear and roared away.

"God, I love Miami," said Gaye Nell Odell.

chapter

nine

The Boss's chauffeur was Pierre LaFarge, whose real name was Joe Wilson, which the Boss thought was entirely too common a name for the man who drove him around in his various luxury cars and also serviced certain of his other needs that nobody ever talked about but that nonetheless lived vividly as rumor throughout the Company.

Pierre had become the Boss's chauffeur quicker than the wink of an eye. One day in the Soaps For Life central warehouse in Atlanta, Georgia, where Joe Wilson was working part-time, the Boss, on one of his constant but random inspections of all departments of his enterprise, saw him bending to lift a small crate and saw too the denims he was wearing stretched tightly over his muscular ass, and without even thinking about it the Boss asked Joe if he wanted a full-time job and a new name or if he wanted to stay in the sweat-and-grunt department of the business.

Joe said he'd take anything that he didn't have to sweat to get as long as it put a roof over his head and food in his belly.

What Joe did not tell him was the secret he had learned to keep to himself. He had just walked off fifteen years in the state prison. And the Boss was so taken with the denims stretched over the hard meatiness of Joe's ass that he did not ask the questions he might normally have asked. And he didn't have an entirely normal (but necessary) deep, detailed check run on Joe, either. Rather, he bought him on the spot in the warehouse, named him, trained him, and kept him in a way that was far better than Joe—now known everywhere as Pierre—had ever been able to keep himself.

From that day to the end of his life Joe Wilson was known as Pierre LaFarge because, as it turned out, Joe liked his bogus name better than the name his mama had given him, too . . . More than that, he loved the job, at least for the first few months, loved watching the Boss sitting there in the backseat reading the papers. That was a class act. To Pierre, the Boss was nothing but class through and through. Maybe it would not happen quickly, maybe it would take the patience of Job, but Pierre LaFarge meant to have the same kind of class someday. But it didn't take long for everything to start to go sour and go very bad. A footrace, a loss, and one swift kick ruined it all.

Across an elegantly designed glass-and-chrome coffee table, opposite Pierre LaFarge, sat the former Mr. Southern California, the former Mr. California, the former Mr. America, the former Mr. World, the former Mr. Universe—whom the Boss simply called Peterbilt for reasons of appearance and affection, but also for reasons secret and sacred, or so he said. Some people, the Boss knew, would have said his relationship with Peterbilt was secret and profane instead of secret and sacred. But the Boss never lost any sleep over that. He did what he did and kept his own counsel. He swore to his dead mother that he would never reveal the reasons for anything that was sacred and secret. And he never had. LaFarge and Peterbilt were in Peterbilt's tiny but expensively appointed office. Pierre was just finishing a Coke.

Peterbilt had just taken down a quart of Carbo-King muscle builder in two long swallows from an enormous Italian crystal goblet and now sat watching the last of the milky substance congeal at the bottom of the container from which he'd drunk. Pierre watched him and was amazed.

"Damned if you don't heal faster than any man I've ever known."

"Had a lot of practice," Peterbilt said. "Ice and heat and knowing when to apply which one will do it every time."

"I thought it might take at least a week for your eyes to open. But here you sit, looking like nothing more serious happened to you than you ran into a door maybe." He stopped talking and looked off toward the far wall. Finally: "But fuck what you look like now. When I'm dead and in hell, I'll still remember what you looked like right after he finished with you."

"It wasn't as bad as you think it was."

"Don't try to shit me. I know what I know and I say it's payback time. Enough is enough. It's not like I mean to go off on him or anything like that. But the ugly little bastard thinks he owns the world, and I say he needs a reality check. If it does turn out I kill him, it'll be for his own good."

"But why now? Why today?"

"My answer is, why not? Better, why not last week? Or why not last month or a year ago? Why not the first time he kicked my bare ass and made me jump over the table as though he had enough leg to send me flying over it himself? I can't believe I've been such a major league wimp. Why?"

"Money."

"True. But I'm tired of talking about it. You said you know where he is. That the truth or a lie? You really know where he is?"

"Well, yes and no."

"That's what's wrong with this country, yes-and-no answers," said LaFarge. "Damned if I wouldn't hate to tell a man yes *and* no if he asked me a question that demanded either a yes or a no but not both."

"Don't burn a hole in your shorts. I intend to explain it to you."

"I think maybe you ought to."

"If you're going to take that tone of voice, maybe you don't need to know."

"Maybe the sorry truth is you don't know where he is yourself."

"Don't, huh? How about this? North Seventy-ninth Street Causeway coming out of Miami Beach."

As deliberately and slowly as possible, he chewed a hangnail from his finger.

"Are you going to tell the rest of the address or am I supposed to tear your head off to get it?"

"You don't have to tear anything off. And you don't have to talk so ugly and nasty either. I hate that."

A little bubble of bile blew out at the corner of Peterbilt's mouth. He had a notoriously weak stomach and everybody in the company knew the right buttons to push to bring a fine lumpy spray shooting out of his mouth with the force of a fire hose.

"Didn't mean to upset you. Just tell me what I asked for."

"How about the Motel Ten?"

LaFarge sat straighter on his chair. "He didn't go back to another of the Tens?"

"If he's not moved in the last twenty minutes, that's where he is now. But he could have moved, he could have done anything. But if he'd moved, he would have called in the new address to me. He always wants to be able to ship me in at a moment's notice. That's why I say I know where he is, but at the same time I might not know where he is."

"That trail's hot enough for me. What are we doing here? I say let's do it."

"Can you get us there?"

"I've had to pick that sonofabitch up all over the country. I can get a plane and one of his pilots. I got authorization."

"He might not like it. It's not as though he's called us to come."

"I might not give a damn what he likes."

"Listen, be serious for a minute if you can. You sure we want to do this?"

"I only know what I want to do. You know, every time he outruns me up the stairs, he gets to kick my ass over the massage table. You know that, don't you, Peterbilt?"

"I've got my own stories to tell," said Peterbilt. "Everybody at Soaps For Life does."

"I already know more than I want to know. So don't tell me. My point here is, he can't kick my ass over a table on the best day he ever had."

"But he can still kick your ass on *any* day he ever has."

"That's what grinds me. He kicks my ass and I got to jump over the table like he did it his own self. The kick don't really hurt that bad. Having to jump over the table like he actually was strong enough to kick me over it, that's what hurts."

"You're lucky," said Peterbilt.

"How you figure."

"When he decides to get down and dirty and work on me, everything hurts."

"I know. I seen. What're we doing here talking about it?"

"You the one been talking. I been listening."

"Every man's time comes to him, and the Lip's time just come to him. I want shit on my dick and money on my hip."

"I'll skip the shit on my dick."

"You never been in the joint, right?" said LaFarge.

"No."

"Then don't knock what I'm saying till you've tried it."

"You gonna make me puke."

"Aim it away from me and puke all you want. I ain't studying puke, I'm studying money and shit. I hope the little bastard's got a tight ass. I want to hear him scream when I slam his dirt track the first time with big six."

Peterbilt's cheeks popped out and he sent a solid stream of puke ten feet on a straight line. But LaFarge sidestepped not a second too soon to get hit with it, and he didn't even look back.

the mulching of america

chapter

ten

The Motel Ten was a salesman's dream. Nothing extra provided, nothing extra charged. There was never any messing around at a Motel Ten. No lonesome husbands doing a quick tap on their secretaries. Everything was on the up-and-up. Everything was in its place and ready to use. It was clean and orderly if you didn't look too close. If you looked too close, the management thought you deserved what you got.

The Boss was returning from the ice machine. He stopped in front of his door and stared out at the yellow dented Dodge that he'd picked up at the regional office here in Miami. It was parked out by the street in the moonlight. The Boss knew the series of mind-sets that kicked in when an average consumption-maddened American saw the old Dodge. It was a nobody's car. It would be apparent that the person driving such a car had no native intelligence, no natural talent, could expect no inheritance from any relative near or far, have no European teeth, and could always expect his breath to smell like a box of Kitty Litter. And besides all that, the driver of such a car had no credit cards, or if he did, the cards were already loaded to the hilt.

But there was something else at work in the blood of even the stingiest, most mean-spirited human being when he saw the car. The old Dodge became an ax to break the ice that inevitably floated somewhere in every human heart. The old wreck was proof aplenty of the opportunity and economic justice in America when a man or woman could get into such a car and go out and chase the pot of gold at the end of the rainbow. Chase it, maybe even catch it, and make it his own. The dirty dented oil-dripping wreck of a car could take any American who had the heart and stomach for it all the way to the top of the business world.

Could anyone doubt it when Soaps For Life started as nothing but a name and ended as a belief, a force spread over every state in the Union? It was all the Boss could do sometimes when he was at the podium at the annual salesman's convention not to scream: *I did it all!* And then bully everyone in attendance into admitting they owed him everything they had. He made the product (without really knowing what he was making), he wrote the Sales Manual (without knowing what he was selling), he was the one who trained the salesmen to enter a house with nothing and leave with the only thing that was real in Soaps For Life: a completed form that guaranteed *money*.

Things had changed a lot since his mother died. She had taught him all he knew about business. And she taught him many kinds of work: how to grow gardens of enormous yield from tiny pieces of earth, how to raise fat chickens in dark narrow coops, how to know and read the seasons of the year, how to avoid Taco Bell, how to eat saucers of ground jalapeño peppers until the tears in his eyes blinded him and his tongue felt walked upon by the split hooves of goats. And finally, to know there was no other road to success but increasing doses of iron discipline and pain, which if used with a full and steadfast heart, would ultimately become love. Or so was the national conviction.

Across the street from Motel Ten, Hickum Looney and Gaye Nell Odell slowly walked around a Hudson Hornet that had been restored to mint condition. They were pretending to examine the finish on the Hudson Hornet and eyeballing the Boss at the same time.

"I'm sure glad you agreed to leave that nasty dog."

"He's not nasty, but he wouldn't do for a job like this. Ida Mae'll take good care of him. Don't you worry about Bubba."

"It's not much chance I'll worry about Bubba. I'm worried about Ida Mae. That dog's liable to take a leg off her. Then again, she may kill the beast. Asking her to stay with the dog did not make her happy. But if she does do something out of character that results in bodily harm to Bubba, remember it's not her fault, it's mine for making her stay."

"Shes' not going to do anything to Bubba. Them two fit like spoons. Never seen Bubba take to anybody like that."

"I got a feeling we won't be here long."

Hickum stopped by the car and gently kicked one of the giant gangster whitewall tires.

"Hey, you!"

They looked around and didn't actually see the man who had called to them until he came out from under the raised hood of a '47 Ford coupe parked under a huge oak tree about twenty-five yards away. He wore Levi's and a Levi jacket with Harley-Davidson wings sewn onto the back. He couldn't have weighed more than 150 pounds with a belly under his belt as round and smooth as a basketball. He walked right up to Hickum until they almost touched. He was what Hickum thought of as a face talker. Hickum did not like face talkers.

"Don't kick that li'l cherry," the man said.

"How's that?"

"Car there. It's cherry."

"Godamighty," said Hickum.

"Yeah," said the little man. "You go on home and circle the date on your calendar. This is the day you kicked a cherry Hudson Hornet. But I don't ever want to see you do it again."

The little man smelled of grease and he had pushed in so close while he talked that his smooth round belly was touching Hickum. If Hickum moved back, the mechanic moved with him. They might have been dancing, the way they moved together. It gave Hickum prickly chills on the back of his neck.

"This cherry yours, big guy?" said Gaye Nell.

The mechanic turned his level, direct gaze on her. "I hear the sarcasm in your voice, lady, which I am going to ignore. But the answer to your question is, yes, I built it from the ground up. You don't see many Hudson Hornets today. They all pretty much died out. But it wasn't the fault of the automobile. It was a car before its time is what it was. The design was like the Studebaker design. Scared the hell out of people. You've got to be lockstep in this country to win."

He took a toothpick out of his shirt pocket and put it in his mouth, expertly flipped it about with his pendulous lips and his tongue while he talked, and stared at the car he had brought back to mint condition from the edge of the grave. He'd never moved from his place against Hickum, and when he turned back from looking at the car, the toothpick very nearly got Hickum in the eye.

Hickum Looney put his hands on the mechanic's greasy shoulders, pushed him gently out of his face, and looked him dead in the eye, a look the Soaps For Life Selling Manual called *We ain't nothing but two regular guys, you and me, but our word is our bond.*

"Could you do something for us?" asked Hickum.

The little man cut his eyes to the Hudson Hornet: "It ain't for sale."

"Weren't thinking of buying it. Here in the good old U.S. of

A. it's some people that think everything's for sale, but we both of us knew nothing like that automobile right there's ever for sale."

"Thank you. I'm obliged. Put your proposition."

"What?"

"Tell me what you think I can do for you and what you think would be a fair price for me to do it if I wanted to do it, which I may not want to. I guess you can understand that."

"Sure I can. But see that fella right over there across the street in front of the first motel unit?"

"You mean the one holding the ice bucket?"

"That's the one."

"Dangerous?"

"Him?"

"Don't play me for the fool. You didn't think I meant the ice bucket, did you?"

"There's nothing dangerous over there that I know of."

"What is it you know of?"

"I like your style," said Hickum. "No way to be too careful this day and time. But to answer your question: It's peaceful as a goddam convent over there."

"What's a goddam convent?"

"A very peaceful place."

"Good, because my old lady don't like dead husbands. What you want me to do over there in that place safe as a goddam convent?"

"When he goes in the room, you go knock on the door."

"Why and for how much?"

"Twenty bucks." Hickum already had the bill in his hand.

"What's he selling?"

"He'll probably call it soap."

"Meaning it ain't soap at all."

"All you need to know is it's not dangerous."

"What if it is?"

"That's why you got the twenty."

"Twenty ain't very dangerous."

"If it's dangerous or it's not, twenty is just how dangerous it's worth to us tonight."

The little man took an unfiltered Camel out of his shirt pocket and studied it as he rolled the cigarette through his fingers.

Just before Hickum thought the Camel might come apart, the little man said, "I take the monkey wrench in my back pocket on just such occasions as these. If he means to fuck with me, I hope he's got a hard dick." He turned to Gaye Nell. "No offense intended, ma'am."

"None taken," she said.

"If he hurts you in any way, we'll take care of it."

The little man looked at Hickum. "You taking care of him won't do me no good if I'm dead. That's the reason I don't usually go on trips like this for twenty dollars."

"Everybody has his standards."

"I ain't only got my own personal standards but I got a turrible short fuse to boot. Think about that while I'm gone." He took another twenty that Hickum had dug out of his pocket. Then he stopped with his back to them. He didn't even turn around as he said, "Of all the shitty things I ever been mixed up in since I got back to the world from the Nam, this has got to have the strongest taint of shit about it of any I can remember." He turned to Gaye Nell. "No offense intended, ma'am."

"None taken," said Gaye Nell.

He turned back to Hickum. "You want me to see if this guy'll try to sell me soap. Have I got it right?"

"Right."

"Seem like ever since I come back from trying to stay alive while I killed a slope or two, I been having to put my mind on shit like this ever' day, trying to figure it out, and I've about decided it ain't no way to figure such as this out. I sure as hell hope I didn't fight in a war to defend this kind of thing."

"What kind of thing?" asked Hickum, who was now convinced that the mechanic was a madman.

"Walking across the street to knock on a stranger's door to see if I can get 'im to sell me some soap. Goddam soap. And doing it in the middle of the goddam night on top of everything else that don't make sense."

"You're right, of course. It doesn't make a whole lot of sense," Gaye Nell said.

Looking back over his shoulder, the vet said. "I'm glad to see both of you ain't crazy."

"How long you think this is going to take?"

"I took the rag off my head and stopped seeing into the future at about the time I started menstrating, Hickum."

"How did you get so dirty mouthed so young?"

"If you think menstrating is dirty, that may be the root of your problem, Hickum."

"There was just no call for it, that's all," said Hickum. "Inappropriate is what it was."

"*Dirty* is what you called it," she said, moving until her face was very near his.

"You weren't whipped enough when you were a youngun," he said. "And back out of my face. I had enough of that from the greasy little devil who just left."

"Whipping me would be a terrible waste of flesh," she said. "And it kind of looked like you didn't too much mind the close talking from the vet."

"Lord help us all, now and at the hour of our death."

She shifted her feet and her face moved as close to his as it could get without actually touching him. "You're not thinking about a whipping or a Lord or a death," she said. "You might as well admit the truth."

"Do not tempt the wrath of God or the wrath of a Looney from east Tennessee, little girl."

"We both know what's little. And it ain't me," she said.

"We ought not to be out here talking like trash where we got no business," said Looney. "We ought to be over yonder in the hospital keeping Bickle company. That'd be the decent thing to do. Decent and kind."

"Seeing as how I'm the one that shot him in the feet I don't think he'd much care for my company. I don't know what he might say to me but I have my doubts about *decent* and *kind*. If somebody shot my goddam toes off, I got a pretty good idea what I'd say to him. And *decent* and *kind* don't figure into it."

chapter

eleven

The two men coming toward them were backlit and so it was impossible to see their faces. One of them was carrying a metal sample case.

"Is that the Lip with the case? I've never seen him touch one of the things," said Hickum.

They passed under a street lamp and they saw that it was the mechanic who carried the briefcase. His walk was a bouncing little strut and his head bobbed as though keeping time to music.

"I feel something weird coming down," said Gaye Nell Odell. "I think I'd just as soon get in the car and get the hell out of here."

"I think you're a little late for that."

"Then you do the talking, OK?"

"If I know the Lip, and nobody does, whatever talking's done, he'll do it."

"I don't even know the little maimed mother," said Gaye Nell.

"He gets out of line with me, I'll tell him to jump up my dog's ass."

"Jesus, Gaye Nell," said Looney. "What's this fixation you have with jumping up asses?"

"*Fixation?* Is that what you said?"

"That's what I said."

"I thought so."

"Well?"

"You can use a nasty tone of voice when you want to, you know that?"

"Changing the subject won't help."

"I don't recall changing a thing. But while we're talking about it, maybe you ought to get you some help. You are a strange individual, but you may only need you a little help."

"I don't need help."

"Them that do, mostly never know it. I read that in a magazine."

"Good for you."

"But you're not going to tell me about your awful fixation."

"Nothing to tell. You've read me wrong, big guy. I'm handy around the house and first one thing and another. But I can't fix much of anything anybody else couldn't fix if they just used the brain God give 'em."

Hickum dropped his head forward and put his face in his hands. "I give up," he said.

"Give up what?" she said.

"Whatever you want me to."

"This will probably come as a shock to you, Hickum Looney, but I don't spend much time thinking about you or men in general. Never have, never will. You do as you like. I'm the one in debt to you, not you to me. I hate to think of where ole Bubba might be sleeping tonight if you hadn't come to the rescue."

"I didn't come to the rescue. It just happened that I didn't have my pants. And that's a real fix if you're a man. A woman? It's come to the place they almost naked anyway, the way they dress. I eat out a lot, being a bachelor, and you'll never know, hell, *I'll* never know, how many dinners I've eaten looking dead into the crotch of a pair of panties. Then it's sometimes nothing's covering it at all, not even panties. I thought more than once I was going to need the Heimlich maneuver. Women are too careless with their hemline."

"I'll do you a favor and give you this for nothing. There's two things in the world that a woman—every woman—knows exactly where she left them. Her hemline and her pocketbook."

As the mechanic and the Boss passed the Hudson Hornet, the mechanic expertly flipped the toothpick from one side of his mouth to the other and said: "Car I was telling you about, Boss. Built her from the ground up. Right by myself. No help from anybody."

He was repeating himself but did not know it, because he was talking about cars, and for him the subject of cars had a movement and a motion all its own that was independent of thought. And like people everywhere he thought, what he loved, the whole world loved too.

Hickum Looney and Gaye Nell might have been invisible for all the attention the Boss and the mechanic paid them. Their focus was on the Hornet.

"Nu can lose ne car now."

"Lose the car? Is that what you said? Cars are my life. I couldn't live if I didn't have a car to work on."

"Mullshit. Dis is ne U.S. of A. Nu'd die if nu didn't have money. Money is what keeps a man alive."

"Never had much of that and I live better'n you'd think. The car is my whole life."

Hickum took Gaye Nell's arm and moved her farther back as the Boss circled the car.

"Nu work on nars cause nu don't know anything else to do. When nu get one finished, nu sell it for what nu *think* is big money, nand it is *big* na nu! The money from one wreck carries nu na ne next wreck. That's your life, am I right?"

"I ain't answering that cause I never thought about it that way."

"Nake my advice nand start thinking nat way."

"That's a loser's way of thinking."

The Boss stopped and put his hand on the mechanic's chest. "I thought I yust bought nu."

"You didn't buy me, you hired me."

"I don't hire anybody or anything. I buy what I need."

"If that's the way you want it. This is your show. You run the team."

The little harelip hopped into the air, turned two full times before he landed, and let loose his peculiar baying cry again. "Whhhhhhoooooooeeeeeee! Nu gone be a good'n. 'Cause I haven't known nu but a hour nand nu done learned a lesson."

"Lesson?"

"I run ne team."

The mechanic's face went flat, without expression. "You mean the soap thing? You mean you own the soap thing? And the people who work for you are the team?"

The little man hip-hopped from foot to foot. "Nu sick? Is dat it? Nu sick? Nere's no *soap* thing. Nand no people work for me. There's oney Soaps For Life. Nand all of us nogether is the *soap* team. I'm like, nu know, the coach. I non't have a title. I yust kinda run it, nu know?"

"Ain't that what I said?"

The Lip showed his tooth in something that was not a smile. "I told nu before. Don' talk. Stay quiet. Talk and nu make trouble for nurself."

The Boss turned and walked over to Hickum where he stood under a street lamp with Gaye Nell.

Smiling broadly, so that the single wide tooth in the middle of his face showed itself unnaturally bright in the dim light, the boss said: "Nickum."

The word was uninflected, suggesting neither anger nor pleasure.

"Boss," said Hickum.

He was suddenly very confused. How had he come to be standing face-to-face with his future as well as his past there in the parking lot with people it would have been fair to call strangers? No answers came to anything he asked himself. His brain felt soft and runny as though it would never function again. Clearly something was expected of him. He felt the expectation not only from the Boss but from the mechanic and Gaye Nell as well. "Nickum, I believe we got a quorum here, if nu feel ne need na vote on anything!" Then he gave his high keening cry as he shot straight up and spun like a top. "Whhhoooooooeeeeee!"

Everybody took a quick step back from the Boss as if caught in sudden fear. Which they were. Even the little mechanic who slipped his hand into his back pocket to take hold of the heavy Stillson wrench that he always carried in there. He had already killed two men with the wrench, one of them a soldier. Unfortunately, the soldier had been one of ours.

He had been court-martialed in the morning, sentenced to life at hard labor at noon, and was back in the field before dark, holding the same rank he'd held before he crushed the young black man's skull with his Stillson wrench when he had come upon the black soldier raping a girl of about eleven.

He kicked the dead soldier off the girl and finished the rape himself, all the while gazing into the dead soldier's eyes that were cast now in a fixed glare. He tipped his helmet to the girl, exhausted from one and a half rapes, but otherwise she seemed to be taking the rape as part of the price of doing business, which she was, and also she seemed pleasantly surprised that her own skull had not been crushed.

The young mechanic had just finished getting his gear onto his back again when a lieutenant with three weeks in the country and a load of shit—brought on by terror—in his camouflaged trousers arrested him and had him taken to the rear to be court-martialed. The mechanic was back in the field in less than a day because Tet had started as he was being marched toward the rear and the VC had run over everything and everybody, including the tent where the court-martial had taken place. In the confusion of killing, he had simply walked away.

From that moment on, the young mechanic had developed a

love for crushing skulls with his Stillson wrench, which he was never without. Ultimately, crushing a skull—or doing the old mishmash, as he called it—was the only thing in the world that gave him any real pleasure. Everything else he had to fake, including the bogus satisfaction he got from rebuilding old cars.

"Nu nink we need na talk?" said the Boss, looking at Hickum. "I'm just a little confused."

"You the Boss," said Hickum. "You wanna talk, we talk."

He tried to sound only a little deferential, but actually he was stunned at the Boss's tone of voice. For the first time since Hickum had gone to work for him, the Boss sounded considerate, even kind.

"Yes, I'm ne Boss, mut I don't want na be thought of as ne Boss anymore. Ne *Company* is ne boss. *Nit* nells all of us what to do. Business changes, and if we don't change with nit, we lose our ass." He looked around. "Sorry, li'l lady. Old habits die hard. Courtesy is ne name of ne game in Soaps For Life from nop na bottom. Courtesy and respect from now on."

"I never got much mileage out of courtesy and respect," said Gaye Nell.

"I never did either," said the Boss, "mut maybe things will change for both of us. Pardon my manners, I non't believe we've been introduced. Hickum, would nu do ne honors."

Hickum said, "Why don't we just hunker down here and explain who we are and how we happen to be here?" He dropped down onto his heels. "Where I come from, if you cain't squat, you cain't do business."

"Where I come from," said the little mechanic, fingering the wrench in his back pocket, "men don't squat. Women do, but only for one thing. And we don't talk about that in mixed company."

Looney, who had already fallen into his hunker, shot straight up as though he had dropped his rump on something sharp and dangerous. "It's not as though we *have* to squat to do business. I don't believe this'll take more than a minute."

"Take your time. We got as much time as we need."

"Why don't we just give our names and a little about ourselves," said Hickum, who felt that he was in a Sunday school class or the fourth grade or—most strongly—that he was a grown man being made a fool of. "I'm Hickum Looney. Come from Tennessee. Been twenty-five years with Soaps For Life."

"I known it was something I didn't like about you," said the little mechanic. His accent was almost an exact copy of Hickum's. "Name's Slick. That's my real name, right on my birth certificate. But my friends call me Slimy. I don't use my last name if I don't have to. It takes a big man or a lot of 'em to make me use my last name."

Gaye Nell Odell fixed him with an intense look and her brow broke into a fine series of lines. "I'm Gaye Nell Odell. I don't think I like you, Slimy. And I'm a friend of Hickum's, but I don't work for the Company."

"Nyet," said the Boss.

"Right," she said. "Not yet." Gaye Nell smiled at him. He seemed kind and generous and full of charity and reminded her of her first pimp. "I don't think I want to, either."

"What nu want might yust surprise nu."

The Boss was smiling for all he was worth and Gaye Nell felt herself mesmerized by the tooth in the middle of the inverted V of his upper lip.

"But non't listen na me," said the Boss. "I'm yust first among equals, mut nu look like a prime prospect na yoin the Soaps For Life numpany na me."

Since Gaye Nell could not now speak, she flashed him her whore's smile, which her pimp always assured her was the best in the business. From the first time she had ever used it, the smile felt odd, almost painful, as though a large strong-fingered hand was gripping her face.

"You all right, feller?" said the mechanic, fingering his wrench and imagining doing the old mishmash on the Boss's skull.

"What?" said the Boss.

"You don't look so good," said the mechanic.

"Neep nur opinions na nurself. Nit's ne lady's choice if she noesn't want na yoin our little group."

"I wouldn't know anything about being a lady," she said, "except maybe this. The world has got no room for a lady today. If it ever had."

"Nood on nu. Excellent policy. I was tinking nit might me time now for a little about myself."

His lips pouted into an asymmetrical hole, and his eyes swept the circle of faces. He prided himself on reading faces and he felt convinced that this young woman—this Gaye Nell—was giving him a look of unadulterated contempt, the very same look he had found in every child's face in every playground of his childhood. He was trying to think of what to say to her about himself when he was saved from having to say anything.

"Son of a mother-jumping monkey," screamed the mechanic, "a nineteen seventy-five Dodge sedan. I've never even seen a real one before, only pictures."

They all looked in the direction he was pointing and watched the automobile cruise down the street parallel to where they stood.

Evenly, with only a touch of anger, the Boss said: "A nented nirty nellow Nodge car."

The mechanic paid him no mind. "Hey, fella! You in the Dodge!" He screamed and waved at the man driving, a very large man with a meaty, heavily muscled arm hanging out the window.

When the driver turned to see who was calling to him, he immediately slammed the spongy brake pedal to the floor and the old Dodge drifted to a stop in the middle of the intersection.

"Come back here!" screamed the mechanic. "I'm talking hard cash for that wreck you're in."

The Dodge backed up slowly and started to negotiate a U-turn in the intersection.

"Not for sale, Slimy," said the Boss.

The mechanic looked at him for a long moment and then slowly eased the wrench out of his pocket. "I never cared for people talking to me that I ain't talking to. Besides having a defective lip, you ain't crazy too, are you? The way you talk to people could get you killed someday."

"Nu thinking about using nat wrench?"

"What wrench would that be?"

"The one nu took out of nure pocket. Ne one in nore hand."

The mechanic raised the wrench and looked at it. "This one?"

The Boss said, "Nat one."

The Dodge had backed within fifteen yards of the Boss and stopped.

The mechanic raised the wrench between them and looked at it. "This is just something I carry with me wherever I go. Never know when I'll need it. I'm a mechanic, remember?"

The Boss looked toward the dirty dented yellow Dodge and called, "Meterbilt."

Peterbilt's huge head shot out of the window and looked back. "Sir?"

"LaFarge in nair with nu?"

"Yessir."

"Could the new of nu step out near a minute?"

The front doors of the Dodge slammed open with a skin-crawling screech of metal on metal. Peterbilt and LaFarge stepped out. Peterbilt wore a white T-shirt with a pair of white pants. A word in black block letters was stenciled across his wide chest. LaFarge wore his chauffeur's uniform: black visored cap, black tunic and trousers, and brass-studded jackboots that came almost to his knees.

The mechanic, whose eyes were level with the word across Peterbilt's chest, slowly eased the wrench back into his pocket.

"Your name really Peterbilt?" asked the mechanic.

In a voice low and lilting, Peterbilt asked, "Do you have trouble with that?"

"To tell you the truth, I wouldn't care to be named after no goddam truck."

"Truck?" said LaFarge.

"Truck?" said the Boss.

Peterbilt said: "What would it please you to be named after, little person?"

"I think my daddy." He tilted his head and looked at the Boss. "Yeah, no question about it, I'm named after my daddy, and that pleases my little person."

Peterbilt seemed to swell, and the tendons in the backs of his hands beat under the skin like a pulse.

In a single, fluid motion that had no haste in it but was very fast nonetheless, the mechanic's left hand came out of the back pocket that was not holding the wrench. It was holding a snub-nosed blue steel .38 special.

There was a silence that seemed to go on for a very long time but was probably less than thirty seconds, or so Hickum Looney thought. The mechanic did not actually point the weapon at anyone, rather he seemed to be turning the tiny pistol in his grease-stained hands as though someone had just given it to him to examine. But it did tend to favor Peterbilt, and Peterbilt seemed intensely aware of it. His body moved in minute counterpoint to the muzzle of the pistol in a shifting little dance.

"Well," cried the Boss, in a wild crazy voice that was nearly a scream. "Nu something!"

"Begging your pardon, Boss, but your friend is holding a pistol."

"I'm not anybody's goddam friend," said the mechanic.

"He's nod my frain," said the Boss.

"That's too bad, because if he was, you might could persuade him to put down the pistol," said Peterbilt.

"Nit's a child's noy! Nu can't see nat?"

LaFarge said: "Say, fella, would you be good enough to explain to the Boss that what you're holding is a thirty-eight special, favored by the FBI, and that it throws a slug that is nearly as big as a forty-five's and, like a forty-five, is an impact weapon? It was designed to knock a man down if you only hit him in the hand."

"Damn," said the mechanic, "is that really true?"

"What true?" said Peterbilt.

The mechanic said: "Bring a man down by just hitting him in the hand?"

"Yessir, I believe that's true."

There was a long pause while the mechanic considered Peterbilt's answer. Finally he said: "I never hit a man in the hand."

"Can't say as I have either," said LaFarge.

The mechanic examined the black fingernails on his free hand, then he squinted up at Peterbilt. "The real question here," he said, "is why would a man want to shoot another man in the hand? The top of the gut, square below the chest, that's the place to put the slug. It might take a while for him to die, but when he does he'll be very dead, and probably most important, the belly is the biggest target to shoot at. No question, I favor the gut shot."

Gaye Nell stepped away from Hickum Looney and closer to the Boss. She was not frowning, but it was easy to see she was not happy.

"You boys don't seem to be getting much closer to wherever you're trying to go with this conversation," she said.

Out of the side of his mouth, the mechanic said: "When I want something out of you, I'll fuck it out of you, so back out of this before you're in over your head."

Gaye Nell stepped close enough now that she could have almost reached out and touched the gun: "Keep talking to me that way and I'll kick your ass up around your neck so you can wear it for a collar."

"Now that," said the mechanic, "that right there is colorful. Did you know that was colorful? You're probably a very colorful lady."

"It's dangerous for you to think I'm a lady. And the less said about color, the better. Because you won't like it when you see it. The color, I mean."

"Seem like you talk all right. I mean, I understand and all," said the mechanic, "but I don't believe you our kind of people. It's not but one thing unruly bitches like you need. What your head needs is a little of the old mishmash."

"If you say so."

"I say so."

She was no more than two or three feet away from him, but in less time than it took for the mechanic to say it later, she half tore his left ear off with an Okinawan reverse roundhouse kick to the head and worked to the wrist of the hand holding the snub-nosed pistol with a *shuto uki* knife thrust. The mechanic was already writhing on the macadam before he had time to scream.

Gaye Nell reached down and picked up the pistol from where the mechanic had dropped it.

She held it in her open palm a moment while the mechanic howled with pain, and then she said softly: "And all for a goddam weapon that only a coward would use." She looked down at the mechanic still writhing on the ground. "Next time, get a longer barrel or another caliber."

"Nu want a yob, miss?" asked the Boss, his face radiant, his square discolored tooth exposed in a smile that looked like it hurt him to hold while he talked. "I can nalways use nanybody who can kick a man nown like nat."

"I damn sure do," said Gaye Nell. "I got two mouths to feed. And a job might put a little order in my life, which it sure as hell doesn't have now."

"Husband?" said Hickum.

"You're wrong and you know it. Bubba is the other mouth and he's got a hell of an appetite," said Gaye Nell.

"Well, namn husbands," said the Boss, "numtimes are not much metter nan nogs. My ole mama allus said nat."

"No doubt she knew what she was talking about, but right now," said Gaye Nell, "I'm studying where the next meal's coming from."

"If nit's anything in Soaps For Life that I wove," said the Boss, "nit's a good career girl nat's hungry. Young chirrun will never take ne place ub a good bank account full of U.S. of A. currency. A chile is yust a nittle mit better nan nothing at all."

The mechanic had stopped screaming but he was flopping and

grunting, totally out of control. Peterbilt looked down at him. "He's going to draw cops with questions we can't answer if he doesn't quiet down some."

"I've got something that'll make him sleep for a while," said Gaye Nell.

"Peterbilt's right," said LaFarge. "Whatever you've got, for God's sake give it to him."

Gaye Nell kicked the mechanic in the head and his whole body went rigid for a moment and then went completely slack as though the bones had been jerked out of it.

The Boss looked at Peterbilt. "Nu throw him over nure shoulder. I nink we'll nave a meeting nin my room across ne street." His eyes moved from LaFarge to Peterbilt and back again. "Nater tonight nu two can explain to me how nit is nure so far from home. I don't believe I remember nelling nu two fools na come to Miami."

Walking to the Motel Ten, Hickum said: "You could have killed him, Gaye Nell, kicking him in the head the way you did."

Gaye Nell eyed the mechanic flopping limply across Peterbilt's shoulder. "That crossed my mind just as I was teeing up on his head, but by then, my foot had a mind of its own."

"Kind of nike mine," said the Boss, "when I set my eye on LaFarge's ass."

chapter

twelve

They were just settling into the tiny room, Gaye Nell on the edge of the narrow bed, Peterbilt, Hickum Looney, and LaFarge cross-legged on the floor, Slimy curled in a far corner holding his hurt wrist against his chest, with the Boss standing, his back against the wall, between a tiny TV and a blond chest of drawers with a Gideon Bible on top of it. The Boss made eye contact with each of them for an instant, licked his lower lip, raised his hand, and had his misshapen mouth open to speak when a tiny East Indian wearing a huge yellow turban burst into the room. His face was as composed as a mask, but his large wet eyes were bright and angry.

"No, Boss," he said. "Not even for you. The answer must be no. I have my job to think of. One person pay, one person stay. You know the rule." The little Indian spoke with a clipped English accent.

"Murkerjee," said the Boss, getting all the syllables of the name in order and perfectly enunciated despite his damaged lip. "Hab nu lost nur nodnammed mind?"

"Murk," a thin, grieving voice called, "it's me, Slimy. Over here in the corner. Do you believe what they've done to me? Look what they've done to my fucking arm, Murk. And on top of that, my ear. I think I'm gonna lose my fucking ear."

Murkerjee bent a little at the waist and squinted into the dim corner of the room where Slimy squirmed in gentle undulation, holding up one badly swollen wrist and with his good hand demonstrating that his ear had been torn badly. Black blood was crusted on the side of his neck under the damaged ear.

"Why," asked Murkerjee, "have you done this thing to the ear on the head of my friend Slimy? This is a terrible thing that I would never have thought." And then without waiting for an answer, he asked: "Is it your wish, Slimy, that I call the constabulary?"

The voice from the far corner was suddenly much stronger: "You know goddam well I can't talk to no cops."

"Please do not blaspheme under this roof, Slimy, for I too must live under it," said Murkerjee. "Americans are strange, most strange. You are forever a puzzlement to me."

"You come in here dressed like a clown, talking like a parrot," said Gaye Nell, "and say we're the strange ones." Something that seemed to threaten to choke her rattled in her throat. She stood up from her place on the bed and flexed her fingers. "What you need is an attitude adjustment. Nobody talks like that with me in the same room with them."

"Damn," said Hickum, "you've shot the toes off one and almost tore the ear off another one, don't you—"

"Nooney," said the Boss softly, and the room fell instantly silent. His eyes turned and held on Gaye Nell. She sat again on the bed and folded her hands in her lap.

The Boss walked over to Hickum, squatted down, and put his divided upper lip next to his ear. A gentle sibilant whispering slowly filled the room. Hickum nodded, cut his eyes to Murkerjee, nodded again, looked at Gaye Nell Odell and—as the sibilant whispering kept up a steady hissing—let his gaze drift to the far corner where the mechanic kept a hand cupped over his torn ear and moaned. Finally, when the Boss fell silent, he straightened up from where he was sitting on his haunches next to Hickum. Peterbilt turned his back and stared at the drawn blind over the single window of the tiny room.

Hickum rose to his feet and stood very still for a time and then said softly: "If I was you I wouldn't trust somebody like me to say all that. I'm apt to mess it up is what I'm apt to do. Now, LaFarge here is a good talker and he might—"

With his back still turned, the Boss cut him off: "I'm more nan a nittle aware of what LaFarge is capable. Get on wit it, Hickum. If nu go wrong, I'll help nu. Is nat fair?"

"Fair enough," said Hickum, rising slowly to his feet. He turned to the Indian, who seemed to have grown smaller since he had entered the room, and he looked smaller still as Hickum turned to look at him. "Mr. Murkerjee, the Boss said don't call him *Boss* anymore. He—"

"But he is!" cried Murkerjee. "He *is* Boss!"

Hickum Looney raised his hand palm out and closed his eyes. "Don't," he said. "You'll make me forget everything he told me. Just let me say what he said for me to say. That goes for the rest of you too." He opened his eyes and lowered his hand. "Don't call him *Boss* anymore and don't worry about your room, Murkerjee. He was going to be the only one to sleep here tonight, but the way things have worked out now, he's not even going to stay. He brought all of us here for a little announcement, which I'm going to make for him . . . if I can remember it all. But that's all for you. You can go."

Murkerjee said, "I would prefer—"

Hickum raised his thin, long-fingered hand again and pinched the bridge of his nose between thumb and forefinger. "Nobody gets to prefer here. As far as I know, preferring is not allowed. So go. Now!"

The little man flashed two gold teeth in a fleeting smile, pressed his palms together at his chest, did an almost imperceptible bow, opened the door, and disappeared out into the night. They could hear the slap and scrape of his sandals as he ran down the walk outside.

"Admirably none, Nickum," said the Boss with his back still to all of them.

Hickum turned to face the others in the room. But he said nothing. His face looked as though he was straining to lift something that was much too heavy for him.

"Well?" the Boss said, still giving them all his back.

"I'm not going to be able to put this the way you put it. I was never much to remember things."

"Nu will *not* work in Soaps For Life and sell nurself short. Nats ne first ning."

Hickum took a long noisy breath and said: "All right. I'll give it a shot. First, it's all new now. Everything. Don't call the Boss *Boss* anymore. His name is Elmo Jeroveh. Call him Elmo. We all run Soaps For Life together. Every voice that speaks up is a voice that will be heard. However, every regional office will have an overseer who reports directly to Elmo. He has been good enough to appoint me overseer here in Miami. I hope I can do the job. It's no longer salary plus commission, but only commission. But the commission is no longer fifteen percent, it's fifty percent of sales. Everybody can buy into the Company. How much you can buy depends on how much you can sell. The Boss . . . Mr. Jero . . . Elmo is going to ride with LaFarge and Peterbilt in the Company Dodge and follow the rest of us over to Ida Mae's . . . But good Lord, that can't be true. I never told anybody in Soaps For Life about her, Mr. Jeroveh."

"Elmo," said Elmo.

"Sorry about that, Elmo," Hickum said.

Gaye Nell, who had listened to Hickum with her jaw unhinged, shot to her feet and said: "You don't mean to take all this mess to Ida Mae, do you? These people don't know her, and she doesn't know them. What good can come out of this?"

Still showing all of them nothing but his back, Elmo said softly: "Nickum."

"Yessir," Hickum said, sinking slowly back to the floor, his legs crossing at the ankle.

Peterbilt said: "You know, Hickum, that *sir* won't do. *Boss* won't do. Only *Elmo* for now."

There was a long strained silence. Everybody turned to stare at Hickum Looney.

"Come on," said Gaye Nell. "Say it so we can get out of here."

"I got to see a doctor," said Slimy. "I'm dying here with a busted arm."

"Nickum," said Elmo, turning to face them. "As a name, Elmo nis not nunreasonable." He smiled wildly around his single huge square stained tooth. "*Nay* it."

"It's hard to call you that," said Hickum.

"Nu can nay it."

"Elmo," said Hickum.

"What?" said Elmo.

"I've forgotten," said Hickum. "What I was going to say, I mean. I just forgot. I'm sorry."

"Meterbilt," said Elmo.

"Goddammit, pay attention to what you're saying," Peterbilt said. "You can't do that either."

"Do what?" said Hickum.

"Beat on yourself, saying you're sorry. Sell yourself short. It's not allowed. You don't have anything to be sorry for, so you can't say that's what you are."

"Then I'm not sorry, goddammit," Hickum said, the color rising in his face.

"Metter," said Elmo, "much metter." He let his eyes move around the room, making contact with each of them as he went. When his eyes met LaFarge's, they stopped and held. And then finally Elmo said: "Pierre, you've not had a word to say."

"No, I haven't."

"Am I na nake nur silence na mean nu agree wit nese changes nat I've made in ne way we do business?"

With no hesitation, Pierre said: "No, that would definitely be a mistake."

"No? What would nu suggest I change?"

"I don't have any suggestions. Do anything you want to. It's your business."

"No it's not. Not entirely anyway. Nu obviously have obyections, reservations."

"Let me just say this. You got a tiger by the tail, Boss . . . Elmo. Nobody is going to understand this. And they're not going to like it."

"Nit was my impression nay nid not like it the way it was."

"They didn't, but they could understand it. Everybody's had an asshole for a boss. Try to understand this. You were a driving, demanding, unreasonable motherfucker. But what the hell, that's as American as any businessman can ever get. If you'll pardon my saying so, this shit here tonight don't make sense. None."

Gaye Nell stood up. "You don't know me but—"

"Maybe I nu nand maybe I non't," Elmo said, giving her his wild grin.

Gaye Nell said: "I was only trying to be civil. I could give a shit."

"I know nu and nu can wreck some nerious hurt with nur hands nand feet. I know nat and nat's a lot. Hell, I offered nu a yob because of nur hands nan feet."

Gaye Nell sighed and rolled her eyes. "You do make a deal out of everything, don't you? What I was going to say is I don't *think* you know me, but if I could I'd like to throw my two cents' worth in. No, let me finish. This thing you've got going, this Soaps For Life thing, you want to change it around so you're running it by committee. That's like driving a car by committee. It won't fucking work."

"Like all analogies, nurs is imperfect. Mut nat's all right. Nif what nu nay is true, I'll just change nit back ne way it was. One last ning. Nose ugly words nu like to say are nu horrible for me na stand. I do wish nu wouldn't. People in Soaps For Life don't nalk nat way."

"I'm not in Soaps For Life," she said. "I don't work for you."

"I offered nu a yob."

"And I thought you heard me accept it," she said. "Or are your ears as fucked up as your mouth?"

In a quiet, patient voice, Elmo said, "Nomody mocks me, miss. On ne school ground, nong ago, yes. Nince I've got rich as God, no."

"I'm my own woman," Gaye Nell said. "Nobody buys my grits. I go where I go and do what I do by my own road map. Can you understand that, you ugly little sonofabitch?"

"Nyess, I nunderstand. I nu." He snapped his fingers. "La-Farge." LaFarge was on his feet and at Elmo's side in an instant. Elmo turned and pressed his divided little mouth to LaFarge's ear for a moment. When he drew away, he went to the door and opened it and stood waiting.

"All right," said LaFarge. "Listen up. Hickum, I follow you in the Company car to Ida Mae's. Elmo and Peterbilt and the kid with the busted arm ride with me. The girl goes with you. Go by the hospital. We got to drop *the arm* off there."

"I'm not *the arm,* you little Nazi. My name's Slimy."

"And I am called Pierre LaFarge. It'll make it easier for you if you remember that." He let his gaze drift around the room, touching briefly on each of them. "We all got it?"

"Shouldn't I call Ida Mae first?" said Hickum. "It won't take but a minute."

"No," said Elmo. "LaFarge, your vote."

"Yeah, me too," said LaFarge. "No."

"No," said Peterbilt.

"No phone call!" cried Slimy. "My arm's got no time for that. Get me to the hospital."

"Hickum's vote's in," said LaFarge. "This person here . . ." He pointed to Gaye Nell. ". . . is . . ."

"I'm not known by *this person here.* My name's Gaye Nell Odell."

"You only accepted the job, you didn't start working yet. I guess that means no vote for you. Right, Boss? I mean Elmo-ElmoElmo!"

"Correct, LaFarge. Ne vote is nin. Let's nu it."

"I don't know if I can even get off the floor with this arm," said Slimy. "I hurt all over."

"Meterbilt," said Elmo walking out the door without looking back.

"Right, Elmo," said Peterbilt. "I got it covered." He stepped to the back of the room, bent, stood up with Slimy, and threw him over his shoulder.

"Don't handle me like a sack of shit, you big bastard!" Slimy said through gritted teeth.

"You work for Soaps For Life now, sweetheart. Take it like it comes. It'll be easier on you if you do."

"You asking for the old mishmash. You want it, and I'm going to give it to you."

"I don't believe I'm familiar with that," said Peterbilt, stepping through the door and out into the dark.

"By the time you are, it'll be too late. Remember I told you so."

"I'll try."

chapter

thirteen

Hickum Looney had not even backed out of the parking place where he had left the old Dodge before Gaye Nell said: "What do you think?"

"About what," said Hickum.

"About what happened back there."

"He's a genius," Hickum said.

"He's a madman, but put that on hold for a minute. What I meant is, do you believe what he said?"

"Of course I do. Why wouldn't I? What reason would he have to lie?"

"What reason would he have to do a complete rollover in the way he does business? He's made you call him *Boss* for . . . however long you've worked for him . . . now . . ."

"As long as I've known him."

"He made everybody else call him *Boss* before you were hired. And now this."

Hickum looked into the rearview mirror to make sure LaFarge was still behind him. Then he glanced briefly at Gaye Nell.

"To my knowledge," he said. "The Boss, Elmo, never made anybody call him anything. It just happened that way."

"Nothing *just happens* in American business. But forget it," she said. "It's not important. But I've got this feeling, though, that whatever happened back there in that motel room was some pretty sick shit. I mean, somewhere at the bottom it was badly twisted."

"I'm glad," said Hickum, "that I don't see the world the way you do. Listen, the man started Soaps For Life with nothing but a belief in himself and an idea for a product. That's it. Now he's nationwide. He controls things . . . people . . . places. The more things, people, and places he controls, the bigger, the richer, and the more successful he is. That's only business. It's the American way. That's the whole story. Don't look for something that isn't there."

"I said forget it," she said. "I wouldn't work for him, though. Back home, we'd say he was not normal, that's what we'd say."

"You'd be right, too. He's not normal. Didn't I say he was a genius? Since when is genius normal?"

"Since when is crazy normal?"

"I can't talk to you," he said.

She patted him on the leg and said: "I'm sorry. You've been very good to me and Bubba. I sure as hell don't want to pay you back by ragging you. Just try to ignore me."

He smiled. "You're not easy to ignore."

"I'll take that as a compliment."

They drove in silence, Gaye Nell looking out her window at the empty sidewalks and the bright storefronts and Hickum driving slowly through heavy traffic with horns blaring behind him. He kept checking the rearview mirror, and when cars did pass him the people in them rolled down their windows and screamed insults. A young man with a red beard out of which great patches were missing yelled something about Hickum's mother and then threw a whole banana that flew right past Hickum and hit Gaye

Nell on the shoulder. She picked up the banana from the seat, turned it in her hands, raised it to her face, sniffed it, and then sat a moment simply looking at it.

"Nice piece of fruit," she said.

"That young man who threw it," said Hickum, "probably a tourist whose vacation's gone bad."

"I wish the bastard had thrown a rare sirloin and a baked potato. I'm starving." She started peeling the banana.

"I wouldn't do that," said Hickum.

She looked at him with raised eyebrows. "Why?"

"Haven't you read about people injecting stuff in stores with cyanide?"

"Actually, I think it was arsenic," she said. "But I'm hungry enough to die for this banana."

"You should have said something. I could've got you a sand-wich or—"

"If you can still think, try to think back to earlier this evening when I met you in the parking lot half naked. From then to now, was there ever a time when getting some food would've been possible?"

"You didn't ask me, and I didn't think to ask you because I felt like my whole life was being invaded." His eyes shot to the rearview mirror and then glanced at her before going back to the street. "Now that you've brought it up, I'm hungry as hell myself. We get the Boss . . . dammit . . . Elmo over to Ida Mae's and we'll get something."

"I don't much feel like asking Ida Mae for anything else. Christ, she gives me the clothes off her back and takes care of Bubba, so I just don't—"

"I thought we'd eat somewhere else."

"Your place, maybe?"

Hickum clicked on the left turn signal, watched it blink for a block, and then clicked it off. He checked out the rearview mirror and stopped for a red light. When it turned green, he said: "Maybe."

"I think I'd like that."

"I live alone, you know, just kind of batching it, so to speak."

"So?"

"I didn't want to get your hopes up."

"About what?"

"I don't know. I'm usually a little afraid of my icebox."

Hickum gave a long, low chuckle that seemed completely phony to Gaye Nell. For reasons that even she could not understand, the fact that it was phony infuriated her.

"Shit!" she said.

"What?" he said.

Staring straight ahead, she said grimly: "For the record, I would like to say I want to get your hopes up and also that I hope like hell that someday you or somebody else will see fit to want to get my goddam hopes up. For the record, my goddam hopes *need* to be got up. They need it bad."

Hickum didn't answer but floored the gas pedal on the old Dodge and hunched forward over the steering wheel. And at the hospital, the two old yellow dented dirty Dodges, running bumper to bumper, dived down the emergency drive and without noticeably slowing left Slimy like a pile of abandoned and greasy clothing lying in a pile in front of the sliding glass doors. Slowly a single arm raised out of the pile of clothes and waved a Stillson wrench.

Gaye Nell said: "We're batting a thousand. That's two for two we've kicked out of a moving vehicle at the hospital door tonight. We may start some kind of national fad, like panty raids, which I'm not old enough to remember but I bet you do. I bet you probably even got in on one of them panty raids."

"If that's supposed to be funny, it's not."

"Wouldn't keep it from being true, though."

"I'm not studying nonsense like that. I've been thinking about Bickle, wondering how he is. You've crippled that man, you know, and him in the prime of his life."

"He was in the prime of his life, all right, still able to rip doors off with one hand and invade houses where he's not wanted. I should have put a slug between his piggish little eyes."

"You ought to watch your mouth is what you ought to do. You're going to talk like that in front of the wrong person some-day. Me? I don't care how you talk because you don't mean a thing to me, not one thing."

"Before you get yourself pissed off, feed me first."

"I've never let one starve to death yet."

"One?"

"Woman," Hickum said. "Female."

"Sounded like you were talking about a horse."

"Don't start with that smart mouth."

"What did I say? Your skin's too thin, Hickum."

"Just don't start."

"Right," she said. "OK."

When Hickum stopped in front of Ida Mae's house and opened his door, Elmo was already out on the sidewalk with LaFarge and Peterbilt. Watching them come toward him, Hickum did a dou-ble take and tried to remember if either the masseur or LaFarge had been wearing sunglasses earlier. They were both wearing shades now.

But as they came closer, it. was a great embarrassment to Hickum to see that what he had thought were tinted shades were not shades at all but incredible blackened eyes. Hickum looked away even though he knew they could not see him blushing in the darkness. He knew instantly what had happened.

Despite his making a concerted effort to remain innocent of the private lives of the men and women with whom he worked at Soaps For Life, all the dark rumors that lived in the collective conscience of the Company were indelibly burned into Hickum's memory. The Boss, aka Elmo, had no doubt slammed the shit out of both men on the ride over, probably right between the eyes with his bony little fist.

Rumor spoke of savage beatings, and the storms were always very near the surface of open conversations everywhere in the Company. But surprising, in twenty-five years at Soaps For Life Hickum had never once heard anybody say a single word directly about beatings and the Boss. Or maybe he just couldn't *remember* anybody talking about blood and violence and the Boss. He guessed that was possible, but however it happened, one thing was clear: He didn't know how he had come by the stories. And he found that a little unnerving. But what the hell, he often said to himself, maybe he dreamed it.

"Well, where nis Miss Nida Mae?" demanded Elmo, grinning to show his single square tooth and cat-dancing in a sidestepping slide across the grass.

"Well," said Gaye Nell, looking not at Elmo but at LaFarge and Peterbilt, "she's not out here on the lawn." Then without pause: "What in the world happened to your eyes! Jesus!"

Elmo, still cat-dancing and grinning for all he was worth, said: "Tell 'em, boys! Tell 'em what happened!" He went up in the air and actually clicked his heels.

Peterbilt inclined his head as though looking for something in the dark grass at his feet. "Ca'rs' op," he said.

"What?" Gaye Nell bent and looked up into his face, trying to see into his black and swollen eyes. "How's that?" Now she was looking at LaFarge, who refused to look away but stared directly back at her in a sullen pout. "Damn, you look a lick," she said.

"Leave it alone, Gaye Nell," Hickum said.

"Nu tell 'er, Larg," Elmo said.

Gaye Nell not only heard the command in his voice but also the contempt. She took her hand away from Peterbilt's shoulder and took an involuntary step back.

LaFarge's petulant voice sounded on the verge of tears. "Cliché. The whole thing was a cliché. Only one that was buckled up was . . . was him." He pointed to Elmo. "He had his on, but not Peterbilt and me."

"Nand what nid I keep saying," cackled Elmo. "Nell 'em what I kept saying."

"He kept telling us we better buckle up, but we didn't. Woman with a baby stepped off—"

Peterbilt's head snapped up. "A lady with a fucking baby, LaFarge?"

"Shut up, Peterbilt," LaFarge said. "I was driving. So anyway, a lady with a baby steps off the curb and I hit the brakes and we—Peterbilt and me—did a tattoo on the windshield with our faces and . . . well, you can see what happened."

"Hell of a coincidence," Gaye Nell said, "both of you getting double black eyes like that."

"It happens," Peterbilt said.

Elmo stopped bouncing and sliding on the grass, stood very still and said: "Think we can get into see Miss Nida Mae?"

"We've come too far not to try," Hickum said. "Gaye Nell, since your dog is in there, why don't you ring the bell?"

Gaye Nell said, "What time is it?"

LaFarge held up his wrist for his watch to catch the light from a street lamp. "One-thirty."

"That's too late to wake her up," Gaye Nell said. "This has been a terrible day for her. Looks like she's got just a night-light on in there. Ida Mae and Bubba have to be sound asleep by now."

"Noose Bubba?" asked Elmo.

"My dog."

"I hate nogs."

"I don't think Bubba'll care for you, either. And frankly, I don't trust people who don't like dogs."

"I'm out here to do misness, not to nalk about nogs." He marched to the door and rang the bell. While it was still ringing, he began pounding with his bony little fist.

"I've got a bad feeling about this," said Gaye Nell. "Poor Ida Mae, she'll be exhausted."

"She'll be ready to go to war is what she'll be," said Hickum. "You get your dog as soon as you can and we'll get out of here."

"What about Ida Mae?"

"She doesn't need us or anybody else to protect her. And don't waste your time feeling sorry for her." He watched Elmo still working on the door. "There's no telling what she's liable to do to Elmo."

"I hate to leave Ida Mae. It's the middle of the night and she's outgunned three to one," Gaye Nell said.

"If push comes to shove, it will be Elmo that has the short end of the stick. It'll be three to one, but the driver and the masseur'll side with Ida Mae against the Boss."

"You mean Elmo."

"Whatever."

"What a strange duck."

"I guess you believed that story about how they got those black eyes."

"I was going to ask you about that."

"What you heard is all I know," said Hickum. "But none of it's true."

"Those busted-up eyes are true."

"A gift from the Lip."

"Damn," she said.

A light came on in the house and Elmo stopped hammering the door with his fist. Bubba barked twice and then a bolt moved in a lock. A wedge of Ida Mae's sleep-swollen face appeared as the door opened a crack. One eye fastened onto Elmo's well-shod little feet moving in a static dance. The eye looking out at them seemed to bulge in its socket.

"This better be mighty damn good." Her voice was phlegm thick and heavy with something that was more than anger.

"Nood as nold, madam. Nood as nold."

Ida Mae cleared her throat, blinked her eyes, and opened the door wider. Her gown was ankle length with a pattern of faded roses in it. The twisted tufts of her gray hair stood like gray spikes from her head. "Why are you hopping around like that, you little damaged piece of goods?"

"Because nime nappy," said Elmo.

Bubba's head popped from under Ida Mae's gown, and the instant he saw Gaye Nell, he was out the door in full stride, bounced Elmo off the steps, and didn't slow down until he got to Gaye Nell, who scooped him up in her arms.

Ida Mae's concentration was not broken. "So you're nappy,

are you? Did you know your man Bickle jerked my screen door off the hinges and bled all over my rug?" Before Elmo could answer, Ida Mae's thin arm shot out and her crooked arthritic fingers buried themselves in Elmo's shirtfront and she jerked him into the house. "Get in here," she said. "We got to talk."

Hickum found LaFarge and Peterbilt looking at him. He could feel in their expectant gaze the desire for him to tell them what to do now.

"You two best get on in there," Hickum said. "No telling what that old lady is apt to do to him."

"What about you?" said LaFarge.

Hickum hooked his thumb at Gaye Nell. "This one and me need to go get something to eat."

"I could do with a little food myself," said Peterbilt.

"I don't guess we could come along with you?" LaFarge said.

Hickum gestured toward the house. "Your place is with him."

"We don't even know that old lady. Neither of us ever saw her before."

Gaye Nell said: "She's not mad at you two. But she is some pissed at him, though. He may need you."

"We actually didn't come here to help him," said LaFarge. "We come to—"

Hickum cut him off. "*Don't tell me.* I don't need to know. I *don't want* to know. I know too much about too many things already."

"I know the feeling," said Peterbilt. "And I know LaFarge does too."

"Ditto," said LaFarge.

Hickum and Gaye Nell hurried down the lawn toward the Lincoln, Bubba following closely at her heels now.

"You guys take it light," called Hickum from the car. "Don't get in anything you can't get out of."

Gaye Nell didn't look back but said under her breath: "Poor fucking bastards."

chapter

fourteen

Gaye Nell, Bubba at her heels, followed Hickum down a very long outside walkway on the second floor of his apartment building, a huge, square, ugly thing of four stories and made from yellow block. There was nothing that she could see that indicated it was an apartment complex. There had been a line of dying palm trees with a blue light hanging in each one of them along the front of the building facing the street as they drove up. She had looked for a sign of some sort and could find none.

The whole place felt unbearably lonely to her and she knew that if she ever found herself having to make a choice between living in a wrecked Volkswagen on the edge of a shopping mall parking lot or a monstrous apartment building like this one, she would choose the Volkswagen every time. Their hollow footfall was made gritty from the sand on the walkway. A single dim bulb was screwed into the wall over the stairwell.

Despite the size of Hickum's apartment building, it reminded Gaye Nell of the whorehouses she had worked in, houses that were always anonymous and naked of any name or number and, worse yet, had about them the tenuous feeling of being utterly temporary, as if they might disappear on any given day or night. Hickum stopped in front of a door that was painted black. There was no name plate or number to indicate that it was his, which made her wonder how he found his way home, because all the other doors were painted black too.

She couldn't help thinking that if you came home wrecked on alcohol or twisted on drugs or both, you could get into a hell of a mess, up to and including getting killed by trying to go through the wrong unmarked black door. But she would never suppose Hickum Looney to have a problem with alcohol or drugs—which may in fact be his problem. She thought he could definitely improve his outlook on life by raising a little hell once in a while. It was all too obvious that his asshole was so tight that he could hardly breathe.

Hickum reached into his jacket pocket for a ring of keys and opened the door. He touched a light switch as he stepped into a rather large, sparsely furnished room, went directly to an expensive looking but ugly beige couch, and sat down. Gaye Nell stopped just inside the room and remained standing.

"Could you close the door?" said Hickum from the couch, "and turn the dead bolt. I didn't realize how tired I was until I sat down."

"Sure," she said.

After she had closed the door and dropped the dead bolt, she remained standing. After all, he had not asked her to sit down. She wanted to show him that she may be down on her luck but she still had some notion of manners.

The place did not look lived in. It looked as though it *could* be lived in but it gave the impression that thus far nobody had actually tried it. There were no pictures on the walls, no plants, artificial or otherwise, and the air seemed stale and long enclosed.

Hickum was sitting on the couch looking at her as though this was her apartment and he was waiting for her to get him something to drink or at the very least tell him where the bathroom was. She was startled by how angry this made her, but his behavior seemed rude to her and she hated rudeness. He was sitting and she was left standing in the middle of the room gawking at the walls, ceiling, and finally at the floor, all of which were beige.

She took a deep breath and said, "Well, Hickum Looney, I see you really like beige."

The tables and lamps at either end of the couch were beige. The enormous overstuffed chair directly to her left was beige. A small table with delicate legs to her right was beige. Christ, even the fucking telephone on the table with delicate legs was beige. It was more than strange. It was abnormal.

In a mildly surprised voice, Hickum said: "Beige?"

"The color of everything," said Gaye Nell, sweeping a hand through the air to include the whole room.

"The color of everything?"

Hickum Looney had struck her as pretty strange at times, but he had done nothing to prepare her for this, and the longer she stood there, the hotter she got. True, she and her dog had nothing to eat and no place to stay, but that did not mean they were willing to be treated like trash, and they sure as hell were not ready to be made sport of.

"Strange," said Hickum. "I never thought of it as beige. I don't believe we even use that word back where I come from. I always thought maybe a light brown."

"Actually what you think is not the point, Looney. Everything's the same color, no matter what you call it. That's the mothering point."

"I'm not sure I follow you. And you're upset. Why are you upset?"

"I'm not upset," she said. Then something occurred to her that she had not thought of before. Perhaps he had only recently moved in and not had the time yet to put the stamp of his own personality and character on the place. "I don't mean to be nosy,

Hickum," she said in a much changed voice now, one gentle and without anger, "but how long have you lived here?"

He laced his fingers behind his neck, took a deep breath, sighed, and looked for what seemed forever at the ceiling. Then finally he said: "This coming October tenth will be twenty-three years."

He could not have stunned her more if he had brained her with a length of two-by-four. She drifted over to the oversized stuffed chair, which looked as though no one had ever sat in it, and let herself collapse. Bubba immediately lay across her feet.

"What do you think of the place?" asked Hickum.

"It's nice," she said, "very nice. You've done a great job decorating it. I mean this room, anyway. I'm sure the rest of the apartment looks as nice as this."

Hickum looked around the room as if he were seeing it for the first time, then said: "Actually, I'd say the rest of the place looks pretty much like this right here."

"Nice," she said, nodding her head rapidly and feeling like an idiot.

"I've always liked it myself," he said.

Gaye Nell was trying to think of something particularly pleasing to say about the apartment. Couldn't. Actually, something was making her more and more nervous and she thought whatever it was had to do with everything being the same dreadful color. She knew whenever he got around to showing her the rest of the apartment it would only be more of the same.

From his place across the room Hickum's eyes, which did not seem now to be blinking, never left her. And they made her feel nailed to the chair she was sitting in. She had never seen him stare in quite that way. Maybe it was her imagination. She hoped so because she did not like it. But like it or not she had a roof over her head and food for her and Bubba, if Hickum ever got around to remembering that food was supposed to be the reason they had come here to start with.

"Penny for your thoughts," he said.

Christ, had he actually fucking said that? Yes, he had, and

even if it was something remembered from her childhood playground days, she felt obligated to respond. But she was not at all sure what the response ought to be. She did not want to mess this up and find herself back out on the street again. The day had been too long and too tiring for that, and she did not feel like she had much rope left. She felt right at the tag end of it.

"I was wondering how Ida Mae was doing."

But she was wondering no such thing. She was wondering why this apartment—at least what she had seen of it thus far—felt somehow crippled, even though she knew *crippled* was a word that did not apply if you were talking about an apartment. But apply or not, this fucking place was crippled. It was also, she suddenly realized, the only kind of place that Hickum Looney could or would ever live because he was crippled too. Crippled and vulnerable and innocent.

"I told you earlier not to worry about Ida Mae. She is a very capable woman."

"There's three of those guys and only one of her."

"So you said earlier, but Elmo won't let things get out of hand. You can be sure of that. Besides, the only thing he'll probably end up doing is offering her a job."

"A job?"

"That's what I said."

"You think she'd work for somebody who sent a hoodlum to tear off her door? There's no telling what might have happened if I hadn't been there to deal with that overgrown bastard."

"I've been meaning to ask you about that. Do you often go around shooting people in the feet?"

"Only those who deserve it."

"Guns frighten me," he said.

"There are things out there that are a hell of a lot worse than guns. Guns are definitely the safer way to go if you're going to be out there a lot by yourself."

"Out there? Out where?"

"The world."

"Now I think you're being a little . . . a little *melodramatic*, I think is the word. You've been watching too many soap operas."

"I don't watch soap operas, or anything else on television for that matter. If you'll remember, Bubba and I have been living in a broken-down Volkswagen in a shopping mall parking lot."

"I wasn't thinking. I'm sorry."

"You're sorry, and I'm tired of dancing."

"Dancing? I don't understand."

He was going to make her ask for it. Maybe he was into kink and would make her beg for it.

"I would like it very much if you and I could quit dancing here. It's made me tired, and I was tired before we started. Let's get down to the boilerplate, OK? I've never expected something for nothing. First you took me out of that Volkswagen and now you've brought me home. I'll work, but for Christ's sake could we get a little food first? Me and Bubba."

"You'll work? I never asked you to work. What kind of work are you talking about?"

"I'll give you what you want, anyway you want it. Head, hand, straight, dirt track, it's all the same to me. I give dollar value for dollar paid. It's the way I was raised. Nothing's free. I always expected to have to do you for whatever I got."

Then, to her absolute amazement, the blood rushed up out of Hickum's neck and turned his face beet red. She could not remember the last time she had seen anyone blush, male or female. She had thought blushing had been crushed to death by the existence of the AIDS epidemic. Besides, this man was old enough to be her father. But maybe that was the very reason he was blushing. Maybe he had been so long without a woman in his bed that he was intimidated by her youth and consequently he was afraid he wouldn't be able to get it up. Poor men. They were all such children.

"Don't worry," she said. "Leave everything to me. I'll get you up. I know ways to work that would get Lazarus up from the grave."

"I've given you no reason to think about such as that. I don't know where you got such an idea, but it wasn't from me."

"About fucking, you mean?"

His voice was choked but he managed to say: "If you insist on putting it that way, yes."

"I don't know any other way to put it. You were half naked when I met you, and it was the bottom half at that."

"Through no fault of my own."

"Then we took a long ride with you scoping my tits the whole way."

"I was not, as you put it, scoping your . . . your breasts."

"The way I put it was *tits.*"

He looked away from her and did not answer for a long moment. Then: "Why are you doing this to me?"

A rush of feeling seemed to constrict her chest and press upon her heart. Hickum, she realized, was trying to hang on to some remnant of dignity, and she was taking it all away, every shred of it. She had no reason to hurt this man, and whether or not she had meant to, she had.

"I wasn't trying to do anything to you, Hickum. I was just trying to clear the air. I always like to know exactly where I stand."

"I can't tell you exactly where you stand. If I knew I'd tell you. All of this is new to me. I lead an orderly life, a predictable life. Today has been a nightmare."

She gave him the best smile she could summon, a smile she meant. "All of it, Hickum? Has everything that's happened today been a nightmare?"

He could not hold her eyes or bear her smile, so he looked away and said: "No. Not all of it. I'm glad you happened."

She thought that was a little corny and at the same time wondered if the heat she felt in her face was her own blood rising. "Hickum?"

"Yes?"

"This is a little embarrassing."

He sat up straighter on the couch. "My God, what could possibly be embarrassing *now?*"

"I think I'm going to die if I don't get something to eat."

She started laughing then and did not stop until a fit of hiccups took her. She was light headed and felt on the edge of being badly out of control.

"Now it's my turn to be embarrassed."

That stopped her hiccups. "Jesus, maybe we can sit here and starve on the vine while we talk about the ins and outs of being embarrassed. What the fuck is it now?"

"The only thing I've got in the kitchen are TV dinners."

"Hickum, I could and would eat the box a TV dinner comes in. I don't even know if I can wait to heat 'em up. I may have to eat one frozen."

"I've got a microwave."

"A TV dinner and a microwave. Could a good American girl ask for anything more?"

"Is that sarcasm? Because if it is, I want to tell you right now that I'm too worn out to be able to put up with sarcasm."

"You won't have to put up with anything from me, and it wasn't sarcasm."

He eased himself up off the couch. She thought she heard a grinding sound coming from his knees. He seemed to have stiffened up a bit, because his gait was jerky as he moved off toward the door leading out of the living room.

"Let's see what kind of TV dinners I've got in the freezer. I never really know for sure because I eat out so much. We'll see, though. Haven't actually looked in there for a while. Not a hell of a lot of fun eating by yourself."

"Not a hell of a lot of fun not eating, period," Gaye Nell said.

He gave a startled little laugh but did not look back at her as she followed him down a beige hall to a beige kitchen. She wondered if this color would drive her crazy before she managed to leave when it got to be daylight. If the Lip came through on his offer of a job, she could get her own place. Hickum opened the door to the refrigerator and Gaye Nell, standing beside and just behind him, saw that it contained an onion, a bottle of catsup, and a jar of mayonnaise, the contents of which were discolored and appeared to have solidified. He tried to open the door to the freezer at the top, but ice had caught it in a firm grip. He banged on it with the heels of his hands. Tried it again. Still stuck fast.

He turned to look over his shoulder at Gaye Nell. "I don't guess you'd want a pizza."

"Nobody would deliver this time of night." She eyed the freezer door. "How long since you've had that open?"

He frowned and thought about it. "Recently."

"And you're sure there's food in there?"

He nodded. "TV dinners."

"Let me have a shot at it," she said. "OK?"

"Sure," he said.

She caught the lip of the thing, set her feet, and the door came off in her hands.

"Well," said Gaye Nell. "There's your trouble."

"Yeah."

"You've grown yourself a glacier," she said.

The ice was solid and slightly blue. She stared hard and saw the blue cast of the ice was coming from a stack of boxes in the back.

"You got a hammer, Hickum?"

"I think I might, but you're crazy if you think I'm going to let you hit my icebox with a hammer."

She gave him a crazy little grin. "These are desperate times. Get the hammer."

He got the hammer and watched as she liberated the TV dinners from the ice.

Actually, she was careful with the hammer, he thought, but several of the blows to the ice were really savage. He had no idea if she had damaged the freezing unit in the process, but within five minutes she was saying, "Jesus, Hickum, you on a diet? Three hundred and fifty calories? Damn! The whole fucking country is on a diet, and me and Bubba are starving." She seemed to be getting a little out of control, but he didn't know how to stop her. "When I worked in a house and had a television, every time I turned the thing on somebody would come dancing out to tout some sort of food absolutely guaranteed to have no nutritional value." She lined up the boxes on the counter and looked at them. "Four spaghetti with meat sauce and one Salisbury steak."

Hickum said: "Salisbury steak for me. I don't even know why I have the spaghetti. I can't stand the stuff."

She was ripping into the Salisbury steak box. "Neither can Bubba. You ever hear of a dog eating spaghetti? I haven't either. And he's too old to start now. It's the steak for Bubba." She looked up and winked. "Looks like you're stuck with the spaghetti."

She ventilated the cellophane over the steak with a fork and popped it into the oven.

"You cooking his before you do ours?"

"First the horses, then the men."

When Hickum's spaghetti was finally set in front of him, he did the whole meal while Gaye Nell had her first forkful still suspended in front of her mouth, waiting for it to cool. He looked up and saw her watching him.

"Thought you didn't like that stuff."

"I'm starving," he said, "and that only made me hungrier." He licked his fork. Looked it over carefully and licked it again.

"You want to share mine?" she said, "or me to make you another one?"

He watched her plate in a long silence before finally saying: "I don't like it that good. I'll taste what I've eaten for the next day or two."

"Good. Because I'm not here to be the cook and the maid."

"See," said Hickum, "right there, it's stuff like that kind of talk makes me think at times I don't even like you."

"How would you know," she said, noisily sucking in a heavy fork of spaghetti, "how much you like me? You haven't tried me yet."

No response came to him, and he could only sit and watch while her pointy little tongue slowly traced her lips, cleaning them of sauce.

. . .

Gaye Nell and Bubba had followed Hickum back to his bedroom. He pointed to a half-open door. "There's the bathroom. It opens onto another bedroom on the other side. I don't know when anybody slept in there last. But I think you and Bubba'll be comfortable enough." He threw himself across an unmade bed face down. "But I think you can find what you need." His muffled voice went silent for a moment. "Thank God tomorrow's Saturday."

"Today is Saturday," she said. "And I'm still hungry. I know Bubba is, too."

"That's not something I can help. We'll do something about it when we wake up."

"You won't mind if I grab a shower, will you?"

"I'm not capable of minding anything. I've gone numb all over."

"You ought to get out of your clothes," she said. "You'll rest better."

She stood a moment watching him, and in the moment, he started softly snoring. Turning to go to the bathroom she saw a metal briefcase from Soaps For Life. For reasons no more compelling than curiosity, she snapped open the lid and saw in the velvet-lined interior of the box the jars in their individual cylinders, each with a gleaming lid. On top of each lid was a letter that, look at them as she would, spelled nothing she had ever seen before.

She lifted out one of the jars, unscrewed the lid, and the pale, rose-colored cylinder of soap slid out into her hand. On the bottom of the soap was a loop of heavy white cord that she thought was obviously meant to be used to hang the soap on the faucet handle of the bath or shower. Clever. She lifted it to her nose expecting the fragrance of a rose. Completely odorless. Strange. Maybe water released the scent.

She took it into the bathroom with her. But when the water was hot she repeatedly rolled the soap rapidly between her hands and was astonished when she could raise no lather. She looked at the soap more closely before finally setting it on the floor outside the shower.

Hickum was dreaming or thought he was. The flat of his hand was pressed against soft wet hair that was smoother than silk. His mouth was filled with a memory, a memory that he could not identify. But it was in no way threatening. It seemed right that it should be in his mouth, and slowly the wet noise that his lips and tongue were making grew louder in his ears, and flashes of light—like fire—started to burst against his sight as his eyelids fluttered, and he knew that he was waking from where he had fallen across the bed and that he was still on the bed but was now pressed against the naked body of Gaye Nell Odell, and that what he had in his mouth was not the memory of woman's nipple but Gaye Nell's very nipple, and that realization caused his pounding heart to drown out the sounds of his sucking, but it could not alter the knowledge that his hand was between her damp thighs, and when he could no longer keep from tilting his head to look up at her face, he saw her smiling down upon him and saw too the flecks of gold floating in her green eyes.

Terror, not shame, caused him to roll away from her, almost falling from the bed as he did. He could not remember when he had last seen a naked woman or who she had been, and he certainly could not remember such a limitless expanse of white skin that seemed to go on forever.

"I don't bite," she said.

But he paid no heed to what she said because he could now see that the flashes of light—like fire—were in fact fire burning from dozens of varicolored candles placed randomly about the room. He felt the skin over his heart go cold. He wanted to ask a question, but the only part of it he could get out of his mouth was: "What?"

In a movement that was so singularly fluid and powerful that it was over before he saw it begin, Gaye Nell, with enough naked skin to cover his entire dreaming life, saddled herself with him, a knee on each side of his face, the place where all known reason ended just brushing his chin as faintly damp as first dewfall, and said: "Soaps For Life do not lather. Neither do they clean. But they've burnt through what was left of the dark, burnt steady and bright."

"Candles?" he said.

"The string at the bottom that they are supposed to hang from makes excellent wicks. In fact I think were put there as wicks. So yes, candles. That's the answer to one question, my poor loveless Hickum. But the bigger, better question is which of us knows the way to go from here?"

For answer, a groan of pure pleasure and pain escaped his throat and he raised his head to meet her, his lips poised to suck and drink before he ever got to the place where she was wet and waiting.

chapter

fifteen

Peterbilt and LaFarge, their blackened eyes swollen to slits now, sat on the couch in the living room looking straight ahead. They could hear Ida Mae and Elmo talking in the back of the house. They could distinguish one voice from the other but could not hear either voice well enough to make out what was being said. Whatever was being said, though, had to be important. Elmo's voice came right over Ida Mae's before she had finished, and in turn, hers would come over his or else cut him off altogether in midsentence. Neither Peterbilt nor LaFarge had ever heard anybody cut the Boss off when he was talking.

"I could drink a glass of water," said Peterbilt.

"Myself," said LaFarge, "I could drink a whiskey. A long whiskey. Straight."

They did not look at each other as they spoke. They sat on

the couch like recently punished children, staring straight ahead, unmoving, and frowning in a slight pout.

"Elmo said for us not to get off this couch. So I guess a drink of water is out of the question."

"I guess."

"Your whiskey too."

"I know. But I still want it."

"Want in one hand and shit in the other. See which one fills up first."

LaFarge's head snapped around to look at Peterbilt. "Where in the name of God did you learn that?"

"From the Boss . . . I mean, Elmo. He said it was from south Georgia, where he comes from."

"Wouldn't you just know they'd say something like that. Fucking lame redneck. Son of a bitch wouldn't last ten minutes on the Rock."

"The Rock?"

"Maximum security. Florida State Prison."

Peterbilt, looking straight ahead, said: "Where you learned to like shit on your dick."

"Shut up," LaFarge said. "It's little enough pleasure in this world. You have to take it where you can get it."

"Don't bark at me. You liking shit on your dick's nothing but the truth. Or if it's a lie, you told it."

"I know who told it and it's not a lie. I also told you not to knock it till you tried it."

"I don't plan on trying it."

"It may be that the day will come to you when a little ass pussy gets to looking mighty good, because things don't always go according to plan. Seems like the plan was for us to come down here and kick the Lip's ass. Get a little payback. But here we sit with our eyes so fucked up we can hardly see."

"It's a damn easy thing to forget what the Boss is like when he's not standing right there in front of you. He throws hate like a stove throws heat."

There was a long silence before LaFarge said: "I got to admit that's righteous."

"Is that a wrecked aspidistra plant I see over there?" said Peterbilt.

LaFarge only turned his head to stare at Peterbilt. When Peterbilt felt LaFarge's malevolent gaze fasten on him, Peterbilt said: "Hey, I didn't mean anything by it. And by God, it *is* an aspidistra plant, or what's left of one, made out of rubber."

A forked vein, blue and ugly, leapt out just above LaFarge's nose and ran up into his hairline.

"You want me to look at a ruined plant made out of rubber? After everything I've been through today, that's what you want?"

Peterbilt said: "Not just any plant, an aspidistra plant made out of rubber. You don't hardly see them any more."

LaFarge's face had turned so red it was tinged in black along his flared nostrils and the line of his chin. His razor-thin lips seemed hardly to move as he said: "Pretty rare, are they?"

"Last one I saw, I was still in short pants—just a little boy— and I saw it in my grandmother's parlor."

A string of drool escaped the corner of LaFarge's mouth and stretched nearly to his shirt before it broke. When he spoke, his voice was a dry, rasping whisper. "Aspidistra? Rubber? Short pants? Grandma's fucking parlor? Peterbilt, I swear to God that if the Lip don't kill you, I mean to do it myself. You're too damn dumb to live."

"Now what? I was only trying to make conversation," sighed Peterbilt, seemingly unmoved by LaFarge's threat of death. "The little bastard only said we had to sit here. He never said we couldn't talk. I think recent events have been more than you can take. Is that it? Is that what's wrong. Or is your underwear too tight?"

But before LaFarge could answer, the voices that had been nearly inaudible in the back of the house now burst into the hallway leading to the living room where Peterbilt and LaFarge sat.

"You've always wanted the salesmen to carry one because you wrote the thing," said Ida Mae, glancing over her shoulder at Elmo, who was following her down the hall. "Just because they carry the Sales Manual doesn't necessarily make it valuable or even mildly helpful. And while we're at it, Elmo, you really ought to spend some of that mountain of money I keep hearing you've made the Company and get that lip of yours repaired. Plastic surgery these days can work miracles."

"Non't change ne subject," Elmo said, his voice rising like a petulant child who has been told his favorite toy ought to be thrown away. "We weren't nawking nabout my lip, which—for nur information, I keep na show nat anything's possible in nis world. But selling na ne max—at least, nat's what I call it—selling na ne max is impossible without ne Sales Manual, which I did write nand I'm namn proud of it."

The two of them were almost nose to nose now in the middle of the living room. Without realizing it, LaFarge and Peterbilt had almost stopped breathing. Somewhere far away a siren started up.

"Being proud of it doesn't make it of any consequence. If it had not been for me, Hickum Looney might not have filled one complete book, much less twelve. Hickum is burned up, burned down, and burned out. Half the time he's on automatic pilot."

"Nif nu've memorized ne Nails Spanual, nu can make a living flying on automatic pilot all ne time."

"I have not memorized the Sales Manual and never will. I was clear about that from the start." She put her hand on his shoulder. "Now listen to an old lady for a minute. Have you ever heard yourself, Elmo? Put your voice on tape and played it back to yourself? *Nails Spanual?* That's what you say, *Nails Spanual,* when you mean *Sales Manual.* And it's really not necessary. But the real tragedy is that you can't get away with it much longer."

"Forget my mouth. I dent fly all ne way noun here na nawk nabout my mouth. I saw nure name on everyone of ne order slips nat were faxed ninto my place in Atlanta, nure name right nair as ne referral agent na every order na ne first one. Nat first one was sold to nu nand den nu took over and guided him through ne city na every other order he filled. Nure a peenom . . . But my yob is *my* yob!"

"*Phenom*, Elmo, *phenom* is the word you want. Your deformity is embarrassing both of us. I told them that from the beginning. Now they're going to cut you out and cut you down."

In an unconscious and instant gesture, one of Elmo's hands flew up to cover his lip the instant she said the word *deformity*. Neither LaFarge nor Peterbilt, sitting transfixed on the couch, had ever seen him cover his mouth in what was obviously a gesture of shame. But then neither one of them had ever heard anybody refer directly to the defective lip. Except the Boss, of course, and he referred to it constantly. At the annual sales convention he often howled about it.

"Ninnything nat culls nu from ne herd is good!" he would cry, caught in the passion of his heated, swirling dance. "I've always tried na play ne nand nat was dealt me. Nu got na play nures. Never get caught trying na play ne other man's game." He would stop and stand very still, and in turn his audience would become hushed, still, and expectant. When everything was as he wanted it, he slowly raised his hand and with the tip of an extended finger he would touch his deformity. He wasn't covering it, but pointing to it, touching it as a shaman might touch a holy relic. "Nis," he would finally say, "nis right here is my ace in ne hole. Nand nu got na find nur own. Find nure ace nand play it *proud.*"

"You might as well not put your hand *over* it," she said. "That lip is still there and it's still ugly."

At the word *ugly*, both Peterbilt and LaFarge flinched as though they'd been hit. And in the same instant LaFarge and Peterbilt flinched, Elmo stopped. Nothing about him moved; not a muscle in his face, not his hands, not even his chest moved to indicate he was breathing. "One of neese times," he said, "nu'll go too far."

"You're not used to people telling you the truth, are you, Mr. Jehoveh?" Ida Mae said.

"Jeroveh," he said, "yust Jeroveh."

"Is that really your name?" she asked.

"Would nat make a nifference?"

"To you I think it would make *every* difference."

"In nat case, I suggest all of us tink of me as Elmo Jeroveh," he said. "It might save nime and rubble."

Ida Mae smiled and shook her head. *"Nime and rubble?"* she said. "I don't want to save nime and rubble, plus I don't know anybody else who wants to save nime and rubble." She looked at the ceiling for a moment and then looked back at him. "Christ, Elmo, get out with a little dignity, get out while there's still time. Being damaged goods won't save you forever."

"This has nothing na do with ne proposition I offered new, mut new mean na rub my nose in it anyway, don' new?"

"It wouldn't even take a good surgeon to fix you up, Elmo. A mediocre one could do it. A little work on the palate, a patch on the lip, and *presto,* you wouldn't have to say *nime and rubble* ever again."

She moved in closer to him so that their faces, since they were almost the same height, were only inches apart. "You could say *time and trouble* like everybody else who speaks the language. And the rest of us wouldn't have to make a goddam fool of ourselves trying to guess what it is you're trying to say. I think the Company might appreciate that." She was a little beside herself now, and a cottonlike froth was gathering at the corners of her mouth. "Do you have any notion at all how much trouble—how much tension and anxiety—you cause everybody around you?" She was panting when she finished as if she'd climbed a flight of stairs. His smile, displaying the single discolored square tooth in the middle of his face, didn't help matters either. It pushed her shortness of breath to the critical stage. "Well, do you . . . you . . . ." She could not go on.

"Nas a matter of fact, I do," he said quietly. He waited until her breathing was settled and slower. "Mut nat was never ne question. The question was, do nu mean na force ne point with me nand ne Company?"

"If you have to put it like that, I think I have to. You know and I know and the Company knows that there won't be a Soaps For Life if you can't change your practices. It's a wonder the law hasn't been down on the operation already," she said.

"Ne law? What's ne law gotta do wit it?"

"How can a woman be a sales*man*? The politically correct word, I believe, is *salesperson,* Mr. Jeroveh."

Elmo started a tiny movement with his legs that looked as though it could easily develop into his famous hotfooted dance. "I refuse na call one of my snaleman a snaleperson, noddammit."

"A good lawyer could make that into a grievous error."

"A namn lawyer good or mad could make anything into a grievous error."

"Only the lilies neither reap nor do they sow."

"What's at nu ay?"

"Just a long way of saying if you're not a goddam lily, you better have a job. And since a lawyer's not a lily, he's got a job and his job is to fuck you up."

"If it was a nanswer in nat, I dent hear it."

"Forget it then. But there's one more thing I've got to ask. Did you give Gaye Nell a job?"

"I offered," he said.

"She take it?"

"She did. She yumped at it."

"There's a lot she might do, but she would never yump. Gaye Nell is not that kind of girl."

"Nu mocking me."

"Why do you suppose I do that?"

Elmo glanced briefly at LaFarge and Peterbilt where they sat on the edge of the couch, their backs straight, their hands planted firmly on their knees.

"Because I'm a nandicap," Jeroveh said softly.

"No, I do it because you're a royal pain in the ass."

"Nure a hard woman with a hard heart na say nat about a nandicap."

"Some of the sorriest people I've ever known were, as you say, handicapped. But hell, I don't want to talk about it. As a matter of fact, just so you'll know, I don't want to talk to you. Talking to you is just about the hardest work I've ever had. And it's all your fault for keeping that mouth. And rumor has it that the Company no longer feels it's a benefit."

Elmo turned his head and said, "Meterbilt."

"Right here, Bo . . . Elmo."

"I know where nu are, noddammit! Get over here!"

Peterbilt was instantly by Elmo's side. Ida Mae looked him over, clucking her tongue and sighing, as if Peterbilt was a prize bull she was thinking of buying. "I hate to tell you this, but you won't do, either. What an obscenity you are. Even your name that is obviously *not* your name is an obscenity. You don't have to tell and I don't have to ask who gave you that name." She looked directly at Elmo. "His sign is on everything that's out of plumb, warped, and basically unnatural. All of that, business can overlook if the profit is there. Without maximum profit, the Company can stand nothing."

Elmo showed her the square tooth at the center of his face. "Nand I new ne moment I laid eyes on nu that nu was one of my own. Nand Gaye Nell Odell is too."

"I don't know if I'd say that to her face if I was you. But I guess you know better, since she's already shot off the walking toes on both the feet of your main salesman and then she stamped the dust out of that greasy little mechanic you had with you—and him with a gun, too. I called the hospital where you dumped him. You'll be glad to know the bone is shattered and the arm won't ever be worth a dime again."

"Meterbilt, nell her what I was nalking about driving over here with nu and LaFarge."

"Before or after you hit us between the eyes, Boss?"

Elmo stamped both feet and he cried: "Nu nummy! Nu fucking nummy."

"Nothing lost, Elmo. Nobody bought that shit about a lady with a baby stepping off a curb."

Elmo Jeroveh breathed deeply and exhaled slowly until he finally looked up at Peterbilt and said very slowly: "After."

"You broke Elmo's heart," said Peterbilt. "Miss Ida Mae, you broke it when you broke his record. And it had to be you, Miss Ida Mae, who broke it, not Hickum Looney. The Boss says the only thing Hickum could break is a promise, and that would strain him."

Peterbilt put both his wide hands over his face and started sneezing rapidly, one right behind the other. Ida Mae had fired off six back-to-back *God bless you*'s before she realized that Peterbilt was not sneezing but laughing.

Elmo kicked Peterbilt hard in the right knee and screamed, "Nawk why, mig mastard!" He looked at Ida Mae and said: "A million-nollar body nand new-nollar mind."

Peterbilt said: "You know how long that record you broke had stood? Forever, that's how long. Since they've been keeping records, that was the record to shoot for. And you just stepped in and sunk that record, boom! just like that, and without studying a Sales Manual or even having one." He hooked a thumb at Elmo Jeroveh. "I mean to tell you, that just walked a hole in his heart is what it done."

"He'll get over it," Ida Mae said. She had quit really listening since she had heard that Gaye Nell would take a job with Soaps For Life if she, Ida Mae, would. And she would, but not in the way Gaye Nell supposed. But then she had no options. She had never had any options. Nobody in the Company has ever had any options. Ever.

"What has nur work experience been nike?" Elmo asked. "Not dat it matters a whole not. Nu can either sell or nu can't. Sell and nu keep working. The orders step, the yob stops. So . . ." He did a little jig on the tips of his highly polished shoes and rubbed his hands together as though warming them before a fire. "Were nu a housewife or . . . yust what?"

"Do I look like a housewife? I can't believe you came here knowing so little about me."

Peterbilt said: "You kind of remind me of my mom."

"You're reading it wrong, Peterbilt, reading it very wrong."

"She was a real nice lady," said Peterbilt.

"I'm not," Ida Mae said. "I'm not a mother. And neither was I a housewife. Educated first as a nurse, and then as a teacher, I walked off twenty-five years in a wretched public school class-room, biding my time. Fifth grade. And listening to a roomful of fifty little savages mangle pledging allegiance to the flag made me the most dangerous kind of anarchist."

Peterbilt took a staggering step back and said: "You're nothing like my dear old mother."

Elmo Jeroveh showed his single monstrous tooth and said: "Nure exactly wike mine."

chapter

sixteen

The heavy beige drapes were pulled over the windows when Gaye Nell woke lying beside Hickum on the bed. Bubba was asleep over her feet. A digital radio clock on a small bedside table stood at nine-thirty. She knew she could not have slept more than four hours or so, and that sleep had been shallow. Gaye Nell had never been a successful daytime sleeper. If she missed a night's sleep, that sleep was gone forever. She had never been one of those who could double up and sleep twice as much as usual and pretend to have got back the sleep she had lost.

She was tired, and when she stretched she found that she was sore. She was naked, and when she looked over her breasts and stomach and legs she expected to find bruises, but there were none, not the slightest discoloration anywhere on her. But then she smiled, remembering. She closed her eyes and saw her twisting heaving body with Hickum, both of them naked in the low guttering light of the randomly spaced, varicolored burning soap that was not soap at all but columns of wax that did not burn well or light well. And the light they did provide made the room a blur of shadows. She submitted to Hickum, whose strength and gasping frenzy surprised her, but it no doubt had surprised him even more, because when he had finally ridden her onto the high crest of his passion, his face suddenly went dark and in a voice a man dying of thirst might have used to call for a drink of water, he cried, "Oh! my God," and collapsed onto her, and with what seemed to be his last breath, begged: "Please, oh please, will you marry me?"

At least she had thought that was what he'd said, but she couldn't be sure because he had immediately sunk into a deep, exhausted sleep from which she had been unable to wake him. She slapped him twice but it had been like slapping a side of beef. He did not even flinch. And so she had fallen asleep wondering if he had said what she thought he'd said and she woke up wondering the same thing.

But by the time she got off of the bed and went into the bathroom and found a toothbrush and some toothpaste, she had another take on the whole thing. Of course he had said what she thought he had said, and, more than that, she knew he had said it out of the rankest kind innocence or ignorance or both. She thought of something that had happened to her toward the end of the first year she had started hooking. A young marine, probably younger than she was, asked her how much it would cost him for all night.

She stopped scrubbing her teeth and simply smiled at herself in the mirror. She had not understood his question.

"What would *what* cost you for all night, honey?"

"You," he said. "What would *you* cost me for all night?"

"Trust me, sugar, you don't want me for all night."

His brow drew together and his jaw hardened. She knew instantly that she had embarrassed him and he was covering his embarrassment with anger. Then she had tried to explain it and had only made it worse.

"What in the world would you do with a girl like me for a whole night?"

"I think I'll be able to think of something," he said. "Maybe I ain't gone turn out to be the sweet boy you think I am."

She looked at him more closely. She was not used to getting sweet little boys for customers, but she sure as hell had run into what she thought was more than her share of men whose preferences ran to the strangest kind of kink, some of which she would indulge if the price was right and some of which she would not indulge no matter the price. But one thing she had learned and learned quickly about the street was to try to get everything settled ahead of time, so that she didn't run into any surprises if she could possibly help it.

Hooking on the street (which she had been doing) without a pimp to protect her (which she had also been doing) sometimes caused surprises to pop out of the night that could and often would get a girl killed.

With the young marine standing on the sidewalk in front of her, shifting from foot to foot and still demanding to know what an entire night would cost him, she did what she had done before and what she no doubt would do again: She had flipped a coin.

She trusted signs. She trusted her instincts. And she also trusted her fate. Whatever was waiting for her somewhere down the road would always be there, and nothing could change that. Or perhaps there was something that could change it if she was willing to pay the price. Unfortunately, her life on the street had taught her that the price could easily be her death.

"Hey," the marine said, startled. "What the hell are you doing?"

"Flipping a quarter," she said, but by then the quarter was back in her purse and she was leading him toward her room.

He kept looking over his shoulder as though he might still see her back there on the corner with a coin in the air.

"What the fuck was that about? I fucking hope it wasn't about me."

"It was," she said. "In a way."

He caught her upper arm so hard it hurt and turned her to face him. "Now hear this," he said. "Let me tell you about in a *way*. In a way the corps is fucking me, the CO is fucking me, the top sergeant is fucking me, the platoon NCO is fucking me. The squad leader is fucking me. I could go on with everybody that's fucking me but the list is too long!" He looked down the street in both directions. He had worked himself into a lather and she could see him trying to chill. "Me?" He struck his chest with his free hand. "Me? I'm just a country boy who got liberty to get off the base and come out here and *do* the fucking instead of *getting* the fucking. That's all I got on my mind: fucking somefuckingbody. So if you got something else on your mind, or you're just a ordinary head case, or a general Section Eight, you'd better cut me lose right here, because I'm nobody to jack around with. Not when I wanna fuck. And you still ain't told me what the night's gonna cost. Got it? You got it now?"

"I got it," she said. "And you can have all you can use for forty bucks. All you can use, anyway you want it. I like your style, so I'm giving you this week's blue plate special. But just remember that I'm not running a social club here or a conversation for lonely hearts. I'm a strictly get-your-nuts-off-and-get-out-the-door kind of girl. OK? Got it?"

He laughed, laughed hard and long. He couldn't get the breath to answer, so he just kept laughing and nodded. When she heard him laugh that way, she knew he was younger than she was and for a second she considered letting him have a free ride. But she considered it only for a second. There were no free rides. Not in this world.

But God he was green and young and sweet, and he reminded her of when she was green and young and sweet, and he ended up being exactly what she knew he would be and doing exactly what she knew he would do. He was so horny he could have bumped into a table and got his nuts off. And he treated her as though she was made of something thin and delicate that might break under his hands, and when she touched his cock that was still wet with her, when she touched his wet cock with her mouth, she knew he had never had his cock sucked, and he reacted to her throat as though his body had taken a jolt of electricity. The tremor that started in his loins spread to take his entire body until the shaking suddenly turned into a rigor that was like death and he screamed one sudden, brief sound that could have been of terror or of joy and then it was over.

She pressed her face against his hard boy's chest and rocked him and made little sounds of pleasure in her throat that she knew he might very possibly remember the rest of his life. She traced his cock, now hardly longer than a peanut and wet, traced the wet wrinkled peanut with her finger while it lay utterly still and lifeless. She smiled, but only because she knew he could not see her face. From the time they were both out of their clothes and naked, she knew, the whole time they were joined together had been something less than ten minutes.

Years from now when her heart was as shriveled and bitter as a turnip, this scene would play itself out again, and she would laugh and ask in her dry, derisive voice what he intended doing with the other eleven hours and fifty-four minutes of the night he had bought, now that he had used up all of six minutes, but for this time, on this night, she only rocked him and let him tell her how wonderful and special she was, what a miracle beyond all understanding she was. But then he was saying the next time he had liberty, they could meet downtown and see a show and . . .

She pressed hard against his chest and did not listen as she realized that already she could not remember his face, nor did she want to remember it. She was not in the business of remembering faces. She dealt in miraculous moments and the sweet motion of yielding flesh. She provided the flesh; her customers had to provide their own miracles. She gave dollar value for dollar paid, and she thought the whole enterprise was eminently fair.

But what she would never get used to, let alone understand, was that in the instant of a man's spent energy, lying naked with a stranger whose name he did not know and whose life at its

very best was a mystery, and at its worst a sinister masquerade—
at such a blind, naked instant an incredible number of men cried
out for love or wife or mother or devotion or fidelity or *anything*,
in fact, as long as it had absolutely nothing to do with the
anonymous whores with whom they had been most intimately
joined.

Gaye Nell got her shower without soap and without shampoo.
There was none in the shower and she was already wet all over
before she looked around and saw that there was none. Christ,
it was bad enough that she was going to have to put back on
the clothes Ida Mae loaned her, clothes that smelled of long
disuse, but she was going to have to put them back on after a
shower with no soap or shampoo. After she had dried off, she
could still smell last night's funk on her. She didn't know if it
was her funk or Hickum's funk or a mixture of the two, but it
was definitely funk. High funk.

"Hickum!" She waited. *"Hickum!"*

That was as loud as she could call. She waited. Nothing. Jesus.
She went into the bedroom and pulled the sheet off Hickum.
He was completely naked and there was something about his
body that made Gaye Nell think of Nazi concentration camps.
His bones were long and insistent under his skin. She had never
noticed before that he was so thin. But, Christ, he was. Old,
too. She took an ankle in each hand. For reasons that were not
entirely clear to her, it was embarrassing that she could reach
almost entirely around them.

"Hickum, dammit, wake up!"

She still had an ankle in either hand, his legs spread so that
one of his feet was at each of her hips. He opened his eyes, saw
her, saw his naked loins, and saw, too, that she was holding his
legs spread, and he opened his mouth and out popped a sound
like a small dog barking.

"What?" she said.

"What?" he said.

"What was that sound you made?" she said.

He snatched the pillow from under his head and threw it

between his legs. "What are you holding my legs like this for?"

She turned loose his ankles, and his legs fell back onto the bed. "I need soap for the bathroom. Shampoo would be nice, too."

"I wake up naked with you holding my legs . . . holding my . . . apart like this right here because you need soap and shampoo? Does that make sense to you, Gaye Nell? Have you lost your mind or what?"

"I haven't given any thought to whether or not I've lost my mind. I still need soap for a shower. You have soap or not? Don't make me dance for soap, that would definitely be low rent."

"You're not being reasonable."

"You're not making it easy."

"You know I have soap. You forget where I work?"

"I didn't forget and it's not what I asked you."

"There are Soaps For Life display cases stacked all over the apartment."

"I found all that last night. That's not soap, it's wax. Don't you remember the candles from last night?"

"Of course I remember the candles. I just forgot the demonstrator cases being full of wax. Special wax, at that. The kind that the heat from the sun won't melt. If I had real soap in the briefcases, the Miami sun would turn it into a puddle of grease."

"Grease? Soaps For Life has *grease* in it?"

"*Grease* was the first word that popped into my head. I don't know what it's got in it."

"You ought not to say what it's got in it if you don't know."

"I only sell it, I don't make it."

"OK. Right. I don't sell it *or* make it." She turned and started toward the bath. "I'm sorry I woke you up."

"My God, you're beautiful," he said.

She stopped with her back to him. She had a towel in her hand but she had made no effort to cover herself with it.

"How well do you remember last night?" she said.

"I remember everything about it. I was exhausted but . . . but no matter how tired I was, nothing could have made me forget how beautiful you were. No matter how tired I might have been, nothing could have made me forget how it was between us. There won't ever be another time like that. That's the one a man spends his whole life looking for. I—"

She held up her hand, cutting him off because it was beginning to look like he was going to babble right on through the morning. "Maybe we're talking about two different things."

"What?" He shook his head gently, as though slightly dazed. "How's at?" His eyes had been bright, his face radiant. Now he looked away from her, letting his gaze settle on the bedcovers. Almost inaudibly, he said: "I'm sorry."

She walked back toward him and sat on the bed. "Do me a favor, Hickum."

He raised his eyes to meet hers. "Anything."

"This is Sunday and we've got nothing to do today but get ourselves back together. Let's not mess it up by being sorry. I'm not sorry. Not a bit. You know why? I got nothing to be sorry for. And you don't either. OK? Will you remember that?"

"I'll try."

"Not good enough."

"You ask too much," he said.

"We probably all ask too much. But trying won't do today." She was smiling. "You've got to do it."

"I'll remember."

"Great. That's great." She gave a little bounce on the bed, put her hands behind his head, and brushed his lips with hers.

He was instantly on his feet. "Don't start that."

"I thought it was kind of nice."

"It's worse than that. It drives me crazy. You don't know how long I've been locked away from such as that."

"You make it sound like you've been in jail."

"I have. In a way."

"Something tells me I'd have a hard time understanding that. It's one of those things I've tried to stay away from my whole life."

harry crews

"Something tells me it'd be totally impossible for me to explain. And I feel like I've been in it my whole life."

"Where is it written that I've got to understand it or that you've got to explain it?"

Hickum Looney thought it was a great question even if he didn't understand it. But one thing he did understand: He didn't have an answer for it.

"I don't believe I've got an answer for that one."

"I'll give you the answer that somebody gave me: It's not written anywhere."

"What?"

"That's the answer. It's not written anywhere. Nothing is written."

He cocked his head and thought about that for a moment. "Good," he said, collapsing on the bed. "In that case I think both of us could do with some more sleep."

She moved closer to him. "I think you're forgetting the last crisis we had last night."

He leaned forward and put his face in the place where her neck joined her shoulder. His breath was warm and it smelled thick with sleep. If it had not been for Bubba, she would have gone back to bed with him.

"Not *that*, you darling. The other crisis. The *big* crisis. It's still with us. In spades, it's with us."

He only looked at her a long time, frowning, and then jumped as though somebody had hit him with a straight pin. "You're starved!" he cried. "That's it, I've let you drag around here this morning, starving to death."

"I'd of let it go if it hadn't been for Bubba. I swear Bubba's at the point of death."

"Sure that's not just a shade over the line," Hickum said.

"Well, hell, look at him," she said, turning to point at him where he was stretched out in front of the overstuffed chair, lying broadside on the floor, his wet, ragged breathing coming in little gargles.

"Right, he does look like mother-I've-come-home-to-die."

"Don't be sarcastic at the expense of my dog's life."

Hickum Looney said: "Actually, I was thinking about getting him some kind of treat for him having such a puny supper last night. But I don't know much about dog food."

"Get a twelve-pound bag of Pro, and for a treat, get a large can of rice, gravy, and boned chicken breasts."

"No wonder you're sleeping in an abandoned VW bus. You're feeding Bubba like the Prince of Wales."

"Bubba hasn't eaten like that in a while, but if he can get it today, why not take it?"

They happened to be looking dead into each other's eyes when she spoke, and he held her gaze when he answered. "If Piggly Wiggly's got it, get it. Stayed around me, Bubba could eat him a boned chicken breast and gravy every night. Just cause we can't eat like a king don't mean Bubba can't."

"That's just sweet as it can be to offer something grand like that. But it'd be too rich every night," she said.

"I bet you could work something out."

"I sure wouldn't mind having the chance to try."

"All right, I'm throwing on a jump suit and getting out of here and popping by the Piggly Wiggly for Bubba, swinging by the Crystal for two country breakfasts—eggs, bacon, biscuit, grits, the works to go. They got the cutest little Styrofoam takeouts you ever saw. Half a sack of juice and two sacks of coffee. That cover it? Think of anything else?"

"Bubba and me's overwhelmed. I don't think we got a thing to say."

Hickum was all cinched into the bright red jump suit and when he got a hand free, he pointed off down the hall and said: "The master bath is down thataway and I think you'll find everything you need in there: towels, washcloths, soap, and all the poo (in the industry, that's what we call shampoo) you can use."

"You may be the sweetest man I've ever met," she said.

"The more you say things like that, the harder I'll be to get rid of."

Hickum stopped very still and gave Gaye Nell the wildest, deepest smile he could manage, so wild and so deep in fact that it conjured in Gaye Nell Odell a feverish memory of the Boss's spectacular smile with a single unthinkable tooth blooming in the middle of it.

chapter

seventeen

The mechanic walked up to the nurse's aid station. There was only one nurse behind the desk, writing on a patient's chart. She didn't take her eyes from the chart but kept writing while she got up and walked across the office to stand behind the counter in front of the mechanic. She didn't look up.

"How may I help you, please?"

"The room number for Mr. George Bickle. As I understand it, he's gun shot."

"You don't need to say that. It's not sanitary."

"OK. That's a big affirmative."

"Yes, that'll be room 319, third floor. The elevator is to your right, about halfway down the hall. I'll have to give you a pass."

"I beg your pardon."

"A pass."

"I beg your pardon."

"You've already said that."

"Yes, I have."

"Then why did you ask me again?"

"Because I don't understand."

Now she put her pen down and looked at the ceiling and took a very slow, very deep breath. And held it. A long time. A very long time. She didn't look the least bit uncomfortable. She smiled. It was a friendly smile. Slimy didn't have the foggiest notion what was going on. He looked around and wished somebody else would come to the desk. But as far as he could see in any direction, the halls were empty. Slimy bet old Hillary Rodham Clinton would be happy as hell about this turn of events. All the primary health givers were free. No grieving friends or relatives in sight. *He* sure as hell didn't have a lot of grieving friends or relatives. From what he'd heard about Bickle, Slimy hoped he'd been unlucky enough to get his gunshot wounds infected so the doctors had to saw both his goddam legs off.

Slimy reached over and took the pass out of the nurse's hand, which she didn't seem to mind at all. "Thanks for your help," he said, "and I hope you die holding your breath like that."

He hadn't taken three steps away from the desk when he heard the nurse say to his back: "You might want to know that the young patrolman standing guard on your friend's room has a mother who is in the terminal stage of lung cancer."

"He's not my friend," said Slimy. "Neither of them's my friends. I don't have any goddam friends."

"You young bastard," said the young nurse.

"Thank you," said Slimy.

He turned on his heel and walked quickly down the hall, got on the elevator as an attendant was pushing a gurney off, and pressed the button for the third floor. He walked slowly down the hall until he found room 319. A smooth-faced cop who looked like he had just made Eagle Scout took the pass out of Slimy's hand and looked at it not very long and not very closely.

"OK," he said.

As Slimy passed the cop he stopped and said: "Hear your mama's real bad off sick."

The cop looked at him, blinked, and said: "The cancer."

"Why don't you step off down there and set with 'er awhile. If your boss man comes by I'll tell him you had to go to the bathroom and take you a tee-tee."

The cop said: "Tee-Tee, you say? I bet you was in the Boy Scouts too."

"Was."

The killer and the cop reached out and gave the secret Boy Scout handshake.

"I'll say a prayer for your mother."

"That's good of you."

"Nothing a white man wouldn't do."

The door was open and the bed was by the window, which had a crack in the glass and leaked the smell of combustion from the bumper-to-bumper traffic on the street below. Everything in Miami was warped, bent, or busted. Now the goddam hospital was coming apart. The very least thing a man could expect from a hospital in the subtropics was a hospital that was sealed tight and air-conditioned.

George's hugely casted feet were elevated, and a tiny grunt slipped out into the room every time he exhaled. When Slimy had been told what Gaye Nell had done to George, he had not believed a word of it. Boosting automobiles as he did regularly, taking a contract on a hand for $500, and even hustling hustlers, he thought he had heard and seen it all.

He knew now that was not the case. But he knew they had given him bum dope the minute he saw Bickle. The bitch had shot his toes off his feet. And for reasons that only doctors know, to fix the toes, they had to remove his feet. If Slimy ever got this straightened out and Gaye Nell was still alive, Slimy would like to hire her. This bitch would give new meaning to the word *collector*.

The hospital staff had the bed raised and Slimy could hardly see over George's chest. He stepped up into a wooden ladder-back chair. Now he could see his face.

"Mr. Bickle?"

Slowly the big man's head rolled on the pillow like a bowling ball.

"What the hell you doing standing in my chair?"

"They got the hospital bed jacked up. I couldn't see you from the floor down there."

"You don't need to see me."

"Begging your pardon, sir, but you're like a man in a shit storm. You ain't in no position to tell what needs to be seen and what don't need to be seen, because you can't see nothing but shit nohow."

"You're a smart little fuck, ain't you?"

"No sir, I'm afraid you wrong there, too. Tell you what I am, though. I'm a man knows I never met a man who needs his toes shot off."

"Who's been talking to you about my toes?"

"This one and that one. Word gits around."

"And I guess you the one that carries it."

"Carries what?"

"The word that gits around."

"Oh no! Oh no, not me! I got enough trouble carrying my broke arm."

"Your broke arm, you say? And who broke your arm?"

"The same split tail that shot your toes off."

"She must keep this hospital pretty damn full, acting that away."

"You can take a deep breath and say that again."

George Bickle lifted his great melon-shaped head off the pillow an inch or two and looked around. "It's a great pot for squat—sit for shit—I'm talking there at the end of the bed, but its empty now, I know for a fact, so if you'd fetch it and put it upside down on the chair you're in, you'd have a good bit more to set on and we might think of something to make us some money to pay for these broke and busted parts that girl given us."

The mechanic got off the chair and looked for the pot but didn't find it until he looked under someone's nightshirt and there it was—the great pot used to squat for nighttime evacuation. It occurred to Slimy that they probably had equipment in Guatemala for patients to shit in while they lay in the bed at night instead of making them get up and squat on a little pot to do it in. Slimy put the pot bottom side up on the chair and then climbed up and carefully set himself down upon it.

"The only way I'm ever going to be comfortable again is to be dead."

"Hey, man. Take that back. Don't joke about death. It ain't funny."

"Tell it to Elmo. Elmo! Can you imagine wanting to be called Elmo instead of the Boss? What a fucking name. Screw it! It's no figgering people. If you happen to get a chance, tell Elmo death's a joke and the joke's on him."

"Not funny. Wouldn't tell my worst enemy that. OK."

"Not."

"Not? Not what?"

"Not funny."

"You say."

"I say."

"You know, we sound like a couple o' goddam parrots."

"That's your opinion."

"Stop that, dickhead. Don't do that anymore."

"Do what?"

"Repeating me with questions and such as that."

"Whatever pleases you. Let me get on with my business here. My business is finding business, and when I heard about you getting your toes—"

"—Feet."

"Whatever."

"It's not whatever, it's my goddam feet."

"Precisely. So I say to myself, I say, You find that man with the feet shot off and you find a man carrying poison for blood and murder in his heart. A man who can't stop and think about doing some serious killing."

"I got to hand it to you, little man . . ."

"Name's Slimy."

"A choice name."

"Mama thought so."

"Your mama named you that?"

"You got a problem with that?"

"Well, I just thought . . . Never mind what I thought. Slimy's a damn fine name. Nearly good as mine—Blackball, on account of my head."

"But your head's not black."

"Not a ball either. But I think it does it fine."

"I believe we might make a team. 'Cause now that I see the look of it, *Blackball* suits you fine. So let me put it right on the table. When I heard the nasty way of hurting people, I thought you and me could work like two mules broke to pull in double harness."

"Don't know a thing about mules or harness. The only question I got is: Is they any money in it?"

"You can't imagine."

"I believe I can."

"Then it's a deal."

They slapped in a handshake that almost crushed Bickle's hand.

When it was over, Blackball said, looking at Slimy's hand: "By God it ain't big, but it's got the power."

Slimy smiled proudly and said: "That's what all the ladies say if they can still talk when I git through with them. Could I use your shitter before I go?"

"Make yourself at home."

Slimy dropped his pants, took the pot he'd been sitting on off the chair, and set it on the floor and dropped down on it, smiling for all he was worth.

"I thought you meant to use that one built over yonder in the corner."

"Naw, this right here just brings back fond memories of home. Hope you don't mind."

"Hell, your shit don't smell no worst than mine."

"You and me's a pair all right, a pair straight out of the barrels of a shotgun."

chapter

eighteen

People all over the country working in the Soaps For Life Company were waiting for what they had been promised, waited with all the fervor of their being, with hope, with a certain anxiety and fear, and, yes, with prayer. The television—through the infomercials bought by the Company—kept them all together across the country. The ones already in the service of soap watched religiously; the others watched in a certain awe and amazement.

When their alarm clocks went off, they rolled out of their beds with the Big Man on their lips. And they dropped to their knees with the Big Man's name still on their lips at night beside their beds. Sometimes in their hearts and on their lips the Big Man got mixed up with Elmo and, for the really old-timers, the Boss.

As will sometimes happen in matters of such kind, the three names became mixed and meshed and confused, one with the other, without the supplicants ever knowing it. Apparently it never seemed blasphemous to them when it all became tightly knotted together, and inseparable, into Elmo/the Big Man/the Boss and—without any of those on their knees realizing it— God.

Over time, when the knowledge fell upon them with something very like a wrath of revelation, their hearts, in their own ways, said softly—for even the most stalwart among them could not bear such a thing alone—their hearts whispered, "Is it such a bad thing? God is All; All is God. God is big enough to contain Soaps For Life and Soaps For Life is big enough to contain the reality of God."

Besides, they heard their blood whispering through their secret hearts, We are on the inside of an enterprise that is monstrously big, big enough to say with God: GO FORTH AND MULTIPLY. The races that crowd the earth today are the result of that command. And inevitably a voice spoke in all the blood that coursed through the veins of those who spread the word, who spoke to every man and woman who would listen, proclaiming: BUY SOAPS FOR LIFE. AND ALL THE BANKS AND VAULTS AND ALL PLACES WHERE WEALTH IS KEPT WILL SWELL AND MULTIPLY IN A WAY THAT MAN HAS NOT EVEN IMAGINED IN THE HISTORY OF THE WORLD.

There will be those who doubt. There will be those who hurl cruel epithets. Sling bloodletting stones at you. Fling all defilement and excrement at you. But why? you ask. Why would they do these terrible things to us? And the answer was given them that these defilers had not yet committed their lives to soap. They were not yet in the fold of Soaps For Life. The word must be taken to them, sold to them, so that they might believe that no matter how filthy they were, they still had the chance to be washed clean by the Soaps For Life.

Everything was as it was, and everything was different.

"That don't make the first damn bit of sense," said Gaye Nell the first time she heard it from Hickum.

"It isn't supposed to make sense, it is supposed to give you something to think on, girl. It'll sharpen your mind and hone your senses."

"You ole turd," she said, throwing a pillow across the living room at Hickum.

It was a playful throw, and they were both laughing.

They had got pretty tight with each other since she moved into his apartment and redecorated to her own taste, with various bright and balanced colors, colors that harmonized and never clashed. Everybody who had seen it had thought it tasteful, having as it did a feminine touch it had lacked before.

"They're just saying that because of my new job with Soaps For Life," Hickum said.

"Hell, your new job is nothing but a name so far. That ugly little freak just give you a new name, that's all. What is a overseer, anyhow? I think it might've been one of them fuckers on the old-timey plantations hired to beat the blood out of nigger slaves."

Hickum stood up. He was serious now. And she knew it. Just by the way he hitched up his pants and took a brief pull at his crotch when he stood up from the couch, she knew it. Men were so sweet and simple. She prided herself that she could sing them like a song and train them like a dog. Still, just because she had decided to allow him to have his say about things and be serious for a while didn't mean she intended to let him talk on too long (which he'd taken to since he had been named overseer by the little freak) or stay quiet and let him talk long and get into stuff he knew nothing whatever about (another bad habit he'd developed since he had come by his title of overseer).

"Listen close now, because I'm not going through this thing with you but once. But it's still important. I took you about as far as I can take you, unless you change your ways some. I mean, I did take you out of a VW bus, you and your wretched dog, Bubba, broke down in a mall parking lot, and got you a job with a future. The time is here when you got to try to clean up your mouth. It won't be easy because it's been dirty so long. But you

the mulching of america   205

got to start somewhere. We all do. You can start by stopping all that incidental loud talking and cussing. I hate that and I think most other decent people with any breeding do, too."

She went to sit on the couch while he talked. She hoped she looked contrite and hoped she was. But she knew she was not.

"Are you listening to what I'm trying to tell you, Gaye Nell?"

"I most surely am," she said, unable to even talk in an ordinary way anymore. Who in the world ever said something like *I most surely am*? Nobody, that's who. But nonetheless she had said it and now she kept her eyes locked directly on his, which he could never bear for long. He turned his back to her and started his monologue again.

"And try to keep your skirt down where it's supposed to be. You're not an exhibition for the gawkers and loungers. You're a member of a select group, a member of Soaps For Life. Now you can start working on that. It's not much but it's something. There's other stuff, but you work on that until you got it down pat, then we can go on to something else. You don't, I'm going to throw you back on the street."

Her hand tipped forward and she said, "I was only playing," but she knew he knew that and knew also that he knew she knew it.

It surprised him how her saying that she had only been playing made him feel. Good and warm and very close to her. A feeling unlike any he could remember.

He made a little clucking noise with his mouth and said, "Anyway you play it, this has been a great two weeks."

"Light work apart and heavy work together." As demurely as she could manage, which was not very, she continued: "But work close and heavy between a man and a woman is always quite wonderful."

He said, a phony frown on his face, "I told you, girl. Get your suitcase."

"You know I don't have a suitcase. But I don't need one. Throw my things out the window, see how much I care." She put a hand on a cocked hip and said: "We could play the game the other way round. Guys I've known liked that flavor. I'll save all my greasy talk just for you, and let you and only you see the great-mother-whore side of me."

"I kinda like the notion of that." But what he truly felt was his heart pumping his brain tighter and tighter until it felt it would explode, and yet at the same time it felt like the most natural thing in the world, nothing to be shamed for or embarrassed about. How marvelously right it felt. He was utterly dumbfounded that there was a time—and it seemed far, far away now—when he would have felt all of this to be an unbearable perversion. "Yeah, I believe I do genuinely love the notion of that."

"Then throw me on the bed and fuck the talk out of me, the good and bad."

"Now you've sealed your fate," he said. And then as an afterthought. "And mine too, by God." She was in the air while he was still talking.

"Show me."

"That's the last thing you're going to say," he howled, going down on her.

And he had almost been able to keep his promise. The sweat was dripping off his face and onto her face when she said, "You've got nothing left to prove. You can give it up."

"Who can give it up?"

"You."

"Why not you?"

"Yes. Oh yes, yes. I can give it up too. Make it a treaty, even, like we saw on the television."

"Maybe I could sign the treaty with you?"

Neither of them said a word. No question. No answer. They only remained so closely joined that the vision of each was deeply lost in the depths of the other's eyes.

Gaye Nell awakened first and had no idea how long she had been asleep. It could have been ten minutes or four hours. She could not remember feeling this good. It was cool in the apartment and, with the drapes drawn, almost dark. She could tell from Hickum's breathing that he was still asleep. They were supposed to go to a movie today, and Gaye Nell tried to think of the title of the picture they both wanted to see. But she couldn't.

Everything in her perceptions seemed pleasantly dim. It was as though her mind was an empty room, without even windows or doors, painted white and filled with a soft blue light, the source of which she could not find. She felt totally comfortable and totally safe and she felt herself slipping back toward sleep when Hickum moved. He didn't sit up, only rubbed his face with his hands and yawned. He was facing her and even his dusky, sleep-filled breath smelled good.

She didn't know whether she wanted to go out or not. Neither of them had what people call hobbies or outside interests. After you got past going to what they both called moving pictures, they lost interest. They both said that the world had been too hard on them to find time to develop hobbies or find outside interests, and they believed what they said. And neither of them felt the need to defend the way they lived.

They did not inquire into each other's lives, either. If one of them wanted to talk, the other wanted to listen, and that was how their conversations started. Almost never with a question. It was as though they were each afraid of the answer they might get if they asked something too personal. As a matter of fact, it was Gaye Nell who had told Hickum from the beginning: Don't ask the question if you can't stand the answer. And he had taken her at her word.

He slowly rolled over onto his back, laced his hands behind his head, and stared silently at the ceiling for a moment. Then still not looking at her, he said: "That's a keeper. We put that one in the record book."

"I can dig it," she said. "It was only slightly short of killing. I felt my heart want to quit there a couple times."

He didn't say anything for what seemed a long time to her and she said: "Is it one you can share?"

"A thought," he said. It was a little thing they had with each other, a way of asking and not asking at the same time.

"Oh?"

"Yes," he said. "About Ida Mae, actually."

"You think of her much?"

"More than I should, probably."

"Me, too."

"I wondered what he wanted with her up there in Atlanta. Hell, I've never even been in Atlanta. Been near it, but not in it. The truth is, I never been anywhere much."

"You've been in me and I'd say that's much, that's too much."

He gave her a easy elbow in the ribs. "Nobody likes a wise ass," he said.

"Depends on whose ass and how wise."

"After a thrash like we just had, talk like that doesn't touch me."

"Whatever he wanted with her it must have been serious business. The salary alone was unspeakable. The perks were unthinkable."

"You're not supposed to know information like that."

"And you are?"

"I'm an overseer."

"Well, kiss my ass."

"Turn over."

She didn't answer but only smiled and watched him for a long time and then finally said, "Wonder what would happen if we called her?"

"She'd answer."

"You know where she is?"

"She's staying at the mansion."

"The mansion? Whose fucking mansion?"

"How many guys you think I know with mansions?"

"The Lip?"

"I think he prefers *Elmo Jeroveh.*"

"Ida Mae in a fucking mansion?"

He turned to give her what passed for his stern look. "I wasn't going to do it. Now I have to do it for your own good and the good of Soaps For Life."

"Sounds serious."

"Are you going to do something about your incidentally filthy mouth, or not? Do you understand me? Do you know what I mean when I say incidentally filthy?"

He waited. She said nothing. But she looked afraid. "You are incidentally filthy when you have no reason. Somebody hits his finger with a hammer and screams *motherfucker!* and everybody understands. They may not like it but at least they understand. But you! Your mouth is full of filth for no reason. Filth of the worst kind. Or at least Elmo Jeroveh thinks so, and I agree. Incidental filth is the result of very bad breeding."

"So that is where you learned to say—"

"It seemed a good way to think about it. You don't agree?"

She did not answer immediately. Then finally she said: "I agree. I'll do something about it. You'll see."

"That's good to hear. Now I don't have to say anything else to you about it. I don't sleep with the hired help. I don't run this bed like a ship. We're equals in the sheets and out of them. I'm not your daddy. I refuse to tell you when, what, and how to do things, including the words to use or not use when you speak. Go figure."

Her lips pressed together and her eyes were suddenly shiny. "Do you mind if I ask you something?"

"Now how am I supposed to answer something like that? I couldn't possibly know the question. But if you want to say something, I'm listening."

"Nobody ever said anything that beautiful to me before," she said. "If you make me say I love you, you're going to be sorry."

He looked over both his shoulders and around the room. "Somebody see anybody making anybody do anything here?"

"No," she said, quickly knuckling her eyes. "And I also don't know where to call Ida Mae in Atlanta."

"Elmo keeps the dish for the downlink for the teleconferences at his estate rather than at the main office of the company in downtown Atlanta. Therefore his private office, from which he runs the Company, is also at the mansion. That is where Ida Mae is staying."

"Big, I guess."

"Sixty-eight rooms."

"You *counted* the rooms?"

"I've never seen the place."

"Then how—"

"We are full of questions today, aren't we?"

"I'm sorry, it's just—"

"Ida Mae told me. Apparently she counted them."

"You've talked to Ida Mae since she left for Atlanta?"

"Remember our agreement. We don't play twenty questions. But, sure. Obviously I've talked to her."

"You never told me."

"You never asked me. No, wait a minute. You didn't deserve that. If you want to talk to her, call her yourself."

"I just got this job. I don't want to lose it. I need it."

"You're not going to lose your job. Elmo likes you. He likes how aggressive you are."

"And how would you know that? You read his mind, right?"

"Because he told me. I don't even remember how it came up. But he talks to me a lot when he's around, which isn't much. I been with him a long time. He doesn't talk much one-on-one, but he listens. A good listener is better'n a good talker. He told me that a long time ago. Nearly all the really good stuff I've got, I got from him. There's nothing criminal or crooked here. It's all pretty straightforward stuff."

"Damn." She picked up the phone. "Give me the number."

"I've got one number, the mansion office. If she's not there, you're out of luck. I'll give it slowly. You dial it."

"Good enough."

He gave it and she punched in the numbers. As the phone rang, he could see Gaye Nell cooling down, go cold even. He thought she somehow had felt slighted for him to know so much more than she knew. Now she felt maybe foolish or perhaps afraid.

"Uh, yeah, hello." She stopped, cleared her throat. "Is Ida Mae there?"

"Why?" She sounded amazed. "Whadda you think? I want to talk to her. Why else would I be calling?" She put her hand over the receiver and said to Hickum, "It's something wrong with the girl on the other end of this line." Then she snatched her hand away and cried: "Ida Mae, you old darling!" Then a puzzled look came on her face and she was quiet for a very long time, speaking not at all, the puzzled look on her face turning to a kind of stunned hurt. Finally: "All right. I'll look to see you. Be happy and remember, we love you."

She didn't even put the telephone back in the cradle but handed it to Hickum and let him do it for her. Then she went to sit on the bed with her hands between her knees. When she did look up at him, she said: "Something's wrong."

chapter

nineteen

"Something's wrong," Gaye Nell said again. "And the worst part for me is that I don't have a clue to what the hell ails her."

"What makes you think something's wrong?"

"What Ida Mae said, and how she said it. How she was. Sometimes it can just be the worst thing in the world. You know something is gone bad wrong but you don't have a bit of a notion what it is. Other times it's nothing."

He sat on the bed beside her and they both looked at the telephone. "I wish I could tell you I didn't know what you were talking about," he said, "but I do. God, I do for sure. The good thing, though, is that sometimes there really is nothing the matter, zero, zip, nothing."

"She didn't even sound like herself."

"She hasn't since the day she went up there. The first time I talked to her on the telephone, I could tell something had gone off track."

"Why didn't you tell me you talked to her? I'm as close to her as you are, she's as much my friend as she is yours."

"I really didn't think I was up to it. I just thought I'd let you find out for yourself."

"Sweet," she said. "That's really sweet."

"All right. Maybe I did everything wrong, handled it badly." His head was tilted forward and he was staring at the space between his feet. "But if you think I did what I did because I was trying to leave you out of something—hell, I don't even know what there is to be left out of—but if you think something like that, you've lost your mind."

She put her hand on his thigh and gently let her palm slide over it. "I just got a little nutty," she said. "But I'll cut it loose and get by it. Don't worry."

He had thought she was about to share something with him, somehow explain it, make him understand it, or at least say she was in it with him. But she only rubbed his leg and stayed silent.

"Something like this comes along," he said, "and you always wish somebody'd take you over in the corner and explain it all to you, and the truth is that if you wait long enough, somebody probably will. Either that or you'll come to understand it right by yourself."

"I'm not real big on waiting," she said. She sat staring at the telephone a minute more before she said: "Maybe I ought to call her back."

"I tried that."

"What happened?"

"It didn't work."

"Hickum Looney, try to make sense. You're confusing me."

"I don't mean to."

"Just exactly what happened? Can you tell me that?"

"I was told she couldn't take my call right then."

"Who? Who told you that?"

"The girl that talked to you just now. She always answers the phone when you call."

"The airhead?"

"Whatever."

"Did she give you a reason?"

"I never tried to call her back but once. It seemed too strange, I didn't want to fool with it."

"So what did the girl say to you?"

"Said Ida Mae was riding her Lifecycle right then and couldn't be disturbed."

"Riding her goddam Lifecycle, was she? Well, fuck me with a limber dick! Couldn't talk to her motherfucking friends because of a bicycle! And don't you dare say anything about me cussing! By God, that needs a little cussing."

"I kind of felt like that, myself. But I didn't want to get in too deep because I don't even know what a Lifecycle is."

"I do."

"Doesn't surprise me. I figgered you probably would. But me? I don't need to know. I've lived this long without knowing and I think I can live the rest of my life being dumb as a stone on the subject of Lifecycles. But it does sound about as nasty a damn thing as I ever heard of. For the life of me I can't imagine Ida Mae . . . well, you know."

"Lordy, you do beat all, Hickum. You think every single thing in the world comes down to a joining of the flesh. Well, you don't have to worry, I—"

A thunderous pounding at the front door of the apartment stopped her. They both turned to look but neither spoke. The same pounding rolled through the apartment again.

"As I recall," said Gaye Nell, "there's a bell out there to ring. It's even got a light on the bell in case it's too dark to see. Wonder why he's trying to beat the door down with his fist?"

"Don't ask me how I know," said Hickum, "but whoever's doing that has quit giving a fuck about what other people think about what he does. Sounds like he might be kicking it, instead of knocking. That's too much noise to make with a fist."

"We gonna answer it?" said Gaye Nell. "Or call the police?"

"Might as well see who's there," said Hickum. "And the police? I'd rather deal with a crook than a cop."

She spoke to his back as he walked to the door. "You know what's wrong with you, Hickum Looney, you're bitter. I know something about bitterness and you're a bitter man."

Answering, he didn't look back. "You got Gypsy blood in you, Gaye Nell. You read my mind like a cheap novel. I could wrap your head in a rag, set you in a carnival tent, and in five or ten years, we could retire in a double-wide trailer the color of your choice. I can see it now, a double-wide on the best piece of real estate in Tennessee."

Gaye Nell pulled him back by the collar of his shirt, stepped close to the door, and yelled, "You sons of a bitches, get away from—" But she never got to finish what she meant to say. The door slammed inward and there stood Slimy behind a wheelchair with Bickle in it. Bickle's huge casted feet stuck straight forward on metal supports like battering rams.

"You called it right again," said Hickum, "sons of bitches all right, and drunk to go with it. Bickle, you sorry bastard, I have to put up with you at work, but not here where I live. Just what the hell do you mean showing up at my place of residence at this hour on a Sunday morning?"

"What are you doing out of the hospital?" said Gaye Nell.

Bickle wiped at his running nose with the back of his hand and said: "You gonna let me answer anything, or just keep screaming at me?"

Hickum saw a tear, or what he thought must be a tear, and said, "You just caught us at a bad time. Actually that slamming on the door scared the hell out of us."

"Speak for yourself," said Gaye Nell. "And you still haven't said what you're doing out of the hospital."

Bickle jerked his head to indicate Slimy standing behind the wheelchair, holding the handles and doing little tricks with a toothpick he had caught between his crooked teeth. Bickle said: "I didn't have no say about it. He took me."

"Did you go in and take this bastard out of the hospital against his will after all the trouble I went to to put him in it?"

Slimy did a few more tricks with the toothpick before he took it out of his mouth, broke it in half, and started mining wax out of one of his ears with the longest piece. "I guess you could say that. I got him here and he didn't want to come. So *against his will* might be one way to put it."

"You can't go around doing shit like that," said Hickum.

"I done it though, didn't I?"

Bickle said: "You still got that pistol?"

"What reason would I have to get rid of it?"

"You might kill somebody someday with that thing."

"Any woman that carries a pistol this day and time knows that sooner or later she'll have to shoot some bastard that needs it." She stepped closer to the foot of the chair, reached over, and and put her palm on his forehead. "Damn, sweat's pouring off you and you're burning up. Did you leave the hospital AMA?"

"AMA?"

"Against medical advice."

"I left against everything I could do about it." He hooked a thumb over his shoulder at Slimy. "Slimy here kidnapped me. He did, he kidnapped me or I might never've come out."

"Why would you do a thing like that?" said Gaye Nell.

Slimy gave her what he supposed to be his fiercest look. "You ain't asked a word about my arm."

Gaye Nell had forgotten working to his arm with a *shuto uki*, or maybe it was an Okinawan roundhouse. Whatever it was, he should have been wearing a cast. His ear didn't look as bad as it should have, either. "Why aren't you wearing a cast?"

"They wouldn't give me one. I didn't have insurance, being self-employed like I am. So they wouldn't hardly give me nothing. Wanted to stick me in a taxicab and shoot me over to the VA is what they wanted to do. But I happen to know about them bastards. They practice hamburger medicine at the VA hospital. And whether anybody likes it or not, it's no hamburger medicine for this old boy. So they splinted me up with aluminum and a Ace bandage and threw me out the door. Why, hell's bells, they treated us better than that in Nam. And even at that, they didn't treat us but a little better than a dog over there. Besides . . . What's your name again? Oh, yeah, it's Gaye Nell. You lemme set your mind at ease, honey, you didn't hurt me. Hell, I been hurt worse than that trying to puke when I was drunk."

"I got a feeling in me there's going to be a next time, and when it comes, I'll try my dead level best to lay a hurtin' on you to remember."

"Do, and I'll sic the Lip on you. He don't put up with no such shit as people like you hurting people like me. Told me that out of his own mouth, such as it is."

"I believe you've mistaken me for somebody else. I don't think you know who you're talking to."

Hickum put his chin in his hand and said: "I think we ought to try to be steady here and figure this out. What exactly is our situation?"

The mechanic took his Stillson wrench out of his back pocket and waved it over his head. "The ship's in port, the anchor's down, we all have duties to perform, but telling the truth is not one of 'em. I seen that right from the first."

"I wish we could try to be serious here for just a minute, that's all I wish," said Hickum.

"Does anybody but me notice we stuck here in the door with this wheelchair?" said Bickle. "This chair's not going on through this door. And it's stuck too far in to back out. We by-God stuck."

Slimy looked at Hickum. "I don't reckon you got a good-sized ax here somewhere, do you?"

"Matter of fact, I have," Hickum said.

"What the fuck you doing with a ax in an apartment?"

"You won't meet many men from east Tennessee without a good-sized ax close to hand. Of course, you won't find many living in an apartment, either. But I had this ax when I moved in."

Gaye Nell said: "You've had an ax in here for thirty years?" The question nearly choked her.

"Twenty-seven, give or take, but not thirty," said Hickum. He looked around at the others. "We wasting time when we could be voting. Everybody thinks we stuck, say *aye*."

Silence. They held it like a measure. "That's what I thought, too," said Slimy.

"What day is tomorrow, anyway?" said Hickum.

"Monday, the whole damn day," Slimy said, "if I ain't miscounted."

"What I thought," said Hickum. "I believe I can find that double-bitted ax in one of these closets back in here, if I look good."

"How come you need a ax, honey?" said Gaye Nell.

"Got to make this door fit this chair is what I got to do."

Behind them on an angle where none of them could see it, the telephone rang. All of them stopped and cocked their heads like deer caught in the lights of a car at night. They stayed that way, stock still, through three rings.

"Telephone's ringing," said Slimy on the fourth ring.

"I think we could have figured that out," said Gaye Nell.

Slimy took his wrench out of his back pocket and shook it in the air. "Keep on with it, bitch, and you and me is going to have trouble again. If you can hear it, how come you don't answer it?"

"Stay out of my business, too-short-to-count! And trouble? I can't remember having any trouble," Gaye Nell said. "You're the one who had the trouble."

"I wish all of you could quit arguing like children for two minutes and act like adults," said Bickle. His voice sounded as though it did not have tears far behind it. "I'm in the wheelchair. Wouldn't that suggest I'm the one who had the trouble?"

"You're just unhappy because you got your toes shot off," said Gaye Nell. "But you're to blame. It's just like you shot holes in your own feet."

"Jesus, are any of you idiots going to answer that telephone?" demanded Slimy. "It's driving me off the deep end."

Hickum turned to look toward the little three-legged table that held the phone. "Nobody ever calls me," he said.

"Somebody's calling you now," Gaye Nell said.

"Probably a wrong number," said Hickum.

"I don't care if it's coming from Mars," said Bickle, slamming himself about in the wheelchair like a huge, crazed baby, "it's still driving me nuts."

"I'll get it," Gaye Nell said. She walked into the corner of the living room where none of them could see her. They heard the phone come out of the cradle and Gaye Nell say hello.

There was a long pause, during which they could actually hear the voice screaming on the other end of the line. When the voice had finally screamed itself out, Gaye Nell said, "Right." And they could hear the telephone being placed back on the table.

When she came back around to where they were, she looked sick, as though she'd looked into a mirror and instead of seeing the image of herself, she had seen the fleshless head of a skull.

Slimy said: "You all right?"

She said, "No, I'm not." Then she quit talking and a thousand-yard stare came into her eyes.

"What ails you?" said Slimy.

"It's for you," she said.

Slimy turned to look behind him, then back at Gaye Nell.

"You talking to me?" he said.

"You go by the name *Slimy*, don't you?"

"Yeah, but my real name is—"

"Don't start with that. Somebody wants you on the phone. And I don't think you want to stand there too long before you answer it."

Hickum, in a curiously stricken voice, said, "But it's not his phone, it's my phone."

"I didn't want to bring this up," said Bickle, "but I've got to urinate."

Slimy said: "Women and babies urinate. Fat crippled bastards like you piss."

harry crews

"Then I've got to piss. I've got to!" His face was red and his strangely narrow tongue stuck out of his mouth while he panted like a dog as he spoke.

"Now you're talking," said Slimy. "Go ahead and piss."

"I can't do that here, for God sake."

"The hell you can't."

"You better answer the telephone is my best advice to you, Slimy," said Gaye Nell.

"I don't need your advice."

"Yes, you do, because I know who it is on the phone and you don't. But you will as soon as you hear him. That lip makes him hiss over the phone just like it does when he's right in front of you."

"Oh Jesus, here it comes," cried Bickle.

"Not on the rug, big guy!" begged Hickum. "It'll smell like piss the rest of my life." His head snapped around toward Gaye Nell. "Did you say the Boss Elmo Jeroveh the Lip . . . Did . . ."

"Every goddam one of them," said Gaye Nell.

Slimy was climbing over the wheelchair trying to get to the phone when Bickle gave a long sigh of relief as a yellow puddle started spreading under him, and Hickum Looney threw back his head and howled like a dog: "How could you, you sorry bastard? How could you?"

Bickle's voice came back in a satisfied spidery whisper: "It was easy," he said. "Believe me it was the easiest thing I ever did."

chapter

twenty

Whatever Elmo had done, and he had apparently done a great many new things for the Company—one thing by itself or all of them together—had thrown everybody who worked at Soaps For Life, from the custodial staff to the highest levels of management, into a dawn-to-dusk frenzy to move soap and still more soap.

A huge chart had appeared as if by magic in every regional office, a chart that was a graphic to show the rising sales of Soaps For Life. A bright red ribbon a foot wide started in the lower left-hand corner of an entire wall of every office across the country and climbed steeply and relentlessly day by day toward the upper right-hand corner.

This wall chart and the wide red ribbon represented the cumulative total of soap sold by each regional office. At the end of August the office that had moved the most soap got to give itself any kind of party it wished, as long as it was not against the law and it didn't cost more than $10,000. There would be nominations by members of the winning region for the kind and place of the party they were going to have, and the nominations would be resolved by vote. A simple majority won.

While every region showed unprecedented sales, the Hickum Looney office in Miami, Florida, and a small, obscure office in Twin Bucks, Wyoming, ramrodded (as the cowboy salesmen liked to say in their cowboy way) by a long drink of water (as the cowboy salesmen described him in their Western lingo) named John Johnson but called High Pockets, were nearly dead even. While High Pockets was overseer to only five salesmen, who covered a territory that was big but sparsely populated, it was still possible for High Pockets and his boys to win it all—the regional sales office contest, that is—because this year the contest, half over now in the middle of August, was calculated by dividing the number of soap kits sold by the number of dwellings—single or family—in the regional territory.

But the daily sales for each individual salesman were still carefully counted and kept posted so that every sales representative knew where he stood relative to the front runner. Now that Elmo was not competing, Hickum should have been winning and winning easily. But he was not. While he was near the top, he was not the top. Slimy and Bickle were. At any hour during the long working day either Slimy or Bickle was leading everybody else. And Hickum Looney was right behind the two of them.

Slimy and Bickle had thrown in together and were working as a team. And that had almost caused an uprising in the Company, a revolt, an outcry for anarchy, until Elmo was asked to rule on whether what Bickle and Slimy were doing was ethical. Within a matter of hours a memo came down. Few salesmen had ever seen a memo from the Boss, as he was called in those good gone days before he had taken Ida Mae to Atlanta and completely reorganized the Company. From that point on, the memos never seemed to stop. And this memo that had come down ruling on the legitimacy of the Slimy/Bickle connection was as direct and authoritative as all the other memos had been. Team spirit, the memo said, had always been at the heart of Soaps For Life, and since Bickle had been wounded in the line of duty, it was only natural and just that he and Slimy be allowed to work as a team: Bickle in the chair and Slimy pushing and maneuvering from behind while they both sold their hearts out.

"Well, I guess that about finishes it for me," said Hickum.

"No guessing about it," Gaye Nell said. "I know it finishes you if you think it does. I never thought I'd live to see the day when you would just throw in the towel and quit like this."

"Who ever said anything about quitting?"

"Maybe you didn't say it in so many words, but you quit, yes sir, mister super salesman, you have laid down and died on this one."

"I've always tried to look at things as they really are instead of how I wish they could be."

"Whether you like it or not or whether you'll ever admit it or not, we all live on dreams. Except maybe you. Maybe all your dreams died one day when you weren't looking, just slipped away and died. You ever thought what it's gonna be like to live out your life in this old crooked and tainted world without a dream?"

He got out of the overstuffed chair he had been in and went over and pulled her to her feet beside the bed on which she had been sitting. He hugged her hard, saying as he did, "Well, bless your sweet little heart, you've been studying the Sales Manual, haven't you?"

She struggled gently, but he only squeezed her harder. "What if I have?" she said.

Her voice was a little shaky and he could feel her push deeper into his embrace. His hands had slipped down her back to cup her taut, rounded little bottom, the part of her that he had found he loved more than any other. Bubba had shredded the tongue in one of the new pair of shoes he was wearing and nearly filled them both with slobber. But he didn't mind. Bubba was part of the price of doing business. And at the moment, he loved the business he was doing. He wondered if he had squeezed the feeling right out of her ass, wondered if it was entirely numb from the deep, twisting probes he had given it.

She pulled her head back so he could see her face. Her lips were swollen and wet, her eyes dilated. "Don't work me up too much," she said in a gaspy little voice, "unless you're horny enough to take me through the rocky white water and round the bend." She sucked in a deep breath and said, "And the good Lord knows I could stand to be taken through some white water filled with sharp rock and around the bend about now."

Bubba had caught the fragrance of her arousal, as he often did, her arousal or her drippings or both, and he had stood up on his hind legs and clamped Gaye Nell's knee with his forelegs and was giving it a vicious non-fuck. It was Bubba's aggressive move on Gaye Nell's knee that jerked Hickum back to his senses and brought him up from the place where he was and made him realize that this was not the time or the place to be doing what he was doing and thinking what he was thinking. There was a subject on the table and they had been in the middle of talking about it. And they didn't just need to talk about it, they had to talk about it.

He turned her loose and stepped back.

"I forgot something," he said and walked back to his deep, stuffed chair and sat down.

Gaye Nell had not moved. Nothing had changed about her in any way except how white she had become. She was very white. Hickum didn't think he had ever seen her or any other woman that pale.

A little voice somewhere in the back of his head, a voice that he was not ashamed of at all, said: I believe if I was you, I would watch what I said and what I did. And I don't think I'd let her see my back.

"Well, goddam, Hickum." Her thin, too-white lips had not moved at all as she said his name.

"As it happens, I was thinking the same thing myself." He tried to make what he said sound normal, as if he got her wet to the knees on a more or less regular basis and then just up and turned around and walked away from her and plopped his ass in a chair.

"I got one thing to say to you," she said.

"Good," he said, "because I got several things to say to you."

"I'll never hear 'em. Where's my suitcase at?"

"Wherever you put it down last," he said and chuckled. "My old ma used to tell me that when I was a little boy."

She turned to look at him. "Go ahead on, if you want to, but I'm warning you, you've got so far on the wrong side of me that you're going to make me say something about your old mama, and I don't want to do that."

She opened a few doors and then slammed them shut. She hadn't been in the apartment long enough to have much in the closets or anywhere else. And her suitcase Hickum knew for a fact to be across the hall in his apartment. When Jeroveh (which turned out to be the name Elmo preferred. Nobody in the Company knew how this preference was discovered or who discovered it. But one day, nobody knew exactly when, it had come floating among them as a rumor and so they had no alternative but to believe) found out Hickum and Gaye Nell were living together, a sealed memo had arrived from Atlanta that strongly suggested that either the two of them get married or else one of them move into another apartment in the building. The building, it turned out, belonged to the Soaps For Life Company, which not even Hickum Looney knew.

The memo had not bothered Hickum at all, but it had thrown Gaye Nell into a fury of screaming and kicking and knocking things about, which got Hickum's blood up a little, because they were in his apartment at the time and it was his stools and wastebaskets and flower stands and whatever that she was kicking about.

"I don't understand the problem," he said.

"Where I live and who I live with is none of his goddam business. Where is it written that I've got to have his approval of how I live?"

Hickum thought: Probably in the contractual agreement you signed with the Company. Hickum didn't know what was in the contract and he was sure she didn't, either. He had never heard of an employee actually reading one of the things. It was thick as the Bible, for God's sake, and written in print that was as small as the print in the King James Version that was in every household in the South. At least as far as Hickum knew, every household in the South had one. Certainly everybody back in east Tennessee had one. When he was growing up he could not remember going into a parlor or sitting room where the Bible, black and thick as a man's wrist, was not prominently displayed. But that didn't necessarily mean that a single person, man or woman, living in one of the houses scattered throughout the entire countryside had actually read the thing from cover to cover. It was unthinkable.

She turned and looked at Hickum. "I didn't leave my suitcase at your place, did I?"

"As far as I know, you didn't leave anything of any account except me, and I'm doing some serious wondering how much I'm worth right now."

"Hickum Looney, don't you dare get corny and hokey on me. If you do and make me cry, you'll be sorry." She had come back and sat in a chair closer to his. "OK. I'm listening. What made you quit right in the middle of what looked like it was going to be a full-tilt boogie? I don't mind being put up wet, but I expect to be rode hard first."

"Your mouth is better than a harem," he said. "If we could bottle it, marriage would be instantly obsolete."

"You could put a cork in that bullshit, too, and tell me why you're automatically whipped now that Jeroveh's come out and said Slimy can push Bickle around in his wheelchair."

"I just don't see any way to beat anybody who's armed with that kind of pity. I've been in this business a long time, and Bickle's casts are a surefire sale at every door that Slimy wheels him up to."

"When you sold twelve books of orders and set a record, you weren't pushing a cripple in a wheelchair."

"I had Ida Mae. She was better."

"I don't understand."

There was nothing to do but spell it out for her, which he'd never done for anybody. "Ida Mae knew where the best batches of dead and dying lived. She knew their names and also had the inside track on what was killing them. They were, after all, her friends. Plus, she had that arm that Soaps For Life had healed that very morning, or so she seemed determined to believe. When she got up and testified for the product it was like Peter testifying for Jesus. I couldn't lose. Under those circumstances, a monkey could have set a record."

"One did," said Gaye Nell.

He looked at her for a long time and then said: "If I didn't know you so well, you'd be real easy to kill."

A little shiver passed through her. "Don't say shit like that."

"I try not to," he said. "You could give me a hand up, if you would. Try to remember that we're only talking about my life here. I've been doing this longer than you've been on this earth. For me, there's no second chance at anything else. Even you're the end of the line for me. You leave, and I'm looking at an empty bed for the rest of my life."

He put his hands on his knees and looked at the age spots between the tiny blue veins just below the skin that the sun had cooked day in and day out until it was as dry and thin and brittle as it would ever be.

She reached over and put her hand on the back of one of his. He raised his head to look at her. Even Bubba had quit chewing and slobbering and looked up at Hickum.

"I usually don't let people do shit like that around me. If you're going to be unhappy and whine, do it on somebody else's time. But you did it, and it's done. Forget it. I have. And forget the suitcase. Sooner or later I would have realized I didn't really have any need of it." She sat quietly a moment. "Well, this is Miami. Lot of people. The least we can do is win the regional ten thou for the party. I believe I could throw a hell of a party with ten thousand bucks."

"That can't happen, either," he said.

She stood up and looked down at him. "Jesus, you've got a bad case of the cain't-help-its. Maybe you are dead and I ought to bury you."

"Naw," he said, smiling, "not dead yet."

"Why the hell are you smiling?"

"Because it's kind of funny, really."

"Not funny," she said. "Not to me."

There was nothing to do but tell her about High Pockets and Twin Buck, Wyoming. But she stopped him before he had barely started.

"Twin Buck? High Pockets? I'm in no mood for jokes right at the moment."

Hickum was still chuckling in spite of himself. He shrugged his shoulders. "Just as cheap to laugh. Cheaper and cleaner than suicide.

"No, wait. Let me tell you what I got to thinking. Like you, I was saying, hell, we might win a ten-grand party. Better than a stick in the eye and quite a thing when you get to thinking about it. Then I remembered John Johnson, High Pockets to you. I don't know how many men he's got working for him, five or six maybe. And I don't know how many dwellings are out there in the middle of nowhere, but I'd be willing to bet there's no more than seventy or eighty. Nothing but a bunch of huge ranches with nothing on them but starving cattle and a horse or two.

"So here's what'll happen. His salesmen will all sell each other six or seven sets of soap and then they'll spread the word to all the sheep fuckers that if each of them will buy a set of soap, they'll be invited to a ten-thousand-dollar party. Maybe even put the deal in writing and have it notarized. There's not another region in the country that can beat that record."

Hickum laced his fingers, cracked his knuckles, and then stretched. "Of course everything depends on High Pockets thinking to do all this. It might just blow right past him and he won't even try for the party money. John Johnson is not quite all there."

Gaye Nell was sitting with her elbow on her knee and her chin in her hand. "Jeez, what a story. How do you happen to know this High Pockets? Wyoming is the dark side of the moon as far as I'm concerned."

"He wasn't always in Wyoming. He worked right here in Miami out of the office I'm in for a while. But that was a long time ago."

"So what the hell's he doing on the dark side of the moon?"

"I'm not real clear on that. Actually, I'm not even a little clear on that. All I know is, he caught the Boss's . . . Jeroveh's eye and became his driver for a while. Same job LaFarge's got now. Then one day he was not his driver or anything else. He was gone. Nobody even knew where. The rumor had it that he was in Twin Bucks, Wyoming. Banished there for the rest of his life. And nobody can do a thing like that except Jeroveh. Gradually we got the rest of it, his nickname, how big the region was he covered. You know how it is around here, somebody tells somebody something and then it gets passed on to somebody else and finally everybody knows what's going on."

"Yeah, I know how it is around here," she said. "It's a weird little place which is completely unreasonable. And the reason it is the way it is goes straight back to the ugly little man with the ugly little mouth."

"It is his company, Gaye Nell. He can run it anyway he damned well pleases."

"That's a fact. He can run it anyway he wants to." She was still sitting with her chin in her hand and she moved to look at him. "Got a question for you."

"Fire away. I'll answer it if I can."

"Remember back that first night—morning, really—I fell asleep with you?"

"Not likely to forget it."

"Remember the candles."

"Sure, but they weren't candles. They were samples out of my display case."

"Right. Your display case. You say you use that case to show what the soap will look like. You show it to somebody, they want to buy, you fill out an order and send the order to . . . where?"

"Up to Atlanta."

"Then what happens?"

"When the customer's check clears, an order of soap is mailed out."

"Have you ever got a case directly from Atlanta, opened it, and looked at it?"

Hickum thought about that for quite a long time. A look of mild surprise took him. "The answer is no. Truthfully, that surprises me, but at the same time, it doesn't. What would I want with a box of that stuff?"

"What does Jeroveh get for a box of Soaps For Life?"

"Three hundred and thirty-five dollars, plus tax, plus three dollars handling and shipping."

Gaye Nell grabbed her own hair with both hands as if she meant to pull it out and gave a short, startled cry. "Holy suffering Jesus! That's a frigging fortune."

"It's great soap," said Hickum.

"You don't know what the fuck it is. You've never had any in your hands. You've had samples. The rest is hope, trust, despair, and the brutal need of the people suckered into buying it. You don't sell soap. You sell the Soaps For Life Sales Manual. And we both know that manual is the biggest string of lies either of us have ever seen."

"Now wait a minute, little girl. You're going too far."

"You've already gone too far, you poor sweet dumb ass. There's no way in the world for you to get back the twenty-five years you've spent shilling for a scam and con game that I'll bet my life is rotten to the core. Your poor, poor baby."

chapter

twenty-one

by agreement, Hickum and Gaye Nell Odell sat at opposite ends of the room for the teleconference late in the evening of the eighteenth day of the contest. This was the first teleconference that had been called since Hickum had had his trousers taken away from him and he had been forced to leave the building half naked. He hated and dreaded this meeting with his fellow salesmen so soon after they had agreed to force him to give up his pants before shoving him out the door half naked for telling a lie that was not a lie at all. And strange even to himself, after only this short time, he was convinced he had not told a lie, and equally convinced that he deserved the humiliating punishment he had been given.

There had even been random moments every single day when he was convinced he should have been made to suffer a greater punishment than had been given him. Say, for instance, maybe a good beating. He knew in his heart that he would feel better, that he would feel a greater release if some of his blood had been left to mark scabby lines over his back from a few quick strokes from a cane. But he couldn't do any of that because while it would make Jeroveh deliriously happy, it would simply make the other salesmen delirious, because if one salesman asked for and accepted a beating, sooner or later every last one of the other salesmen would be expected to ask for and accept the same beating. That was just how things worked at Soaps For Life.

So it was not only absolutely mandatory that he take what was given him but also mandatory that he pretend that suffering it made him a better human being. Such thinking made no sense and he realized that. But the Company and how it was run made no sense, either. The retirement and fringe benefits were particularly good, though. And that made very good sense indeed. Beyond that he could not bring himself to care one way or the other. Let the others save the Company. And the world, too, while they were at it. In the meantime, he would walk off his retirement and end up in some great place, like California, maybe.

But right now everyone's attention was focused on the fact that this teleconference had been announced only four days before it was being held. Very strange. But equally strange, the rumor that lived in the Company had nothing to say about it. Rumor had been snookered by the early announcement and therefore was totally incapable of rattling anybody's cage. But that was all right. His (for reasons nobody questioned but everybody understood, rumor had always been thought to be a male) victory would come. Winning was rumor's nature. A natural law like gravity.

Rumor could not be beaten. It was inconceivable even to think such a thing. That was why everybody tried to act so casual in the face of rumor; everybody was so terrified. Conventional wisdom had it that anybody who was not terrified of rumor was soft in the head.

And besides all the other stuff to cause high blood pressure and irregular heartbeat, for the first time there were the women at this meeting. Nobody seemed to know quite how to treat them because it seemed like just about everything a man could think or say or do or wear was sexual harassment, and the men were scared to death of it. Sexual harassment meant loss of wife, children, home, job, and it meant using every dime you had or could beg or borrow to hire a lawyer who would ultimately lose your case. (Had anybody ever heard of a sexual harasser being found innocent?) The judge would sit there trying not to yawn from the boredom of looking at your dumb, defeated ass and finally tell you to go on and get in the jail cell and learn to like it quickly because you weren't ever, ever, going to get out and teach little children to be sexual harassers.

Besides Gaye Nell, there were five other women present, all of them blonde and blue eyed and all of them taken out of the secretarial pool. Gaye Nell was the only female who did not have blond hair and blue eyes, but she had agreed to get her hair bleached and have blue contact lenses put into her eyes although she did not need them. Her vision, uncorrected, was twenty/twenty. But so far she had not got around to doing her hair or getting tinted lenses.

Hickum had thought she would raise hell about having to have her hair bleached, but she only shrugged and said she did not mind. The truth was she had once had a pimp who had her hair restyled and dyed a different color every two weeks. The pimp said she would turn more tricks and she had. She, of course, did not tell Hickum any of this.

Hickum was frightened and totally unnerved by this teleconference, not only because it was the first time in memory that it had been called days ahead of time rather than coming about randomly and spontaneously, but also because there were women present. How would the women act? More important, how would the men react to working with women? They had been encouraged to bring their questions, thoughts, and feelings to this meeting and to allow Jeroveh to have them, to lay them at his feet and forget about them.

The very thought of bringing the truth to Jeroveh and speaking it straight and simple so anybody could understand made Hickum feel his bowels loosen. There were simply too many unpredictable quantities factored into this equation. There seemed to be no stability anywhere in what Jeroveh was doing. Craziness and unseemly behavior could easily break out in this tightly packed room, break out and spread like cholera.

Among other things, teleconferences in the past had never occurred during contest month, except for the one they had on the first day. During the rest of the month, every salesman's nerves were shredded. Ulcers were flaring. Tics always developed. Strange rashes, resistant to all medication, developed. Insomnia was rampant. The sound of salesmen grinding their teeth could be heard throughout the Soaps For Life building. To Hickum Looney, it seemed a particularly bad time for a teleconference. Men were losing their hair, their teeth, their wives and children. They sure as hell did not want to lose their jobs along with all the other losses they were suffering.

There was another mysterious and awful problem during this time. During contest month a large number of salesmen would simply disappear. A firm, undisputed rumor had it that contest time was a way for the Boss, now Jeroveh, to get rid of all those who could not measure up under pressure. The effect was for every salesman's job in every region to be on the line the last day of each week during contest month. Poor showing, gone. Vanished. And it was considered bad form to ask after the disappeared ones. So nobody did. Ever.

A uniformed security guard stood at the front of the room beside the door. He was a very large man whose pleasant, relaxed face smiled as his friendly eyes moved slowly among the sales force gathered in the room. But despite his friendly eyes and pleasant face, there was something ominous about the way he rhythmically pounded his left palm with the foot-and-a-half-long truncheon he carried in his right. Hickum knew that *truncheon* was not the word for whatever the guard was using to beat the hell out of his left hand, but it was clear enough what it was used for.

But his mind had seized on *truncheon* and would not turn it loose. An embarrassing tremor—a hunching of shoulders and a ducking of heads—ran through the men and women every time the truncheon struck the security officer's thickly muscled palm. Nobody had ever seen the security guard before and everyone sat staring straight ahead at the darkened television screen, waiting for the meeting to start.

Hickum Looney held a remote control for the television and he kept an eye on the clock, round and big as a basketball, affixed to the wall directly above the security guard, who was still smacking his palm with considerable force. Win, lose, or draw, it had to be done. The clock on the wall said he could wait no longer.

"Say, pal," Hickum called to the security guard, "you'll have to quit making that noise with your . . ." Hickum simply could not make himself say *truncheon*. But it didn't look like the nightstick cops carried, sometimes in their hands, sometimes on their wide belts. It looked like what his mind had seized upon: a truncheon.

This fucking thing the guard was pounding his hand with did not look like anything Hickum had ever seen. Just having it in his hands made the guard look like a psychopath, which, if Jeroveh had anything to do with recruiting him, he probably was. ". . . noise, yes, that noise you're making will have to stop."

The security guard, who was looking right at him, seemed to increase the intensity with which he rhythmically beat his palm. Hickum turned his head and looked directly into the savagely derisive gaze of Slimy, who was standing over by the wall, half propped against George Bickle's wheelchair.

"Hickum, why didn't you tell me we were going to have gash in here too? Wall-to-wall pussy is not a subject a man ought to keep from his friends, especially the men in the trenches. Keeping them in ignorance will ruin all the chances you have for winning."

"Shut up," said Hickum. "I don't know what you're talking about and you don't either."

"What I want to know really is when they're bringing up the

damn food," Slimy said. "Lots of food and drink is what we need." His head spun on his neck as though on a swivel as he spoke. He winked at Hickum. "I love me a good food fight," said Slimy.

"Good Lord, you're put together like a bad onion. Every time you peel off a layer, you run into a more rotten one underneath," Hickum said.

"You're not as straight as you might think you are," Slimy said, and then slid so close to Hickum that he could have kissed him. "You are not as rare as you think. Every morning you shave, you see one twisted freak who doesn't even realize he's a freak."

In an attempt to try to avoid Slimy, Hickum looked at his watch and cried: "It's time."

He had thought he would have to call for the silence that fell, but the room became as still and quiet as the inside of a coffin. The huge screen in the front of the room wavered and flickered for an instant, but finally out of the flickering light came the sharp, still-as-death image of Jeroveh. He was at a desk, not a podium.

The podium was reserved exclusively for the annual sales convention, just as the desk was always used for a teleconference. There he sat now, ramrod straight, his arms stretched and his clawlike little hands gripping the edges at either end of the desk. He did not say anything, nor did he look like he meant to do anything.

Then everybody in the room gradually became aware of a figure that moved behind and just a little to the right of Jeroveh. Hickum instantly turned to look at Gaye Nell, but she was already looking back at him, mouthing as rapidly as she could *Ida Mae, Ida Mae* over and over and over again. She also seemed to be struggling—successfully so far—to suppress a shout, or wild yell, or maybe only laughter. But Hickum was horrified. More so than he could remember for a very long time. There was something— he had no notion what—that was very bad and very wrong about all this. To begin with, he did not think anybody besides himself and Gaye Nell even recognized Ida Mae as a woman. Turning

the mulching of america   237

to look at Bickle, Hickum could tell that even Bickle, whose bleeding and damaged feet had been bandaged by Ida Mae, thought he was looking at a man. Hickum did not blame Bickle for that. Her change was a miracle.

And Hickum did not believe in miracles unless he was caught by circumstances larger than himself, which always scared him into becoming an instant, raging believer. At that moment, Hickum would have followed anybody who would save him, followed him anywhere: onto the wheel, up the steps to a gallows, into the funny little room with the ugly massive lethal chair, or into the equally funny little room where he would be strapped down on a gurney while a man pushed needles into his veins as though he were giving Hickum an instant drug addiction, which Hickum, of course, knew was the addiction of death.

Slimy and Bickle started a whispering, hissing exchange.

"God, what killer clothes!"

"Killer clothes? What an awful thing to say."

"On my block, when I was growing up, any of us would of killed for those clothes. With what those threads cost, you know what kind of old neglected automobile I could buy and build back into mint condition? The kind of machine you couldn't even put a price on."

"No, I don't. And I don't care either."

"You damn right you don't. You don't have the soul for it."

"What difference does that make? It's still a rotten way to talk."

"Watch your mouth or I just might push you and this chair off a curb in front of a car, make scrambled eggs outten you. How you think you'd like being scrambled eggs? In this chair, you nothing but a baby, you know. Nothing but a goddam baby with two busted feet."

Hickum did his best to shut them out and focus on listening to the street noise outside instead. But he could still hear them despite his best efforts not to listen. They were for all the world like two flea-ridden, yellow-gummed monkeys in a tiny zoo cage. The security guard, still smacking his hand, moved across the room and stopped between Hickum and where Slimy leaned against Bickle's chair. Hickum knew something was about to happen.

He didn't think he could take much more happening. Shit coming out of left field. That was life. Sometimes he thought that was all of life: shit coming out of left field and nailing you solid when you weren't looking and hadn't done anything besides. To stay as far away from Bickle and his filthy little partner chattering over by the wall, he concentrated on how Ida Mae was dressed.

Since the screen was black-and-white, he could not be sure of the color of her clothes. But it was not black and it was not white, rather something in between, a merging of the two, probably something like pearl. Everything she had on was of the same color, pearl, if in fact there was such a color. He wasn't really sure.

On her head was a low-crowned, wide-brimmed hat that looked like it probably belonged on a man's head. It was cocked just a tad to the left and pulled low over her face, shading her eyes and hiding the quilted, bleached, translucent skin on her broad forehead and high flat cheeks.

If he had not known it was Ida Mae, he would never have recognized her. He thought she looked like what the lead horn in a tight, hard-driving jazz band might look like. It was all fantasy, though, because he had never seen a jazz band except on the album covers lying on sofas or coffee tables in a few houses where he'd been trying to sell soap.

Her jacket was long and cut tightly over her thin frame. Her trousers flared over thin-sided, narrow shoes and they reminded him of the sort the young Sammy Davis Jr. had tapped in long ago; except these exquisite shoes were light colored rather than coal black.

Nothing she wore was off the rack. Everything that covered her looked as though it had been imagined and fabricated by a single designer of pure genius who made clothes for her and only for her. That, of course, could not possibly be the way it happened, but however it was accomplished, somebody had managed to fuck up his miserable life so badly that he had been condemned to read Ida Mae's ruined, arthritic body the way a blind man reads Braille.

Her end-of-the-road, can't-get-any-worse body lived in some blind bastard's fingertips in precisely the way some other poor devil's fingers carried around the living experience of *Crime and Punishment*. The contemplation of such joys was so delicious as to force the most hardened Christian into the act of suicide, even though the Christian would spin rapidly toward his death knowing that all his friends would have their fun with his final act by calling it a kind of pleasure sweeter than masturbation.

Ida Mae was rapidly shuffling some papers on the podium in front of her. She did not raise her head to look at the sales force when she started talking.

"To the densest of you, I'm sure it has become obvious that changes have been made here at Soaps For Life and are still being made. It is in your best interest to pay closest attention to these changes. Jeroveh did not hire me as vice president in charge of production and sales to have everything remain as it was. Change is in the air. We will have change. Those of you who cannot identify and benefit by these changes will not suffer; your services will simply be terminated. No letters of recommendation will be issued from these offices on anyone's behalf. When you go, and many of you will go, you will go without any support from the Company."

She stopped talking and shuffled her papers some more. A buzz of conversation stiffened in the room. Again, when Ida Mae spoke she did not look up from her papers or make eye contact with anybody.

"I hear your presence, and I do not want to hear your presence. I do not want to know you are in the world with me, much less in this room. I am perfectly aware that many of you will go home tonight and breed. More's the pity. But in the meantime, shut up."

She finally stopped whatever she was doing with the papers

in front of her and looked out at them. One of her seemingly boneless hands drifted up and pushed the wide brim of the hat up from her face. When they saw her eyes, their breathing stopped in their collective throats as if a single loop of piano wire had been jerked shut on them.

"Better." She stared at them for a long moment in silence. "Yes, that's better, but just remember that as long as two of you exist to rub up against each other, it can never be good enough. Never."

She dropped her head toward the stack of papers in front of her and shifted through them. Then she smiled, her false teeth moving slowly in her mouth. "This is the last time we'll meet on teleconference until the contest is over on the last day of August and the winner is determined."

Jeroveh had not moved during the entire meeting. Now he looked up and let his eyes move over his employees. "I wish I could see all of nu at once, see nu together at ne merry same time. Ne only opportunity I've ever had for nat was at ne annual sales convention. Nu and nu may or may not have noticed I've never naken the nadvanage of nat nopportunity na really nook nu over, na really examine each of nu close. Nis year I will. Really, I mean na check nu out nis year from nead na heel." He paused. "Make of nat what nu will." He looked at Ida Mae.

"Ditto," she said.

The screen went to black and they all sat there stunned. What had been said? What did it mean?

chapter

twenty-two

Slimy was having a cup of coffee in the living room of Bickle's town house, which had been modified to accommodate a wheelchair powered by a DieHard battery. It was still early morning but rays of sun burst through the high wide windows and splintered on the chrome that edged the rough leather furniture.

"So did you think it out?"

"I spent the entire night thinking, and I hate thinking."

"It's because you stay mad. One of the mysteries of life is why theoretical men—I'm talking about people like you, the mysterious ones—are always so mad all the time."

"I'm not goddam mad all the goddam time."

"I always think about how damp and strange you are, too."

"I'm not damp and strange and I'm not fucking mad, either. I haven't been mad in almost a month."

"Whatever you say," said Slimy. "But don't think I'm pointing fingers. With your smarts and your experience, you must know by now that people who are rich and prestigious enough to shop for what they want in the very best and hottest meat racks in the world make my teeth ache with longing."

"Talk on. Talk the ugliest shit you can think of. It will never hurt me. My heart is pure. I'm very nearly never angry. Anger is for losers with nothing else to do."

"You've been mad since the moment I met you."

"I think that wins the argument."

"What does? What argument? I didn't know we were having an argument."

"Discussion, then, if that makes you happier. That better? After all, try to remember, big feller, we're partners."

"I didn't ask to be your partner."

"It doesn't seem like asking's got much to do with anything around here. Hell, I never got much mileage out of asking, anyway. Can't see what difference it would make, anyhow. We've still had the same thing in mind, making money."

"Speak for yourself. All I'm trying to do is make me another built-from-the-ground antique car, one of a kind. One that nobody has bothered to look at in the last thirty-five years or so." He was excited now, flapping his arms. Drawing imaginary cars on the air. "By God, when I get through with it a king wouldn't have the nerve to fart on the seat covers. When I rebuild a car it buys me the slack to do whatever I want to do. And what I want is old whiskey, young women, and fast horses."

"You stole that."

"I ain't stole a goddam thing. What is it you think I stole."

"That's John Huston's line."

"You're apt to drive me crazy talking like this. I don't know a John Huston." He looked around the room as if somebody with that name might be hiding somewhere. "The least a white man would do would be to tell me what I stole."

"Old whiskey, young women, and fast horses is what John Huston said he had loved most in life."

"I can trash-talk any fool who ever stood on a corner curb to death, put 'im in his grave. Only a fool would have said a thing like that and cop to it in the public press."

"John Huston was not a fool."

"If he went around saying shit like that so people could lay it on his name, he was crazy. Sounds like something a sissy who had too much money might say, now that I think of it. It's not even good trash."

"Do me a favor."

"What?"

"Shut the fuck up."

"You forgetting we're sitting in my place."

"I ain't forgetting nothing. One of the things I ain't forgetting is you can't walk around in a fine apartment if you messed with the wrong person and left your feet something else because of it."

"Two feet do not mean much."

"Unless you haven't got 'em."

"There's other things."

"Damn straight. This apartment, for instance. How the hell did you get so fat walking from door to door selling whatever it is we sell."

"You got doubts about that soap, too?"

"Soap? Bullshit."

"I haven't figured it out," said Bickle. "After all these years, I've never figured it. And I've put some time in on it, too. I'm talking the soap we know about. Or maybe think we know about. Me? I think it's near about as close to soap as candy is to horseshit. And the man himself is crooked as a snake." He held up one of his huge fingers. "Contradiction one. He treats us like fucking dogs, working us in this sun until we're fried like bacon. Then something bad happens to one of us, me in this instance, and he covers us like a tent. Takes care of everything."

Finger number two shot into the air.

"Contradiction number two. The split-faced motherfucker has never let a woman get higher in the company than using her fingers, then out of the blue—out of nowhere—not only do we have women selling product, we got a woman running the whole fucking company."

Third finger.

"Contradiction number three. The guy's fucking names! What is that? Maybe that's the whole enchilada right there, in a nutshell, as they say. Then the final contradiction, after which you can't find one because we've reached the bottom of the barrel. Maybe! But I wouldn't even bet on that. These names are gonna drive me bugfuck. Maybe he wants to be God. If he does, he's nuts and we don't have to think about it anymore. But I don't think that for a minute. I could go on. Anybody who's worked for him ten minutes could. From any direction you look at him, anybody in the world can see somebody seriously lost it on God's assembly line and he got made into a human being, or at least something that looks like one, instead of a corkscrew."

"You shoulda been a comedian," said Slimy.

"You think I been joking here?"

"Hell no, I don't think you joking. I think we all hip deep in something we don't understand."

"But the money is good," Bickle said in a mincing little voice he thought whores must sound like if anybody ever asked them how it come to pass they were doing what they were doing.

"Now you take this apartment here," Slimy said, setting his empty coffee cup down and sweeping his arm in an arc meant to cover the large, comfortable apartment. "Now how in the name of sweet Jehovah could a guy afford to live in a place like this peddling soap?" He smiled. "You want to give us another finger and explain that to me?"

Bickle only sat in his Sears DieHard-battery-driven wheelchair and smiled.

Slimy said: "I can feel it, big guy. I'm onto something. Am I right or am I wrong?"

He took a sip of his coffee and then stood there smiling for all he was worth.

Bickle sat with his back to a huge bay window in the apartment, absentmindedly playing with the controls of his well-padded but medium-priced chair, and gave Slimy back his own best smile.

"You can tell me," Slimy said. "Whatever it is, it'll stay right here in this room between me and you."

"That's good," Bickle said, "because you're not onto a goddam thing. Not even close."

"Good, play that shit if you want to," Slimy said. "But tell me this. How does a guy live in a place like this going from door to door with something that we're not even sure is soap?"

"I can't."

"Why the hell not?"

"Because I don't know."

"You playing with my head, you footless fool? And that's a dangerous game."

"Anybody who gets off on doing the old mishmash has got to be dangerous."

"I'm glad you didn't forget."

"Not likely."

"Good. So let's start over. What does this place cost you?"

"Nothing."

"Oh, we are cute today," said Slimy. "I—"

"Hold it a minute. We both know that it's got to cost somebody something. Maybe it's Jeroveh, maybe not. But use your head . . ."

"I'd rather use my fucking Stillson. More results and faster. It only looks like a messy way to control your life, but in the long run it's actually quicker."

"Whatever pleases you. But if you'll use your head for just a second or two, you'll see that this place is built throughout to accommodate a guy who lives in a wheelchair. You know how long it would take to build a place like this? Not to mention the money. I was still walking around on my feet for a hell of a long time after this place was finished, and I didn't need it."

Before he went on, he let a silence stretch between himself and Slimy as the color changed in Slimy's face. "But when I was released from the hospital, this is where I was set down. Doped up, at first I thought I was home. Then I thought I was having honest-to-God hallucinations. Didn't take long before I realized that I didn't know where the hell I was but wherever it was I knew it was not my rank quarters. It could be courtesy of the Boss."

"Jeroveh."

"His fixation on names for himself has done got tiresome to me. We've played that game too long."

Slimy said: "Maybe. Maybe not. Told myself I had to learn not to jump too quick. I started to think a good long while ago that everything about the strange little mother is a concern to us. Or ought to be."

"Pretty much what I've been trying to tell you."

"You've got a strange way of trying to tell somebody something. Actually I just said *strange* to be kind. *Crazy* is the word I should have used."

"You wouldn't know the right word if it come up and bit you in the ass."

"So you say. But it's one thing about me. I still got both feet."

"I'll remember that."

"Seems like you got a lot of practice talking about what all you're gonna remember."

Bickle hit three little levers on the armrests of his mobile chair and it silently whipped around so that Bickle was looking out the bay window at the street outside, leaving his back to Slimy. He took a cigar out of his shirt pocket, bit the end of it off, and said: "Light me."

"Light yourself, crip. At least you still got both hands. Fuck around with the wrong people long enough and you might not even have them."

Bickle took a slender gold lighter from a little side pocket on his chair and fired up his cigar. He took several heavy puffs, looked at the end of the glowing cigar for what seemed to Slimy to be a very long time.

When Bickle looked up, he said: "You just became replaceable."

Slimy's hand went suddenly into his back pocket, but then just as suddenly came out empty. "It ain't nobody that can't be replaced. The trick in life as I see it is that it is not you that takes the hammer."

Bickle's heavy face lifted into a broad, good-natured smile. "Yep, that's the trick." He tapped the top of the little side pocket on his chair with his forefinger, which was big as a banana and very nearly as yellow. He held up the cigar he was smoking. "Smoke one of these with me? Sorry about that *light me* business. Hell, I'll light you. I got several handy right here in my carryall casket." He made a sound that might have been a laugh if it had not been so thick with phlegm. "Carryall casket, little joke of mine."

"Yeah, for a guy that lost his feet, you one fucking laugh after another. But, sure, let me have one of those." He threw out his little chest and said: "Light me up."

Bickle opened the lid to the little casket-shaped pocket on the side of his chair, and when his hand came out it was balled into a huge fat fist. Slimy didn't know what was going—Bickle's fist was empty. Bickle's heavy face held his simple smile because he knew that Slimy thought his fist was empty.

But it was not, and he simply waited until Slimy finally saw the very tip of a huge bore of a short-barreled, heavy-caliber automatic pistol that had been modified especially for Bickle's peculiar sense of humor. You could knock down a charging thousand-pound bull from twenty feet away with the deadly piece of ordnance concealed in Bickle's meaty fist.

Slimy did not know what caliber or make of pistol Bickle was holding, but he knew from what he could see that if Bickle dropped the hammer on that thing he would be killed all the way into the next street. And he definitely had not planned to go that way. He had not planned to go at all.

"*Mano a mano*," said Bickle.

Slimy squeezed his cheeks together and stiffened his spine. If Bickle meant to kill him, he was a dead man already, so he knew the only way to play it was to talk shit.

"What is that? This *mano a mano*, that out of the kosher deli your old mama runs? Because that ain't American. I know American, and that ain't it."

"It's Spanish, actually, but you don't need to know that. What you need to do is put your hand in your back pocket."

"My back . . ." He could not go on and he forgot to close his mouth.

"If we're going to do it, it's time," said Bickle.

Slimy's face brightened immediately. "Then let's don't do it."

In one single sustained roar in which one exploding round could not be distinguished from another, Bickle shot a Star of David in a tight group no bigger than a teacup into Slimy's chest. The rounds blew him all the way across the room and spread-eagled him against the wall. Little bleeding holes slowly formed the Star of David on Slimy's shirtfront.

But Bickle knew, when they came out on the other side, they had taken Slimy's entire back with them. As Slimy slid slowly to the floor neither his eyes nor his mouth closed, and he looked to Bickle as though he had one last sentence he desperately wanted to say.

"Not in this lifetime, sweetheart," said Bickle. "Not in this lifetime."

He took a portable telephone out of a cradle on the side of his chair and watched a little girl standing on the street corner just outside his window with an enormous woman who was undoubtedly her mother. The little girl was trying to lick ice cream out of a waxed paper cup. Somebody picked up on the second ring.

The little girl was having a terrible time getting at the ice cream, now that all that was left was in the bottom of the waxed paper cup. The voice on the other end of the line with Bickle was loud and rough. Bickle glanced over at Slimy, whose eyes were still open but whose mouth was now closed. His blue lips were tightly, almost primly, pressed together.

The voice in Bickle's ear repeated: "Hey, you doing business here or not? This is mulching. We got business or what?"

Bickle watched the little girl struggle with her waxed paper cup and said in a bemused voice: "Whatever became of ice cream cones anyway, the kind you can eat? Why all this paper?"

The voice again said this was mulching and fairly screamed when he asked if they had business.

Bickle asked his original question while he watched the little girl throw her paper cup by the curbstone, which was already nicely littered with crushed paper.

"You got the wrong number, buster, and I got no time for bullshittin about whatever you got on your mind."

The voice was fading on the other end as if the man was putting the telephone back in the cradle.

"Probably mulched, wouldn't you think?" asked Bickle.

Whoever was on the other end was suddenly attentive again. "Did you say *mulched*, sir? Were you referred or are you an old customer?"

"They don't get any older than me, you motherfucker. Nobody's got more years in the firm than me and I'm still working."

"Jesus, is this Bickle?"

"It ain't Santa Claus."

"Hey, listen, Bickle. I'm sorry. I really am. I didn't mean nothing. It was a slip. You know what I'm saying?"

"I know you made a mistake."

"Yessir."

"Not to worry. It'll stay between us."

"I owe you and I'm grateful, I really am."

"You've owed me a long time and I'd think you'd be grateful now for more than a few years. I don't suppose you'd much like to become your own product."

"For Pete's sake, don't even make a joke about that."

"It's happened before, you know."

"I wish I didn't know, but I do. I know."

"Just stay loyal to me and nothing will ever touch you."

"I appreciate that and I'm sorry about fucking up when I picked up the phone. It's been—"

"You said."

"Yeah, I did, didn't I? Got a bad habit of repeating myself. But enough of that. How can I help you?" His voice dropped an octave and became very solemn. "Were you calling about your feet, sir?"

"Well, I've got another matter, but that can wait. But since you mention it, are they doing well in your estimation?"

The same solemn voice came back: "In my experience, going back almost as long as yours in the Company, I've never seen better. You know the tiny rose garden on the west side of the building by the avenue? That was where I thought best to honor them, and never in my life have I seen better results. The roses honor your feet and your feet honor the roses."

"Splendid. Wonderful. And you followed my instructions?"

"To the T. An extra trip through the grinder, twice more through the pulverizer, then mix from my private stock, and the result was fit flour to make bread for the gods."

Rumor had it that the chief mulcher (who himself existed only in rumor, as did the process of mulching the Company grounds with the remains of what rumor chose to call Company problems or Company honors) always used the phrase about the gods at least once, sometimes more, but rarely, when speaking of an honored mulching.

The phrase *fit flour to make bread for the gods* had been brought by rumor and no one could find its source. It sounded Elizabethan, but it was not to be found in the concordance to Shakespeare's work, or in any other concordance any number of people had taken the time, energy, and patience to search through. Perhaps rumor himself was father to the phrase. In any event, Bickle was pleased to hear it again and especially pleased to hear it spoken about his poor severed and lonely feet.

"It would be my prediction, sir, that those roses mulched by your feet will win the grand prize from the Greater Miami Florist Association."

"If I were you," said Bickle, "I'd expect a little package in the mail."

"Thank you. My wife thanks you. Now, with your permission,

sir, on to other matters. I believe you spoke of another bit of business."

"Indeed I did."

"Are they honorable remains, sir?"

"*Wretched bastard* is the term I think I would use."

"How does one through the grinder, mixed with fresh cow manure and mulched about in an ugly cactus patch that never grows no matter what you do with it?"

"Excellent, unless you can think of something worse."

"I'll do my very best to make it very bad."

"I know you will."

Bickle glanced at his watch. "My watch has the time as just after twelve noon. No doubt you know that I'm staying at the quarters for the incomplete."

"Yessir."

"I have a car and a driver. As soon as I take care of a few more bits of business, I'll be out of the apartment for a couple of hours. Will that give you time to tidy the place up after you remove the debris?"

"More than adequate, sir. And you'll have nothing to tidy up when I'm finished. It'll be a delight to do this little service for you."

"Good-bye and my very best to the missus. Remember the little package coming your way."

"You can be sure of that, Mr. Bickle."

Bickle replaced the telephone in its cradle on the side of the chair and spun round to look out the window again. The same little girl was working her pointed little tongue into another box of ice cream, the same kind as before. He would have given a year's pay to have about five minutes with the child's mother, a shapeless mound of fat who had wet an entire muumuu from shoulder to hem with sweat. And she was heedlessly making a replica of herself by allowing the child to have unlimited quantities of ice cream. There really ought to be somebody—or perhaps an agency—to control people like that.

He hit some little levers and rolled himself over to the wall where Slimy was sticking to the plaster and still had his lips pressed primly together. Bickle shook his head. It did make a man think. To absolutely no consequence, of course, but it was cause for thought.

There was not going to be any package in the mail to anybody. Bickle was not sure there was anybody. But rumor said there was, and nobody talked about it. The gardens around the office were magnificent and immaculate, cared for by a single very old man who seemed to always be pushing a wheelbarrow.

One needed to stay away from the plants and always stay on the sidewalk. Or else the smell of drying blood was overwhelming. Or rumor said it was drying blood they smelled. Whatever the source of the odor, no one could deny the strength of it. Quite naturally, though, the smell never, never was mentioned by the employees, so its strength and source were irrelevant.

He could not for the life of him remember where he got the telephone number he had dialed to get the mulcher. He assumed sometime; a long time ago, he had been issued the number by personnel. Of course, he could assume anything he wanted to, because nobody ever talked about it. Rumor assured every head and heart that every single employee of Soaps For Life had such a card to be used when necessary. The simple truth was, however, that he had never asked any other person about the telephone number and nobody had ever asked him. Rumor said that to do so would show disloyalty to the firm and distrust to its officers. Rumor spread the same kind of appeals for the same kind of trust during the Vietnam War. It was quintessential rumor work.

On the one hand rumor quietly admitted that Soaps For Life was making Agent Orange as a side product, plus a nerve gas with an unpronounceable name, BUT (and this BUT was always in all caps when rumor was spreading the gospel) since it was patently dishonorable to admit to anything that put our fighting forces as well as Pentagon news releases in untenable positions, every employee must remain quiet. And every soul was quiet as only a soul can be.

chapter

twenty-three

bickle had the right-turn lever pushed all the way forward and the left wheel lock pushed back, which caused him to turn slowly round and round on the same spot. The heavy woman in the sweat-stained muumuu with the child, who had yet another cup of ice cream, turned before his eyes and then was replaced by the wall where Slimy had been shot dead. The mulcher and his people had been very thorough. Not only had the body and the blood been removed, but the wall had even been faultlessly repaired. Nobody would ever guess a hole the size of a washtub had been blown out of it.

But Bickle was not happy, not with anything. Perhaps he would never be happy again. He could not remember a time in his life when everything about him was not buried in doubt. He seemed an enormous doubt to himself. And it was all because everything he thought he knew he did not know, and everything he had taken for granted had dissolved before his eyes. He kept turning and gradually it seemed to him that the large woman busily making a replica of herself by keeping ice cream in the hand of the child and the spot across the room where Slimy died were at different ends of the same spectrum. But he did not know the nature of the spectrum or why he should think they were at opposite ends of it.

Lost as he was in doubt and confusion, there occurred to him a totally improbable course of action. He took the cordless phone from the side of his chair and dialed a number. Across town the phone rang on the little table at the side of Hickum Looney's bed. Hickum, sweating and breathing in little gasps, turned his head to look at it.

Gaye Nell Odell, sweating and breathing hard, said: "You wouldn't."

Hickum looked at the phone. "It could be important," he said.

"And what we doing isn't?"

Hickum stretched and picked up the phone. "Hello."

"Hickum?"

"Bickle?"

"Yeah. Just had a call. Don't ask why I was asked to relay the message, instead of them calling you, because I don't know. I don't know anything. You didn't get a call from Jeroveh, did you?"

"Jesus, Hickum," said Gaye Nell, "you were just about to take me around the bend. Ditch the phone and get back to work."

She had hardly got the first word out of her mouth before Hickum slapped his hand over the phone.

"Is somebody there with you?" asked Bickle. "I thought I heard another voice."

"The truth is, Bickle, I'm right in the middle of something."

What he was in the middle of was Gaye Nell Odell. She glared up at him where he lay between her knees, both of which were stretched wide and pointed toward the ceiling.

"Well," said Bickle, "I'm only relaying a message. I wasn't asked to explain it. You're to get the first flight out to Atlanta. You go up there and talk to Jeroveh and then come back here and tell me what it's all about. I want to know what it's all about, and he said he wanted you up there anyway, and that you could come back and tell me what it was all about."

"What's what all about?"

"He didn't say. He just said you'd come back and tell me."

"Since when do I report to you, Bickle? Besides, it's the weekend."

"Did I say you were reporting? They only said you'd tell me what it's all about. And, frankly, that's all I want to know, what it's all about. And as far as it being the weekend, did you ever know the weekend to count for anything at Soaps For Life if the Company needed you?"

Gaye Nell had pushed herself away from him and was now sitting in the far corner of the room.

"Maybe I'll call him."

"The word given to me was that he wouldn't accept a call. Certain key people are being summoned to the mansion. You're one of them. My advice is to go."

"I don't need your advice."

"Maybe you do, maybe you don't. You don't want it, don't take it. But he said it was a turnaround trip. You'll be back before you know you're gone."

"Bullshit."

"That is not what Jeroveh would call the proper attitude. And I have to tell you, I don't either. Since when don't you answer when the Boss calls? You know what's good for all of us, you'll go. We're all in this together."

Hickum dropped the phone back into the cradle and looked across the room into the very angry eyes of Gaye Nell. He glanced at the phone. "I told you it could be important and it was. Bickle."

"I got ears. I also got feelings. You took me to the water and didn't let me drink."

"That's not fair."

"What's *fair* got to do with anything? You ever hear me saying

h a r r y   c r e w s

anything about *fair? Fair's* just another four-letter word. What's Bickle doing calling you on a Saturday morning?"

He told her.

"Does that make a hell of a lot of sense to you?"

"That's the way business is sometimes. But as one of our great presidents said: 'The business of America is business.' "

"How utterly goddam depressing."

"Maybe, but it's the truth, or the president wouldn't have said it." Hickum had been quoting from the Inspirational Section of the Sales Manual, and he wished he could remember the name of the president he had just quoted, but he couldn't. "I got to see what clothes I can throw in a bag and get out to the airport."

"Maybe picking up the phone wasn't so bad after all. Would you believe I never been on a plane before."

Hickum, already on the way to his closet, stopped. His back was to her. Without turning, he said softly: "Don't start, Gaye Nell."

"I already started," she said.

"Bickle didn't mention you. Jeroveh didn't mention you. You got to stay here. Besides, something like this, I wouldn't be surprised the cost of this trip didn't come out of my own pocket."

"It wasn't Bickle and it wasn't Jeroveh I had in my saddle five minutes ago. It was you. And you left the job about half done. But I understand how you are, and I forgive you. Hell, we pulling in double harness now, and both of us have to forgive everything we can."

Hickum was genuinely touched by her saying the two of them were pulling in double harness. It was a common enough saying in the part of Tennessee he came from, but he had never expected to hear a woman say it to him. For a very long time he had hoped one would. But one day or night over the long years while he was busy with soap and not paying attention to much of anything else, it felt as if his heart had turned to a turnip, and quietly and without even marking the loss, he had buried the hope.

the mulching of america   257

She stood up from her chair and came across the room toward him. She put a hand on each of his shoulders. "Old son, I can't risk something happening to you. I'm coming with you to run interference. I'd be afraid to send you out on a trip like this by yourself. You need me to take care of you on that airplane."

"But you said you'd never been on an airplane."

"I lied," she said. "Give me your credit card."

He reluctantly took out his wallet. "I don't think I ever had more than seven, eight hundred dollars on this thing in my life."

"What's your credit limit?"

"I don't know."

"We're about to find out. I've got to call a kennel to come pick up Bubba. Hate to do that but it can't be helped. I'll get us reservations on the first plane to Atlanta. You get in and out of the shower while I'm doing that and I'll be right behind you when I get off the phone. Hop to it, Hickum! Hell, we may get a chance to sit down awhile and chew the fat with Ida Mae, find out how she managed to stop being a little old woman in a dusty house and become a mogul of soap."

"You're going to get us both in trouble if you don't mind your manners."

"I'm going for one reason, to keep you out of trouble, not get you in it."

"I'll believe it when I see it."

She headed for the telephone and he for the bathroom. He was always quick in the shower because in the Miami heat it didn't matter how well he bathed or if he bathed at all. He was always wet with sweat after the first hour away from air-conditioning of one kind or another. And he was even quicker at getting dressed because if it was business, it was always the same uniform: jacket, shirt with tie, and trousers. So he was dressed before Gaye Nell had found a kennel that would come for Bubba. He threw an open suitcase on the bed. He hated to go off without a change of clothes. One never knew in this world. He was still staring at the suitcase when his doorbell rang.

harry crews

Gaye Nell looked up from the yellow pages she was searching through.

"Who can that be?"

"The usual way you find out is open the door," said Gaye Nell.

Frowning, Hickum walked to the door and opened it. A man who in size and dress could have been a double for Jeroveh's chauffeur, Pierre LaFarge. The black visor of his cap was polished bright as a mirror, as were his boots. Hickum had never seen him in his life.

"Mr. Hickum Looney?" he asked pleasantly.

"Do I know you?"

In the same pleasant, even voice, the man said: "Mr. Hickum Looney?"

"That's me," said Hickum. "You mind telling me who you are?"

"I was sent to give you this." He handed Hickum an envelope. "It is a first class ticket to Atlanta."

Gaye Nell, wearing a bathrobe, walked up beside Hickum. "What's going on?"

"My instructions were to fetch you immediately to the airport." He shot back the sleeve of his jacket and looked at his watch. "We'll have to hurry, and even then the traffic will have to be on our side ro make your plane." He smiled pleasantly.

"Calm down, junior," said Gaye Nell. "I'm going too, and I haven't even had a shower yet."

Still smiling pleasantly and looking at neither of them, but rather at a spot between the two of them as though he were reading his message off a wall behind them, he said, "You'll not need a bag, not even a dop kit for the gentleman. I was told to tell you that you'll be taken care of, entirely taken care of."

"You're just about to piss me off, sweetheart," Gaye Nell said.

Hickum put a hand on her shoulder. "Be still. Hush." Over the man's shoulder, he had just spotted a dirty dented Dodge car, a yellow one, parked by the curb behind his Lincoln Town Car. "It can't be helped."

"What can't be helped?"

"Nothing whatsoever," he said.

The back of Hickum's neck had gone cold. Something unthinkable spread by rumor long ago was trying to form itself somewhere behind his eyes. But he had buried it so deeply in himself for so long that it would not quite form, and for that he was deeply grateful.

The pleasantly smiling, immaculate little man, who would not meet his eyes, said: "When you come off the concourse at the airport in Atlanta, you will see a man dressed just as I am holding a sign with your name on it. He will take you to your destination."

Hickum said nothing. He knew there was nothing he could say that would make any difference at all. He turned to Gaye Nell and embraced her.

With her face pressed against his chest, she said, "You're going to leave me and Bubba and go off to God knows what? Just leave us like this?"

"It can't be helped," said Hickum.

"Anything can be helped. Just don't go."

"They'd just come after me."

"They'd what?"

It was as though he had not heard her. Instead he spoke to the man in black. "Just let me throw something in a bag."

"Begging your pardon," he said, "but I wouldn't do that if I were you. No indeed, definitely no suitcase."

"Why in the hell not?" Hickum said. He could, at least for the moment, show anger.

"Because those were my instructions to be given you, instructions from Ms. Ida Mae herself."

Hickum brightened immediately. "From Ida Mae? Well. Why didn't you say so? I could come in Bermuda shorts and she wouldn't care."

"They were made with the consent of Jeroveh down to the last detail."

"Do I look all right to go as I am?"

"You look splendid, sir."

Gaye Nell, who had been listening to all this with her lower jaw slightly unhinged, said: "Jesus Christ, this sounds like the goddam army."

The little man, his boots tightly together at the heel, his hat squarely on his head, said: "In that you would not be far wrong, but with a difference. The Company runs a very tight ship, the army . . . Well, to put it kindly, their ship is slack, very slack." With that, he reached through the open door and took Hickum by the tie and jerked him through the door. "My watch says it is time to make a move, a rather desperate move if I may say so, if you are to catch your plane."

"I don't want to catch a plane." He was trying to scream but the cinched tie made his voice a squeak that shamed him.

The jackbooted little man, with amazing strength, pulled Hickum along behind him. He did not even look back when he said, "But the Company wants you to. Now I know you've been with Soaps long enough to know that in differences like this, Soaps always wins."

Hickum found the last breath in his constricted throat to call in a whispering voice: "Good-bye, Gaye Nell. Good-bye, sweetheart."

"Have a good trip, Hickum."

He was not going to have a good trip and he knew it. But even if he'd had the breath and time to explain, he would not tell her the truth about what he knew was going to happen. The one-way ticket had said it all. Rumor had told them all long, long ago how this was played out. No use to tell Gaye Nell, she'd find out soon enough. Even if he could have, he would not have alerted the Atlanta police. They were all paid or afraid. It amounted to the same thing. They would be somewhere else when he needed them most.

The man the Company had sent to put him on a plane was a model of efficiency. Hickum had fainted from being hauled around by the necktie, and when he began to regain his senses, he was being wheeled by an attendant down the boarding ramp.

He turned his head as best he could and told the black man pushing the chair that he could walk.

"No trouble at all, sir, no trouble at all. That's what I'm here for, to help people who can't help themselves."

"There's been a mistake. I really can walk."

"I'm only doing what I was told to do, sir. You understand. But I tell you what, after I get you out of this chair and into your seat and you fly out of my city, wherever you're going, you can walk out tall and proud. But as long as you in my city, you ride in my wheelchair. You understand, sir, just doing what I'm told."

In a depressing revelation, it occurred to Hickum that everybody was only doing what he was told, and most depressing of all, that included himself.

At the door he was allowed to walk onto the plane by himself. A pretty blond stewardess with blue eyes directed him to a seat in the first cabin. This was a first for him. In his entire life, he had never flown first class. About the only observation he'd been able to make before the stewardess was bending over him with her blinding smile was that there was a hell of a lot more room to stretch his legs.

She set a long-stemmed glass in front of him and poured from a bottle wrapped in a white linen towel.

"Your employer insisted you be served this champagne. He arranged to have it put on board himself. We don't ordinarily carry anything nearly this fine." When the glass was filled, she looked up at him, her long-lashed eyelids blinking like a hummingbird's wings. "Once we're in the air, what might your pleasure be for an hors d'oeuvre? I suggest caviar, the real thing, the best in the world, also put aboard the plane by your employer." She giggled fetchingly and at length and then said: "You must be quite special to your company."

Hickum had been watching the little bubbles rise in the glass while she talked. The champagne made no sense to him. None of what she said made any sense to him.

harry crews

He looked up at her. "I never had any champagne in my life. I'm pretty much a beer man myself."

Her pretty face fell. "Oh dear. This will never do."

"It won't?" said Hickum.

"You've got to understand, sir, that my company is responsible to your company, and my company told me you were to drink this extraordinary champagne. Please don't be displeased. I'm only doing as I was instructed to do. We also have an assortment of exquisite lunches for you to select from once we're on our way and at altitude."

"If I ate anything, I'd throw up," he said.

"Oh my," she said.

"That wouldn't do, right?"

"I'm afraid not, sir. I just started with the company and I'm doing everything wrong."

She looked at Hickum as if she was ready to cry. "Don't you worry," he said. "There is always a solution among people of goodwill, right?"

"Of course you're right, if you say so. But my instruction did not include a solution, only the best service you've ever had. The very best. Anything you wish. Of course that might have to wait until we're on the ground and in the limousine I understand is meeting you."

"I don't understand," said Hickum. "What would have to wait?"

"Head."

"Head? I'm afraid you've lost me."

"The best blow job you've ever had."

Hickum was shocked that he was not shocked, and neither did he blush. It was just more instruction she had been given on give dollar value for dollar paid. Nothing very unusual in that. He was on a plane to Atlanta for reasons he wasn't really sure of, wasn't he? He was doing what he had been told to do. So was she. But it occurred to him that between people, between him and this lovely child, there might be a way to short-circuit the Company's plan for both of them.

the mulching of america   263

When he looked up from his linen-covered tray, she was still hovering right there nearly touching him.

"Do you want to please me very, very much?"

"Oh, yessir. The company does and I do."

"Then here's what we'll do. I don't know your company. I've never met it. For that matter I don't know my company. I've never met it. I know the man who gives me orders, that's all. But he's not the Company, is he?" Her dazzling smile was gone and she looked very puzzled. "Please don't be upset. This will please everyone concerned. Take away this glass of wine. Bring another long-stemmed glass and a bottle of beer wrapped in linen. Pour my glass full. Everytime it's empty, fill it again. I don't have much capacity for alcohol, so I drink it slow. And about the a . . . a . . . the backseat of the car waiting to pick me up . . ." He put his hand low on the right side of his abdomen. I'm just getting over an operation and . . . well, you understand."

"Oh, my poor man," she said.

"This is going to be a piece of cake for both of us and for our companies. And the best thing will be that we are telling both companies to go fuck themselves. Oops, sorry."

"Don't you dare be sorry. It's only too bad we can't figure out a way to make the companies go fuck each other. My, my, you're blushing. How absolutely endearing. You sit tight and I'll take care of everything."

And she did. He only drank three beers and a part of another on the entire trip. And he got off the plane feeling better than he'd felt in a long time. His stewardess waved to him walking away from the plane and called: "I owe you one." He suddenly felt very, very clean, as though he had just had a scalding bath, and he couldn't for the life of him understand why.

Again, a jockey-sized black man, dressed the same as the other driver, was standing at the end of the concourse holding a neatly printed sign that read MR. HICKUM LOONEY.

Hickum walked up to him and said: "I'm Hickum Looney."

"Very good, sir. Do you have bags?"

"No. Not a thing."

"If you'll follow me, sir, I'll have you out to the mansion right quick. It's only a short drive."

It may or may not have been a short drive. Hickum did not see much of it. He was too busy being scared. He knew they had to be twenty miles over the speed limit all the way and the driver completely ignored every traffic sign he saw. Hickum kept thinking that to die anywhere was bad enough, but to die in Atlanta, Georgia, would shame his entire family back in the noble state of Tennessee.

Hickum did even not know they had arrived until the driver whipped the Rolls into a long tree-lined drive that led to a singularly ugly three-story building of sharp angles and an absolutely flat roof that had a sign that ran all the way across the top of it. Everybody in the Company who had seen it thought it was too ugly and gauche to bear. But it was their company, so they looked at it and carried it forever in their memory. The sign in red letters six feet tall read: THE HOUSE THAT SOAP BUILT.

The massive doors swung open as they crossed the marbled porch, and another man, black and inexplicably turbaned and wearing something that might have come out of the film *Lawrence of Arabia*, said, "How good of you to come, Mr. Looney. Would you follow me please?"

The mansion was designed after the manner of the regional office or vice versa, Hickum didn't know which, but it was about four times as big. And the decor of the mansion was the same as the office. No pictures, either originals or prints, no plants or flowers, either real or artificial. And the scent that was in the office hung in the air everywhere. Jesus, where did he get that shit, and why did he put it inside every building he owned, even the one he slept in?

Two doors swung open as he and his escort approached them, swung open by some mechanical device, apparently, because Hickum saw no one touch them. The two doors opened onto a very large room with a fireplace that, curiously, had a low fire blazing in it, or maybe it was a fake fire—Hickum couldn't tell.

His escort had silently disappeared and he was left alone staring at Ida Mae and Jeroveh. Jeroveh seemed somehow shrunken and his color was bad, a faded color of gray.

"Come closer, dear boy, come closer," said Ida Mae.

Hickum came into the room, but before he was within two strides of where they were seated, Ida Mae said, "That will be fine," which at first Hickum didn't understand, and then, from simply the look in her eyes, he knew it meant, "Stop where you are." Hickum stopped, puzzled and afraid for no reason he could name. He turned to look at the old man for whom he had worked for twenty-five years. "Good to see you, Jeroveh." He wanted to tell him he was looking well, but that would be a lie, and he knew somehow the old man would know it. Somewhere he had a mirror and if he had looked into it recently, he knew he looked as though he was dying.

Searching desperately for something to say, because the fear that he could not name was growing, Hickum smiled and said, "Well, I'm here."

"So you are," said Ida Mae.

"Good to see you, Jeroveh," he said again.

The old man turned watery eyes on Hickum but said nothing.

"He prefers to be called Roy now," Ida Mae said.

"Roy?" He was supposed to call the man who controlled the lives and destinies of men and women across the entire country *Roy?*

"Don't look like that, for God's sake. It's the name his mother gave him."

Hickum had never thought of the Boss having a mother. And try as he would, he still could not form the thought.

In the silence that stretched after Ida Mae's voice, he tried to think of something to say, and then he thought of what he had wanted to say ever since he had heard she was in Atlanta.

"Ida Mae, can you—"

"I am called by Ms. I. M. Milk now. By everybody."

He was stunned, and the back of his neck went cold again.

He could not bring himself to call her anything but Ida Mae, so he just left off the name.

"Yes, well, can you believe just short of a month ago I walked up to your house to sell our product, and now here we are at the headquarters?"

"Do you really believe, Hickum, that you just *happened* to walk up to the house I was in?"

"Of course I do. It was on my route for that day and—"

"No. It was all planned. Everything in the Company is planned. Do you really think we can just let things happen? We make things happen and then make it look as though it could have been no other way. There are no accidents, ever. A company with integrity and honor controls everything. Go to your grave with that word in your ears: *everything.* There were high hopes for you in the Company, and in a little over three short weeks you failed them all."

"Jeroveh," cried Hickum, "or Roy, or whatever I'm supposed to call you, what is she saying?"

The old man stared at him with watery eyes.

"I'm afraid he won't be saying much. You see, he failed too. Everybody fails sooner or later. I will too. But in the meantime, I'll have the world ordered as I like it. That's quite a lot when you think of it. Some of us think it's worth any price."

"But what's to happen now?" said Hickum.

"You know as well as I, but you want to be told . . . No, you have to be told, don't you? It doesn't matter now, but just so you'll know, that is part of the reason you failed and we've had to bring you here to meet the mulcher, which is an honor. If you were an ordinary failure, we would have had the mulcher take you where you fell. For the superior failures, we bring them here to headquarters and . . . Well, you know."

"Good Lord, Roy, can't you do—"

"He's going with you, I'm afraid."

"But he's a legend, the founder, an inspiration a—"

"And I shall be a legend, a founder, an inspiration, and so

on. And the one who comes after me will be too. That's the way the Company works." Hickum staggered over to a chair and fell into it. Finally he said: "But what about Gaye Nell and her dog and Bickle and—"

"Don't trouble yourself, dear boy. It will all work out. The world grinds on."

To no point whatsoever, Hickum saw that the fire in the hearth was, in fact, a fake, not fire at all, only colored light.

about the author

Harry Crews is the author of nineteen books and numerous articles and columns. He lives in Gainesville, where he teaches at the University of Florida.